SEAL Team 7

I0658273

Danni's Return

For my husband who always believes in me,
has given me so much support in following my
dreams...

I love you!

Acknowledgments

I want to take the moment to thank you all for being here for book four! I have to tell you that I am so humbled by the love, and support of the first three, and I really hope you enjoy this instalment of SEAL Team 7!

This book, I have to admit, is my favorite. I fell in love with Jamie and Matt which spurred the series, but when I began this book, it was originally not meant for the SEAL world, one of the reasons it isn't set in the usual San Diego, is because of that. I loved living in New York, it always felt like I was home, so I wanted to draw on that. Danni and Brad, their history, and their connection spoke to me; it was so very easy to follow them, allow them to tell their story to me.

I hope you enjoy!

I'd like to thank those who continue to help and support this.

Grandma, Lori, and Kathleen, I hope I am getting better with all of your hours of editing!

Mike, you make this possible xo

Dad, whether you know it or not, you are super important in my daily life!

Bren, your friendship, love, and smile makes every visit so very special! Thank you! xo

My family, friends near, and far.

"Mr. Johnson." He looked up to see his assistant standing at the open door to his office, important paper work before him on the desk and in his hands; a headache that had been brewing for hours furrowed his brow and made him roll his neck to the right.

"Yes Maggie."

"I just wanted to let you know before I leave for the Anderson meeting that your mother called while you were on the conference call."

"I'll have to call her back from the plane." He checked the time on his wristwatch. "Just be warned she was asking a lot of questions about tomorrow night's gala and who you were taking."

"As a date?"

"You got it." Maggie smiled at her boss knowing this would make his gut of steel churn. "I gladly informed her for you that you were going stag."

"Gee thanks." He let out a deep sigh. "I bet that brought about more questions."

"A few; I let her know you haven't seen Amber in months and the connection the papers made to you with Tiffany Rice were just rumors."

"Please don't tell me you have the feeling she was asking because she's using her guest invite to bring a female to set me up with."

"If she is, she never let on." Maggie smiled at him. "She did the same type of thing to your father all the time."

"She set him up with women?" He deadpanned as he reached for his briefcase and set it to the side of him on the desk. "No, played this mental game of course.

The only good thing is that she does it out of the kindness of her heart."

"The only saving grace."

"Well, I'd better get to this meeting, any messages for Anderson?"

"No, do me a favor, call me when it's over and let me know how the proposal went over."

"Anderson won't be able to say no, you know he's going to love this package."

"God, I hope so. We have the board of directors meeting next week and I have an ulcer just thinking about what they're going to say when they see the quarterly figures." He placed the files in the leather case. "The figures I saw are up almost ninety percent."

"Anything less than a hundred percent is less than what my father would have achieved." He got up pushing his heavy desk chair back and reaching for his suit jacket from the back. He was wide but lean, what you would refer to as any young fit American men who had a history of football.

"You don't give yourself enough credit," he heard Maggie say and he looked over to the woman a few years younger than his mother, and also his father's trusted secretary for the last thirty-five years. He had known Maggie and her family for years, ever since he had been small and his father had brought him in to his sanctum after school two afternoons a week, so he could show his son how the family business worked and Maggie was that motherly comfort in a dark decorated interior of the office he now sat at the head of behind that large oak desk that never felt completely his.

"There's no room for self-praise when you're constantly ensuring you aren't smearing the good business sense your father had."

"Brad." Maggie rarely used his first name, and never would in any company other than between the two of them. "Stepping in after your father passed away was not something anyone expected you to do."

"He did."

"He was very proud of the career path you set for yourself. It's your own determination to do good for him and your mother that brought you here."

"I sometimes wonder if I shouldn't have just let the board appoint an outsider and stayed where I was."

"Bite your tongue young man. You know anyone outside of the organization would have run this into the ground."

"We don't know that."

"I do." She stepped closer in to the office. "When your father had to take leave, he thought he was leaving everything in Darren's capable hands. Even I was sold on the twit's abilities, but you saw the numbers when you stepped in; not only was he spending more on himself but he trusted the wrong people with a lot of the financial resources we have." She paused a moment for emphasis as she watched Brad fiddle with the cuff of one sleeve. "The best thing you did was to fire Darren."

"The board gave me two years to turn this all-around Maggie." He finally fixed the damn sleeve on the suit he hated having to wear, almost as much as he hated a lot in life these days. He never wanted a job sitting behind a desk twelve-plus hours a day, but this is where life had led him. "We have two more quarters to report before we can arrange a ticker- tape parade in my honor."

"You can do it."

"Mom has the same faith in me too." Picking up his case he looked back knowing he was forgetting something, and realized it was his iPhone. He couldn't catch up with calls or return his own mothers without it. "Smart women can always see past the handsome strong man and see his worth."

"Okay, with that fortune-cookie fodder I'm leaving." He let out a short laugh touching Maggie on the shoulder as he went past her. "Make sure you take a couple of aspirin, because you know if you don't, that headache of yours will only get so bad you'll be grouchy tomorrow night." The last of her words followed him down the hall.

CHAPTER ONE

"Daisy, who was that on the phone dear?" Daisy heard her boss shout from the living room where she had been tinkling on the baby grand piano as she did most afternoons, especially when it was raining out and they couldn't go for their usual stroll around Central Park.

"It was just the doorman saying your dress is downstairs Mrs. Johnson." She came in to the living room carrying the glass of water she had asked for ten minutes before. "I was hoping it was Bradford."
"Maggie told you he was going to call you from the jet."
"I'm just excited about everything." Mrs. Johnson took the glass and a couple of sips before passing it back. "I still don't think he'll be happy if he even thinks there's a hint of a set-up."
"I'm just trying to make things right."
"But right for who?" Daisy took a step back as Mrs. Johnson pushed back in her wheelchair from the piano. "Bradford just needs a little nudge in the right direction."
"And every time you try making him do something you think is right he goes in the absolute opposite direction; he did it when he was three and he'll do it now at thirty-five."

"Daisy, I just want him settled, and some grandchildren before I'm too old and frail to appreciate them." She was wheeling her way around the living room towards the main door of the penthouse apartment she had lived her entire adult life. She had married John Johnson at twenty, a perfect pairing as their parents had said, and in some respects it had been, the love had been there, they had made a son together, but after her accident, the one which left her unable to use her legs she had only been able to be half a wife to a man who had loved and adored her, no matter what her disabilities but she had held a small amount of anger inside, knowing because of her he had missed out on so much.

She wouldn't allow her son to miss every single thing he should have in life. If she had to meddle then so be it.

"I'll go and get the dress, you stay here in case he calls, and if he does do not let on."
"I'll try Mrs. Johnson."
"No, you're right, that won't work." She stopped midway down the hall. "You go; I'll sit by the phone."
"Sure." Mrs. Johnson waited as Daisy left and she wheeled herself back down the hall to the room which had been her husband's for almost four decades but now only held the lingering smell of his expensive brand of cigars. She had asked Daisy to remove the desk chair a while back and she wheeled herself behind the ostentatious desk and opened up the photo album she had pulled out a few days before after a call from an old friend.

The pictures inside where old and not as good a quality as the ones she got from her digital camera or phone now. Most of them were a little bent or marked as they had lived crumpled inside a shoe box inside Bradford's childhood closet for so long; but once he had officially moved out thirteen years before she had found them and placed them there for safety.

Her son, the miniature version of his father when he was small was now far more handsome than John had ever been. His thick dark brown hair as luxurious and soft looking as any melted Godiva chocolate, and his eyes matched just the same, they were deep, and filled less these days with the golden sparkle they had once held, but they fitted the strength of his face. None of the best sculptors alive or dead would be able to find an equally stubborn stone to carve him out of. Bradford had always been a skinny boy until he had hit the age where girls were more than just innocent friends. His determination to be muscular had started, he'd gone on to play football through high school and even when he was down at the academy in Annapolis he had played for the team there.

Most of the pictures inside the album were of Bradford and the one person who he had confided in when they were young. They only saw each other during the six weeks of summer vacation down in the Hampton's and a few weekends while the weather held out, but their friendship had been strong. All the adults had seen it from the beginning just like when they'd noticed how, in their early teens, it seemed more secretive, where no one knew where they were going and what they were doing during the days and nights, and it hadn't been until her son had been fourteen, almost one year older than his friend when concern came in to the equation.

His father had caught him kissing her.

Talk started, plans discussed that the two of them were a good pair; that like the two sets of parents whose own pairings had been planned for the good of their families the two of them would bring the two oldest and wealthiest families on the East Coast together in marriage. A joyous plan that was kept from the children, ensuring that when the time came for Bradford to be brought in to the idea, he wouldn't fight it but rather welcome it as well.

A plan that seemed to be flowering as the two of them got closer and closer each summer, until the six weeks between high school and going off to Annapolis, the Morgan family had spent most of the spring in the Hampton's, their daughter spending the weeks in the city going to the same high school but a year behind Bradford. At the beginning of summer they were still a pair, but it was halfway through when the plan became something that would never come to fruition.

Tragedy struck; a weekend sailing trip the Morgan's had scheduled to the Kennedy compound, their cousins up in Hyannis, Massachusetts. Their sail boat had been destroyed in a 'freak accident' one reporter had written; the authorities concluded it was a faulty wire that once the May-day was called and responded to, all there was left were pieces of the wooden boat floating in the ocean in the morning; some people had whispered it was part of the Kennedy curse, and it had been Teddy Kennedy himself who had called their house in the Hampton's to tell them the bad news.

Theresa Morgan had been lost to both the ocean's mysterious depths and more than likely her injuries, her body never to be found. Ethan Morgan and the ten-year-old son Peter had been found by the Coast Guard inside an inflatable life raft, while their daughter had suffered severe injuries and was airlifted to a Boston hospital.

The summer had gone on without them but always in their thoughts.

Bradford had never been the same after a trip up with her husband to Boston to see the girl he probably would have married without their little plan, but the girl he had known for so long, the one he had probably loved at eighteen had not been the same pretty young thing he had known.

She knew a part of her son had died along with their dreams.

The last picture on the page of the album before her held the last picture ever taken of the two of them, both looking at one another, the summer breeze whipping her long blonde hair while he touched her cheek.

Seeing that picture always made her eyes water.

When the house phone started ringing beside her she had to cough before she picked it up, so that her voice held nothing to show any weaknesses; she had an image to uphold whoever it was calling. "Johnson residence." She said.

"Mother."

"Bradford, I was just thinking about you." Her face lit up, she knew she had a smile now. Her son was her life, her pride and joy, and she didn't care who knew.

"All good things I hope."

"Always, are you in the air?"

"About twenty minutes from O'Hare."

"Is it business or pleasure which takes you to Chicago, dear?"

"Business mother." She heard that clipped tone he used when he knew why she asked, but he had absolutely no idea.

And that's where the shock would come in.

"Maggie tells me you aren't seeing Amber anymore."

"No."

"How come? I was beginning to like her."

"You hated her, you made sure she always knew that, and anyway, we wanted different things." He sighed deeply.

"Which were?"

"Is this why you wanted me to call you mother?"

"I just want to know what's going on with you dear, don't be mad with me."

"I'm not mad."

"Then tell me what Amber wanted and you didn't."
She waited patiently as there was a pause from his
end in answering.

"Amber wants marriage, children, the entire white
picket fence thing," he finally said with an audible
sigh. "And you want to keep this bachelor phase of
your life going?"
"Nothing wrong with that mother."
"A man has needs."
"Ones I'm not going to agree I have or don't have
while on the phone with you."
"I thought you loved her."
"I liked her sure."
"Well if the love's not there then I suppose it's good
to let her go now."
"You aren't leading this conversation in to some sort
of set up tomorrow night, are you?"
"So suspicious sweetheart." She chuckled. "I have
nothing planned to backdoor you or embarrass you."
"Who are you bringing?"
"Just Daisy."
"And there's no secret guest to set me up with?"
"No one I know of; of course, you and Maggie
invited everyone, so only the two of you would know
who will or won't be there."

Letting that sink in a moment she went on to say. "I
was hoping you would join me for dinner at the end
of the week if your schedule allows it."
"I'll have Maggie let you know. I'm not sure exactly
what my schedule is after tomorrow's gala."

"Good, then I'll call her later and we'll spend the evening. You can decide what we'll have and I'll order in."

"Sounds good, how are you feeling today?"
"A little bored. We couldn't get out because of the rain but Daisy just went down to get my dress and after dinner Clive is coming up to enjoy some after-dinner drinks. Of course, tomorrow I'll be busy getting ready and everything."
"Maggie said she was coming over with you in the limo."
"It will be nice; I always loved Maggie, you're lucky to have her."
"Don't I know it."
"You know I was thinking about this summer, going out to the house for a few weeks."
"The fresh air will be good for you."
"I was hoping you'd take some time off and join me."
"We'll see mother." She heard his voice; it softened slightly as it also tightened and knew, all the way down to her toes she no longer felt that he would never go back to that house, the house he hadn't stepped inside of since he was nineteen.

CHAPTER TWO

The first time that day he could really shut off and relax came on the flight back to New York. The meeting over in Chicago and the papers signed inside his briefcase, and in less than two weeks the largest hospital in downtown Chicago would break ground on an extension wing to accommodate not only the veterans from every branch of the military it had been giving free care to since his father had instituted a yearly monetary payment some twenty years before, but now it would help some of the new issues these kids came back with. A first of its kind, state of the art prosthetic wing. Full 3-D printing capabilities would be used for the first time in that kind of setting. John was actually very proud of what he and the team had created on paper.

That's what his family business had been for generations. Helping groups help others while the other side of the business made millions daily with their conglomerate of smaller businesses.

Resting his head back on the leather of the chair he sat in, he left the paper Maggie had passed him earlier that morning unread on the small table before him.

Even with the sound of the engines, the hum of them filling the small Lear jet cabin he was able to relax and let himself think.

He didn't believe his mother was innocent in not trying to set him up.

She had been trying to set him up for years, when he'd been stationed overseas, in other states he'd had an excuse to stay out of her radar but now, after being in New York permanently the last year and a half since being a teen, he found it harder to dodge her attempts at aiming cupid's arrows towards him.

Needing to forget the nagging fear his mother really was setting him up Brad took the paper before him and opened it up. Normally he had the paper finished before ten every morning, but he'd be lucky to get past the business section before the next was hot off the presses.

A name on page four stopped his reading as he looked at the face of a man he hadn't seen since they were both young. Sitting in the middle of the society page was a picture of Peter Morgan, who, it seemed, was recently engaged to Felicity Spencer who was a few years older than her fiancée, and she had been in John's year at school. She was also the daughter of the second term mayor, a mayor who didn't need a wage as like his own family they were all independently wealthy.

The Morgan name, the family name brought back images he had tried to suppress, memories he couldn't cut out physically from his brain but had to live with until the day he died.

He would have Maggie send a congratulations note, maybe a bottle of champagne too, but he wouldn't call, couldn't because even with this professional picture staring back at him from the paper he could only see the young kid, eight years younger than he was the last time he'd seen him at the hospital in Boston.

He closed his eyes and closed the paper sharply before reaching for the two fingers of Scotch sitting in the glass, neat, beside him.

Would there ever be a time he would forget the past? He'd seen men killed in combat, blown up, shot and maimed right before his very own eyes but nothing could compare to seeing her connected to all those horrid machines, her head pretty much wrapped like a mummy, only those black and blue swollen eyes, closed and taped, visible against the whiteness of the bandages.

The burn of the Scotch did nothing to help and he cursed himself for being unable to forget, get over the past.

Thankful to the sudden shrill of his cell he picked it up pressing the talk button at the same time without even opening his eyes. "Johnson." He said.
"You just got yourself an open invitation to use a certain villa out in Vale this winter." It was Maggie's voice filling his ear. "Also a rather large bottle of aged brandy, and signed papers."
"He was happy then?" He used his free hand to rub his left temple, he had to take those aspirins like Maggie had suggested or she'd be right within

twenty-four hours in her prediction. "That's an understatement."

"Well what choice did he have? It was either our company bought him out or he retired, leaving it to some half-wit to run in to the ground."

"Any ideas who you'll have head up the company?"

"I don't know, who do you think would want the responsibility of a publishing company?"

"I'll have to get back to you on that." He knew Maggie was frowning; weird how you knew from the way someone spoke.

"I called my mother." He announced.

"Ooh, so is there some scheme?"

"She's denying it but I don't buy it."

"I wouldn't either."

"Do you know something you aren't telling me?"

"No."

"Because you know, if you did and I found out, I may be tempted to rethink my father's wish to keep you around Maggie." He joked.

"You would never."

"You're right."

"She asked me about having dinner this week, I told her I would have you call and arrange it, seeing as I'm just the corporate head and I go where I'm told."

"Your only free time would be Friday if you want to spend time as well as dinner."

"Let her know for me, oh, and also Maggie, I need you to send a bottle of champagne and a congratulations card down town to Morgan trading."

"I did this morning."

"You did?"

"On your mother's orders."

"You never mentioned it to me."

"I'm sorry Brad. Your mother called and asked. I didn't think it would be a big deal."

"It's not; it's just...." He paused. "You didn't say anything."

"I didn't say anything because I know what your feelings are when the Morgan family are mentioned."

"What are my feelings?" He wanted to know because he sure didn't know himself.

"She meant a lot to you Brad, and I know why you left early for Annapolis, why you never go to the house in the Hampton's; why, whether you understand it or not, you insist on being a bachelor."

"God Maggie, don't you start with the bachelor thing too."

"That's the only comment I get out of you?"

"Everything else you said was right."

"You know we sent an invite to Ethan Morgan?"

"We have every year. None of them ever come."

"Then you better prepare yourself. Ethan accepted."

"He did?"

"Your mother had a call from him. He wanted to make sure you would be okay if he accepted. I'm presuming he and Peter will be coming."

"Who else would Ethan bring?" Through the grape vine, rumors and whispered conversations between his parents he knew what had happened to Ethan's daughter, how she had spent so long inside the hospital, first in a coma, then with rehab. From what he had determined that had been tougher than anything else. Last he heard she was living in California.

"True."

"How was your meeting?" He wondered if Maggie was changing the conversation for his benefit. He appreciated that. "The hospital will be able to accommodate thirty new specialists and over two hundred permanent patients in a year and a half when it opens."

"Your father would be proud; that hospital was one of his pet projects."

"If only we could get Mayor Spencer to allow us the same in New York."

"Maybe you could use Peter and Felicity as your in. Didn't you once have dinner with her?"

"Back when I first returned, she was campaigning to me on behalf of her father. She acted like we had been best friends in high school but, we never got along."

"That's right, she was the same year as you. So as long as it wasn't a personal dinner, otherwise Peter would hold that against you."

"The fact Peter and I have eight years and everything between us, is bigger Maggie."

"Either way. So, you're on your way back to the city?"

"I should land before midnight. What time is my first meeting in the morning?"

"Nine."

"I better get some reading in or I'll be up all night going over those notes."

"Remember, I won't be in until ten and Cindy is going to cover my desk."

"Lucky me." He laughed. "Thanks Maggie and thanks for tonight, well, for everything you do."

"You're welcome."

The remainder of the flight he did go over the files, so when the limo he'd moved in to after they'd landed at La Guardia, pulled up outside his own building on seventy-eighth between first and York, he was ready to go in and just crash.

The four-story brownstone had been completely gutted when his father had bought it five years before. He'd had no plans on coming back to the city but it had been convenient when he had. What had been a basement apartment had been turned in to a one-car garage on one side, and a home gym he frequented when he could, on the other. The main floor held his living room, a dining room he never used unless his mother was over, and a modern kitchen which had mainly seen take-out except for a couple of occasions Daisy had cooked for him and his mother.

On the second floor was his study and the guest bedroom his mother had used a few times, two smaller ones as well. A chair lift was fitted to the stair railing to that floor. The third floor was where his sanctuary was; almost the entire floor was his master bedroom and a bathroom bigger than most New Yorkers' apartments; leaving the fourth floor as an open space, a loft with its own tucked-away tiny washroom, and more windows than the entire house.

After locking the door behind him and setting the alarm he left his case at the table inside the entryway and hung his trench coat in the small closet, before turning the light on for the staircase and going straight up to his room. He would love a shower but his body cried out for sleep, so inside the quietness of his room he slipped out of his suit making sure it was in the dry-cleaning basket. His housekeeper would be able to find it and drop it off at the cleaners when she came in. Sometimes he wondered why he bothered having a housekeeper when he was hardly there to make a mess; but he liked knowing the place was always ready in case he wanted to make a mess.

Once he felt the comfort of his large Californian king bed under him he adjusted the pillows, and laid back closing his eyes. The soft cotton and luxuriously expensive sheets his mother had bought for him feeling good against his naked length, and smelt familiar and like home.

As sleep took over, that face, the one from so long ago came back to him again, the face of a female whose laughter was unlike any other females he'd ever heard.

CHAPTER THREE

"It looks like you need this." Maggie appeared as he stood looking over some blueprints they'd hoped would be there a few days before, of a building they were proposing to construct in Philadelphia as part of the urban redevelopment the city was going through.

Turning, he saw in her hands a brown bag and a cardboard cup. "If that's the strongest black coffee from down the block then you'll get a raise."
"What do I get if this bag contains something even better?"
"A promotion," he joked. "What is in the bag?"
"Turkey on whole wheat."
"Lettuce, tomatoes, pickles and mayo?"
"Of course."
"Then you can have a promotion as long as it isn't my job."
"I'll hold you to that." She teased back as she handed both items over.

"What do you think?" Brad asked her, noticing her looking at the plans as he took the first swallow of scalding hot dark liquid. "I can't really tell, I've never been good at putting these drawings in to a building inside my head, I like it better when the architect sends those little to-scale models."
"I'm not too sure about it, and I can."
"Want me to call Bob up?"
"He's already on his way."
"Oh, so you know." Maggie moved towards the main door to the office where her desk sat. "I called over to

speak to Ethan Morgan's secretary; played the 'did Peter get the gift and card' trick."

"And?"

"She happened to let slip that Ethan is going with Peter and the new fiancé tonight."

"And not?"

"No, she wasn't even mentioned."

"Oh."

"Oh?" That had made Maggie stop. "What did that response mean?"

"I didn't sleep too well last night; seeing Peter's picture brought up a few old memories for me."

"You've been thinking about her?"

"A little."

"You cared a lot for her as I remember."

"I was besotted." He sat down, putting his brown bag on the desk, his coffee which he kept in his hands. "She was my best friend."

"When was the last time you saw her?" Maggie moved back to sit on the chair on the other side of his desk. "In Boston."

"A very long time ago, can I ask why you never contacted her after?"

"She was in a coma for a very long time."

"And after?"

"I'm sure my father told you." He took a sip wishing the coffee was something stronger; little rattled him but the subject of her did.

A very foreign feeling for him with everything else in his life.

"I remember she was in a coma for a few years, the doctors thought she would never wake up but she did."

"Dad said she had no memories, nothing about who she was, what she was."

"And no recollection of you or your relationship together."

"Correct." He coughed trying to expel the lump in his throat. "Her father sent her to a rehab in California, I stopped trying to hear any news or gossip about how she was, and that's all I know."

"Then I know a little more." Maggie paused waiting for him to make eye contact. "If you're interested?"

"Do I get a choice?"

"You know you do."

"Sure." He said softly.

"Norma, Ethan's secretary and I have dinner every Christmas together, and everything gets gossiped about, so I know a little."

"I didn't know you were that friendly with Norma."

"Both of us have worked in our companies for the same length of time, and with your families so close back then there was hardly a day when we didn't speak at least once on the phone."

"Dad did spend a lot of time with Ethan."

"Even your mother and Theresa were known for their shopping sprees."

"I did know that."

"But you don't know about their daughter."

"Are you going to tell me or are you waiting for me to beg?"

"You beg?" She tried to lighten the moment.

"I've been known to but the person doesn't normally live to tell about it."
"Should I leave now?"
"No, please, I am interested."

"Ethan sent her to Los Angeles; there's a clinic just north of the city, where they specialize in traumatic brain injuries, memory loss and other related physical problems. Like you said, she couldn't remember anything of her life and it had to be rebuilt. Norma said Ethan let her get the help, her strength back, she took classes and got her high school diploma and then took a college course while still living at the facility. Once Ethan was able to find someone capable of holding down the company, he moved out there. She'd regained her intellect but not the memories. She didn't even recognize her own father Brad, which could be why sending her away was easy for him to do as she couldn't miss him. He was there a year and then came back while she chose to stay there, Ethan bought her a place and she started working building her own life the way she was comfortable with."

"Was there any residual brain damage?"
"Norma said occasionally Ethan mentions what he refers to as bad days, so maybe there are, but I don't have the answer to that."
"Do you know what she does for work?"
"No." Maggie got up. "You should talk to Ethan or Peter; you know maybe it would help you to know, to even talk about it with someone who loved her just as much."
"Love?"

"You know you loved her." Maggie said leaving the office.

Having Bob come in moments after his conversation with Maggie had alleviated some of the thoughts flowing around his head, but as he entered his house with two hours before the gala he knew he would have to struggle to control them.

After his shower, he took the tux covered in plastic from his closet. He hadn't worn it since the gala the year before. The rest of his closet still felt foreign to him, aside from the basic jeans and sweaters he preferred to wear. The rest were suits he had to wear to the office. Sometimes he missed the old uniform he had to wear and tucked in the far end of the closet were a few of them. He might be working his father's life but he didn't know if he wanted it. The board of directors didn't either.

Those white uniforms represented not only the life he put on hold for his family but also where he wanted his working life to end.

Checking himself in the hall mirror as he waited for Charlie to arrive with the limo, he was glad he'd stopped for a quick trim on the way home, that he hadn't shaved that morning so he could shave tonight and be smooth. He took in how pale his skin looked against the darkness of the tux and his hair; the skin around his eyes even more gave it away. He missed working in the open, for as long as he could remember he had a tan pretty much all year round, but these days he spent the majority of his day inside.

When Charlie honked the horn outside he left his jacket off and carried it over his arm. The weather for April had yet to feel spring-like, the sun rarely made an appearance and so far, the rain had yet to take a day's vacation but for the last few hours it had stopped, and a slight warmth had blanketed the city.

Settled in the back of the car he called Maggie to see where they were. She was in another limo which was just pulling up to his mother's apartment, so doing the math he would be arriving at least ten minutes, if not more, before they would arrive.

This evening was important for the company; their charitable donations came from the money they raised during the gala. Over a hundred upper-crust New Yorkers would be there as well as members of the board; and unlike the year before when he felt like a fish out of water, this year he was determined to show all of them that he could do the job just like his father had taught him.

CHAPTER FOUR

The gala had been held inside the opulent interior of the Plaza Hotel's Grand ballroom for the last fifty years, aside from the two years when the ballroom was being redecorated.

It oozed money to anyone who heard, and those column writers for the New York Post always flourished their articles the next day with at least two paragraphs on how it was decorated and set for the evening. Little changed over the years. There was always a string quartet playing; the round tables set for ten were around the open dance floor, and the hotel usually held at least half if not more of the guests who opted to stay overnight, so as not to have to worry about getting home after the event was over.

Being the first to arrive Brad entered the ballroom seeing how his mother had laid out the decorations. She was always a big part of the night, overseeing every aspect; she took a great deal of pride in doing that, and tonight she had outdone herself.

The round tables seemed to glitter. The deep red table-cloth covered with a golden one was set with the finest bone china by Wedgewood, and crystal glasses which sparkled and shone when filled with water. The center pieces were a mixture of blooms he couldn't name, but flowed with the theme of this red and gold. The chandeliers were glistening casting light off the cream marble columns and gold railings which looped like balconies between each. The wooden dance floor gleamed with the fresh coat of wax and he felt comfortable knowing he wouldn't be made to dance; it wasn't a grace issue but a hatred of being made to do something he had never enjoyed doing.

As he took a flute of champagne from a waiter dressed perfectly in his own tuxedo he looked around as the first couple came down. He knew there were place cards on the tables informing them where they would be sitting and with whom, so he stayed off to the side waiting for his mother to arrive. Really this was his mother's shining night, and she had more right to greet them than he did, especially as he had no idea who half of them were.

Coming down the special ramp not more than ten minutes after he arrived was his mother, being pushed by Daisy. His mother looked as good as he would expect, Daisy was dressed as she always was at occasions like this, just enough to fit in, but enough that if anyone was asked to give a description of her they couldn't. Maggie was trailing behind typing something in to her blackberry; he wondered what was making her frown.

"You look wonderful mother." He leant down, kissing her cheek.
"And you get more handsome every time I see you, I swear." She gave him her biggest smile as she took his hand, which made his heart widen. He felt complete as long as he knew his mother always cared

for him. "Daisy." He touched the woman's arm and then said. "Maggie; problem?"

"Ah, no." He didn't buy it but didn't have a chance to ask, seeing as guests were coming over to his mother and he had to start paying attention. After the first few they moved over towards the couple of stairs which led to the ballroom. You could see the people coming from the other side as they walked the corridor around the pillars, and the line was starting to build.

It was like the day of his father's funeral except there were no condolences from those they greeted, his mother first then him. Both Maggie and Daisy were standing back a few steps behind them. His mother's face had a new light to it since the evening started and he wondered if maybe he should figure out how to get her to help more with the office, she'd always been a social butterfly and it showed with every name she remembered, every child and grandchild each person she welcomed had.

"Peter and Felicity." He heard his mother's words while he finished speaking to one of his father's old golf club buddies. He turned to see the older version of the young boy he'd last known. "Mrs. Johnson, Brad." Peter simply said while Felicity leaned in and air kissed his mother's cheek. "I heard your father was coming too." Brad mentioned to him.

"He's on his way, we took separate limos." He felt the slight curtness from Peter. The kid held something against him. "Felicity." Brad went on to say, the young woman smiled to him and as quick as the 'hellos' to them had come they moved on towards a table where they found their names. Brad watched for a second, unsure if he should bother now to ask Peter about his sister; there had been no 'thank you' for the congratulations gift so something was amiss.

Hearing his mother's voice beside him again he was in another little world as he looked around the room. The sounds faded in his ear as he spotted faces he knew, shared a smile with a few people from where they were sitting, the ladies in the most expensive dresses, and the men in tuxes of all ages and styles, but all basic black. It wasn't until his eyes scanned to see how many more people could possibly be waiting to come in, he saw the line was gone from across the way but there stood a woman looking just like he had been, scanning the room, a look of confusion on her beautiful face.

A face he recognized and would never, could never forget.

As he held his breath, taking in the woman with blonde hair, wondering if he were mistaken, it happened. Her hair was down and curled softly in the way only a professional stylist could accomplish, the golden waves contrasted with the black dress she wore which was reminiscent of the one Audrey Hepburn had worn in Breakfast at Tiffany's. Sleeveless and long, showing off toned arms and the slight scoop at her collar bone exposed her neck where an expensive diamond necklace lay. A small clutch seemed to be her security blanket from the way she gripped it, and a shimmering black shawl hung from her bent elbows.

As he gazed he prayed silently two ways, he wanted it to be her yet he also didn't.

Seeing Ethan walk up behind her and put a hand on her shoulder as he leaned in close to say something seemed to tell him who she was.

She was there.

"I'm sorry Brad." Maggie's soft voice sounded beside him over the noise of the talking and the music. "When you asked what was wrong earlier I had just found out."
"So, it is her?" He turned slightly but kept an eye on them as they started moving towards the entrance, and again his breath caught, knowing in mere seconds he would come face to face with her.

XXX   XXX

"Ready sweetheart?" Her father's voice came from behind her as his hand touched her shoulder. She was looking out at the sea of faces, wondering if there was anyone who would stand out to her eyes.

The entire day had been surreal.

She had arrived in the city that morning, the city she'd seen pictures of, seen in movies and was told about but couldn't remember. Even after her father had picked her up from the airport, and on the way in to the city pointed out things she should know, nothing stirred a memory or a recollection.

It was frustrating.

Her comfortable bubble of California was burst being out of her world, the place she had built around her.

But not knowing anything wasn't completely true, as she did remember a few things, and would dream at night about faces she didn't know. She would wake smiling, knowing she had been able to conjure up something to recall to herself.

She was only at this party because of her father; he wanted more than anything for her to be the daughter he missed. She knew that, years of being in the care of a psychologist had reaffirmed her damaged self. But her father had always been there, made every sacrifice to ensure she got better, so she saw this week on the East Coast as a small sacrifice back.

Letting him steer her with his hand cupping her elbow, they walked around the ballroom. The pillars hid people as she kept watching, like when you're staring too hard in to a fan, but the faces were different seen from different angles, and it was one, a man in a tuxedo watching her, that made her heart skip a couple of beats.

There were a few couples before them who were waiting in line to say hello to the woman in the wheelchair who screamed out familiarities to her and the man who was still watching her. She wished she knew their names without being told, could recall them on her own to show them she was as normal as anyone else in the room, because she knew from her brother who was speaking with their father, that the gala was being held by old family friends.

Feeling her palms get warm as she held that clutch, she turned to hear something her father was saying about the ballroom, its history, when a flash of something came to her. She closed her eyes for a second and turned away, looking towards the marble pillar beside her. "You okay honey?" her father's calming voice asked.
"I'm good." Even when she opened her eyes something else showed itself in her mind, and when she smiled her father thought it was for him, which she let him believe, but it was a memory or image which had made that emotion come to the surface.

Coming to the people greeting them, she stopped, feeling her father's hand on the small of her back. "Mrs. Johnson." She saw the shock in the older woman's face.
"How wonderful to see you, dear." Her hand she had held out to shake with the woman was now clasped between the two withered old hands. "It's been too long." Actually, she wasn't sure in years how long but she would certainly check on the actual figure once they were seated.

Moving on to the man who had been watching her, she held out her hand again. "Mr. Johnson." He took her hand but said nothing, just kept looking at her more intently, which unnerved her almost as much as how handsome he was.

CHAPTER FIVE

"Danni." Brad whispered as he held her hand. There was no way this was all imaginary now as he looked closely, trying to see if there was anything different on the grown-up face, but even with the light powder and mascara on her face, he could still see the bridge of freckles across her nose.

"It looks beautiful in here," he heard her say.
"Yes it is." She looked at him; she was still processing the use of Danni and not Danielle like everyone called her these days. It was far more familiar than she'd ever known. "Bradford." Her father's voice beside her made her take her hand back from the man the same age as herself, and stand to the side while they spoke. Her father hadn't stopped smiling since the airport, and even now he was joking and laughing. She took the moment to look around more. She caught sight of Peter and the woman who had looked at her as she imagined some would, as if she were a nutcase. Her brother was like a stranger also. Of course, he had come out to visit with their dad, but he was dealing with his own issues about everything that had happened in the past.

"We should take our seats, dinner will be served soon," Mrs. Johnson announced to them and to Brad's shock they were sitting all together at the main table. As they made their way through the other tables with Danni in front of her father, he knew the looks of wonder were the old friends trying to see if the rumors were true; was the damaged and crazy daughter back? The only spaces left were at the table where Peter and Felicity were cozy and laughing at something until they saw the six of them coming towards them. The look the couple shared before glancing up at the woman in front told Brad that the underlying emotions ran from Danni's presence and probably less from himself.

With his mother to his left, Maggie on his right, he was pleased to have Danni opposite. The centerpiece between them also allowed him to look at her unnoticed. She said little as the conversations flowed and her brother on one side of her didn't seem to want to encourage any type of conversation out of her. Ethan now and then would say something to her and she would smile sweetly, silently, and then take a sip of her glass of champagne. Someone should tell her the drinks were free, Brad thought, but he didn't want to say something that would have her admit something embarrassing about herself, if she couldn't drink because of medication or something.

Danni ate her food as if it was tasteless, because her other senses were on overdrive. She saw the looks as she took her seat, the leaning postures of couples whispering, wondering if she were the one they had heard about, the one who had been hidden from public almost like a distant great- aunt who had been locked up in a mental institute her entire life as she'd had a lobotomy; and thankfully she could say she had never been given one of those.

"How long are you staying dear?" Danni let her eyes focus on those around her and looked in the direction of Mrs. Johnson who had asked the question. "Just a week." She didn't know why her voice sounded so hoarse and quiet. She was known by her friends at work as the clown, the funny one who could make you smile when you were down. "And how are you enjoying it so far?"

"Everything's a little overwhelming." Brad just about heard her words. He tried hard not to but he was making mental notes of the Danni he knew at eighteen and the one now seventeen years later. She'd always been a quiet girl around their parents and adults, people she didn't know; but he remembered those times they went out, the bike rides in to town where they'd buy a soda from the drug store, and when they took their boogey boards out in to the always cold Atlantic Ocean; how he made her laugh by just a word, or some silly joke she made up.

He couldn't imagine what it would be like to lose all those wonderful memories, how to deal, knowing everyone sees something you don't like as an inside joke.

Danni was grateful when her father stepped in to talk to Mrs. Johnson. They had finished their aperitif and were waiting for the dessert and coffee. A waiter refilled her champagne and she was tempted to down it. She picked it up, planning on going through with it, except she had half of the flutes contents going down her throat when her eyes connected to Brad's again. Letting the glass sit in her hand she smiled to him as she felt the blush rise up her cheeks.

Brad had seen her embarrassment and smiled himself. He picked his own glass up and held it up in a salute to her. Unlike her, he did down the entire glassful, noticing a few of the people around the table had seen the wordless communication. Then as their attention, but not his, left Danni, she also finished the last drop.

That earned her a wider smile.

Once the coffee was being served people began milling around, and a few had gone to the dance floor to dance to the music still being played by the small orchestra. Peter had taken Felicity up, and the opening at the table was used by one of the men Ethan worked closely with down on Wall Street. Stuck in the middle Danni looked lost, bored and confused and he wished he could take her somewhere, get her away from whatever it was she was thinking. "I think you should ask her to dance." His mother whispered.
"I don't dance mother." He turned his head sideways so no one at the table could hear or lip read. "Not even to keep that smile on her face? I've seen how the two of you have been eyeing each other all through dinner."
"I still don't dance."
"I'm not asking you to do a line dance. Just take her out there and hold her, move around the floor and get a chance to speak with her a little."

"You're pushing; this must have been the thing I suspected you had planned."

"Nonsense." She scoffed. "I had nothing planned about anything."

"Of course not."

"Look, I'd ask except I'm a woman and in a wheelchair."

"Smooth." Brad shook his head laughing slightly.

Looking up to see her looking back, made any other argument stick in his throat.

"Danni, would you like to dance?" he asked across the table, and her movements stopped as her eyes widened. "I err...." She paused, looking towards the dancing people behind her. "I don't dance."

"Good, neither do I." He wasn't going to have his mother bug him, but she was right: a chance to hold her and talk to her was appealing. "Oh, okay." She remained in her seat until he walked around to her side and held out his hand for her. The shawl had been placed over the back of her seat, and her clutch was left on the table next to her father. So when she took his strong hand she had to remember she didn't have them.

Being walked to the dance floor Danni let herself relax a little; she wasn't sure why, but the man exuded something which put her at ease. Once on the wooden floor he gently took her in his arms. One hand on her waist, the other holding her hand, while her spare hand she placed on one of the wide shoulders hidden by the tuxedo.

"You've been watching me all night," she said in their privacy.

"You've been watching me." He countered, copying that smile.

"I've been searching you for any changes from the boy who gave me my first real kiss."

"You remember that?" He frowned slightly and then regretted it when she avoided his eyes slightly.

"Forget the boy who also introduced me to sex as well?" Another blush rose in to her cheeks.

"It's just earlier you called me Mr. Johnson." He tried hard to explain without insulting her somehow. "To be honest I didn't put two and two together until we came face to face. I've had your image in my head a very long time."

"You never asked anyone?"

"What would you have asked? Dad, who was the boy I kissed so passionately my feet felt like they hovered, and when we were on the beach naked. Well, that's not something I feel comfortable asking my father about."

"I see your dilemma." He laughed.

"I have a lot of images of you in my head. I guess we were friends."

"For a long time we were best friends, but we only saw each other during the summer until we were older and went to the same high school for a year."

"Were we in love?"

"Our parents wanted us to marry." Once the words left his mouth he wished he'd kept some things to himself, still not sure what care he should use when telling her stuff.

"Wow, we must have been." She looked thoughtful and he leant in slightly closing the few inches separating them. "We both joked we would only agree to keep them off our backs. I was leaving for college and you, well there were things you wanted to do."

"Like what?"

"You wanted to live in Paris for a year."

"Whatever for?" Her frown was deep as she looked at him like the idea of frivolous trips to Paris was stupid, as if her life was filled with more meaningful things these days. "Something to do with shopping and acting."

"I sounded shallow?"

"No, you were just young and idealistic."

"Can I ask you a personal question?" she asked him.

"Of course."

"Why, if we were friends and in love like you say; then why haven't I met you before in all this time?"

"Good question." He started thinking leaving a silence as she watched him, and he had just figured out how to explain when he heard. "Do you mind Brad if I cut in?" It was her father, and he graciously handed her over to him. He stepped back as she gave him another look, and then he returned to the table. His mother was speaking to a woman at the table behind, Daisy was missing and Maggie was speaking with Felicity while Peter could be spotted over at the bar.

"That was a beautiful sight." Maggie told him.

"It's so good of you to be seen with her." Felicity said. "Poor thing has less marbles than a kindergarten playground."

"Felicity!" Brad said, shocked at Danni's future sister-in-law.

"Well it's true, you know she freaks her brother out so much. We had to make excuses to leave before them tonight, so we didn't have to share a limo."

"How does she freak him out?"

"The way she acts; as if she's not all there and has no clue what any of us are saying."

"Maybe she's just bored with what she's hearing." Maggie spoke up and Felicity's perfectly plucked eyebrows rose. "She's severely brain damaged. Come on Brad, you must see the differences more than any of us."

"I don't see any differences outside of age."

"Don't tell me you still think she's the one?"

"Danni's a beautiful woman," was all he replied, using his need for a swallow of champagne to hide any more.

"Did I hear you speaking about my sister like you still want to do her?" A drunken Peter pulled his seat out and sat back down. "I don't think that's appropriate conversation to be sharing with a room full of people," Brad heard himself say.

"Do yourself a favor and get a woman who can actually remember your name in the morning." Peter started laughing loudly. "From what I hear though, most women you bed aren't the kind who stick around till morning."

"Peter Morgan." Brad heard his mother's voice. "Felicity, do yourself and Peter a big favor and get him a coffee. There are two of the three column writers from the New York Times behind you. I'm sure no one wants any rumors hitting the morning edition of the Times."

"He's just telling the truth Mrs. Johnson." Felicity said loud enough that the returning Ethan and Danni heard. "Telling the truth about what?" Ethan asked, and Danni looked to her brother and the woman she really didn't like meeting. She knew the discussion had been about her, the undercurrents of tension had been boiling all evening. The fact they'd come separately had been a big 'flashing in your face' neon sign too.

She knew exactly what the score was, and she'd gone to the stupid gala for her father anyway.

"You know father, I should go. There's those ten psychotic drugs I have to drown myself in before eleven, or I turn back in to a revival of 'One flew over the cuckoo's nest'." She picked up her purse and shawl as she tried to avoid looking at anyone's face. She'd basically just shut them all up with her sentence, shoved it up the end where sun rarely shone, and from the sudden dip in conversation, not only from their table but the others around them, she knew they'd understood very well. "It was nice seeing you both again." She spoke to Mrs. Johnson and Brad who was getting up. He felt guilty even though he had defended her. Both Peter and Felicity looked embarrassed, and they certainly should. "Why don't we go for a walk?" Brad suggested, walking around to her. He gently took her elbow inside his cupped hand again, and they walked to the nearest space between the marble columns. He had to disconnect the rope keeping people from using it, but once through he directed her this time in the direction of the bar.

"This isn't the direction I was thinking about heading." She stopped in the entrance; the main exit for the hotel was to their left through the hotel lobby, the gala patrons still encapsulated behind them in the ballroom. "You really want to go home?"
"Pretty hard when this city isn't my home." She looked from him to the exit she felt like fleeing to, and then back. "LA is your home?"
"You sound shocked by that."
"You once loved this city."
"If you hadn't heard, I'm not the same girl you keep referring to." She gently left his hold and put some space between them. "I know what Peter and that woman said. I know what the truth is. I'm an embarrassment to my family." Brad watched as she tried so hard to hold back the tears collecting in her eyes. Their blue hue distorted but shimmered from the moisture and only one escaped not ruining any of the make-up which had been delicately applied.

"You aren't an embarrassment." He said softly.
"I know I am, I'm a freak, I'm the one who has to be told who people are, the one who has been shut away for fear someone might find out how damaged I am." She turned her back to him. "I thank you for leaving

there with me, for your support, kindness but I'm just going to hail a cab and go back to my father's. You should go back in there before I ruin whatever image that handsome face has earned you."

"Danni." He said wishing the words to tell her, stop her, would come to him. The last thing he wanted was for her to leave. "Your girlfriend is very lucky Bradford Johnson." On an impulsive move, Danni turned back and on tip-toes kissed his cheek lightly. "Cherish her."

CHAPTER SIX

He stood there watching her as she walked down the main staircase to the doors. All the men she passed stopped to look at her and who wouldn't? Danni, whatever she thought about herself, she was a knockout. At seventeen he'd lusted for her with all of his adolescent hormones, he'd been besotted beyond reason half the time and the other half he'd been even more so.

"You couldn't make her stay?" Ethan's voice made him snap back.

"She was determined to leave."

"I had a feeling she may freak out by some look or comment but I had hoped neither would happen."

"It can't help her that it came from her own brother."

"No, I doubt it can."

"I've never felt it appropriate to ask, like it was none of my business but how bad is she these days?" Brad stood there waiting for the man who was like a second father; one he didn't see often or in a long time but Ethan and his father had been so similar.

"Danielle is healthy, strong and aside from having the first seventeen years of her life erased by the accident she doesn't have any problems."

"So, she doesn't have spells or problems with her memory?"

"No, only the memories before the accident are missing Brad."

"Then why does Peter act as if there is a problem?"

"Peter I think is just a little jealous of the attention I give his sister."

"He sounds a lot more than jealous."

"I gave him and Felicity a piece of my mind." Ethan sighed. "I'm going to leave and make sure she gets in okay." He held out his hand. "It was good to see you Brad and thank you for being kind to Danni."

"I should have made an effort years ago; I suppose I'm guilty of that."

"You have nothing to be guilty about. Your dad would have been proud tonight."

With Ethan retreating also Brad walked back to the gala, there were toasts going on and he took his seat as inconspicuously as possible.

The speeches ended and the conversations picked up. Noticeably both Peter and Felicity looked completely scolded and they should. Maggie had flagged down a waiter, and there was a new glass of champagne put before him. He gave her a small smile as thanks she rubbed the top of his arm in that fashion she did when she knew he was probably thinking a lot more than he should. The woman was like a second mother, knowing him too well.

"Can we all go home in the same limo?" His mother asked.

"Sure; you feeling okay?"

"Of course honey, it's just after the nastiness of those two." She nodded to the two across the table. "I want to be able to hold your hand on the way home."

"Always." Brad rubbed her back.

"It was very nice you went with Danielle."
"I was just doing the right thing."
"You are a wonderful man just like your father."
"Nah." He smiled. "Dad was one in a million."
"And you aren't much different."

Once their duties as hosts were completed and everyone was done, he wheeled his mother out to where the limo had been waiting; and theirs pulled up, Charlie coming around to help with his mother, who insisted on sitting on the leather seats and not her chair in a special limo. Both Maggie and Daisy were inside too, and it was Daisy, the normally quiet one, who said. "I wanted to strangle that ungrateful brat." The three of them looked at Daisy. "I liked him when he was little; there was always something special and innocent in his little eyes, but he's grown into a real son of a." Her words stopped as she realized what she was saying. "I agree." Brad listened to his mother continue as he did what he promised and she sat wrapped in his arm holding his other hand. "What a way to be made to feel." Even Maggie stepped in. "You did the same thing your dad would have done." She gave him that look from the side facing seat where she sat beside Daisy. "Let's hope it was the alcohol speaking more than his real feelings." Brad rolled his neck a little.

Maggie was dropped off first, Charlie then drove over to his mother's penthouse and he went up with her, Daisy making sure they got in okay. After a kiss on his mother's cheek he went back down to Charlie and within ten minutes, a little after eleven–thirty he walked back inside his house. Closing the door, he decided on a scotch before bed.

He had taken his bowtie off, stuffed it inside the jacket pocket and then hung the heavy black fabric over the bottom curve of the railing.

In the kitchen, scotch in hand, he leant his elbows on the counter and replayed everything from that night, the parts with Danni anyway.

"I know I'm a freak, I'm the one who has to be told who people are, the one who has been shut away for fear someone might find out how damaged I am. I thank you for leaving there with me, for your support, kindness; but I'm just going to hail a cab and go back to my father's. You should go back in there before I ruin whatever image that handsome face has earned you."

He certainly thought she was wrong labeling herself that way. He would have protected her tonight with every fiber of his being. No one deserved the way Peter had been talking, and he certainly didn't have an image to uphold, because, like her he had been missing for some years while he served in the Navy. But then, people openly knew about his military career and commended him on that.

"Your girlfriend is very lucky Bradford Johnson, cherish her."

Now why hadn't he told her there was no one?

XXX   XXX

"Danielle." Ethan shouted as he entered the Brownstone he had bought ten years before. It faced the Washington Square Park on the North side, a nice neighborhood, and in warmer days a perfect place to live and walk to his office down on Wall Street. Peter had lived there in his own apartment in the basement studio which now was rented out to a college student. But his daughter had never lived there. This had never been a home for her, but there was a room especially for her on the top floor.

"I'm just cleaning up." He heard her shout, and he began climbing the stairs wanting to get out of his own penguin suit. "How about we have some hot chocolate after I change?" He called back. "Sure." He went in to his room on the first floor, and was just leaving, wearing jeans and a sweater when he caught up with Danni coming back down the stairs, a robe over her pajamas, her hair in a ponytail, and her face free of make-up.

"I'm sorry about Peter and Felicity." He apologized, as they reached the main floor turning to head towards the kitchen. "Don't worry about it."
"He had no right to say anything."
"Then he should be grateful I don't have a memory of him being any more than what you tell me, my brother."
"Half-brother."

"Right." Danni took a seat at the counter, knowing her father when she was working through who everyone was after the coma had explained that his first wife, her real mother, had died in child-birth. Theresa Morgan had been her step-mother; the only one she had and even that woman was still a mystery to her, like the one who gave birth to her. How hard it must have been for her father losing both wives and then almost losing her. In a way he still had, because she didn't recall the little things which made him a father, was he always around, was she a daddy's girl?

"Did you have any fun tonight?" Ethan set the mugs of milk in the microwave and turned to her. "Getting dressed up and pampered wasn't so bad, though I don't know where I'll wear a dress like that again."
"Never say never."
"Yeah, I can see me wearing that in LA."
"How about the people, did anyone stand out to you?"
"Are you asking if I remember anyone?"
"Slyly, wasn't so subtle, huh?"
"No." She laughed and she liked that he smiled.
"There were many faces that seemed familiar, a few people I recall."
"Like?"
"I know Brad and I were good friends when we were young."
"Yes, you were." God, he looked happy she knew that, she thought to herself.

"I'm guessing without going into detail, you know how close we were to each other."

"I certainly don't need that." With those words, he turned his back to the sound of the microwave calling. He passed one of the mugs to her, and the Hershey syrup and a spoon. "He got very handsome with time."

"Do you know we all planned on you two getting married?"

"No, but Brad said supposedly we were going along with your plan, but really we were going to do separate things."

"He was off to Annapolis."

"The Naval academy?" She pictured the movie she had seen a few weeks ago. Set to cadets in that very school. The lead male was, of course thoroughly handsome and swoon worthy…

Just like how Brad had looked in that tuxedo.

"Yeah, you had another year of high school and wanted to go to Paris very badly." Thankfully her dad's words returned her from her wandering mind. "To shop?" She asked as she stirred the hot chocolate mixing in the syrup. "And for school."

"What did I want to be?" Though Brad had told her she wanted to see if her father had been aware of this dream or desire because no one had told her she had dreamed of something different in life. "A movie star."

"That's what Brad said." Danni laughed. "Was I really?" She had picked up her mug, but lowered it in shock. "It's all you talked about."

"How was I going to do that?" She had to ask seeing as she lived in LA, the birthplace of Hollywood and in the years since living there, being notorious and famous had meant nothing to her. "NYU drama degree."

"How come you never told me that?"

"What you do with your life is up to you, your decision, and I wasn't sure if you'd want to anymore."

"Obviously I didn't." Danni blew a little on the drink in her hands. "And Brad went to Annapolis?"

"Worked through the academy and came out and served eleven years."

"And now he works his father's company?"

"When John Johnson got sick it was a hard time for both Brad, and Louise."

"What kind of a man was he?"

"Not much different from me, we were good friends too."

"How come Mrs. Johnson's in a wheelchair?"

"Drunk driving accident."

"Did the culprit go to jail for it?"

"No, Louise did it to herself."

"Why?" That got more shock from her.

"She got pissed off at John one night when they were first married, not long after Brad was born. She drove off drunk, and ended up crashing into a tree."

"How long have you known them?"

"All my life, John and I went to school together and Louise was a few years younger than us."

"Sounds like two old friends were trying to set their children up."

"We never needed to set you up; the two of you did everything without us having to get involved."

"You were planning on me marrying him."

"Because we all figured you and he would."

"Why didn't he ever visit me in hospital? I mean, if he loved me, and you guys thought we'd get married, shouldn't he have come to see me?"

"Brad did, the first day you were in Boston." Ethan hated bringing this up; his daughter had always had a lot of questions on the subject, so for her he revisited it, but unwillingly. "You didn't look like you, he got upset, the doctor's prognosis wasn't good and he left. He went to the academy early."

"But I got better, I woke up."

"Danni." He reached and took her hand in his. "He had to get on with his life; he was a successful Navy commander who I haven't spoken to in years. I don't know the answer to that question; only he does."

"I tried asking him but he didn't answer."

"You know how hard this was on all of us; just remember it was hard on him too."

"You know dad, I think I'm going to take this up to my room. I wanted to call Sam and see how everything is." She got up as her father came around, kissing the top of her head. She knew her father had taken the week off, it was Wednesday and she was going back the following Tuesday. "What are we doing tomorrow?"

"I got tickets to see Hamilton up on Broadway."

"That's supposed to be phenomenal."

"So I heard. If it's okay with you, Louise asked if we'd like to join her for dinner Friday night."

"Are we going to see the Empire State Building and the statue of liberty?"

"Yes."

"Okay, I'll agree."

CHAPTER SEVEN

Thursday was like a whirlwind of meetings and calls, and he didn't get a chance to stop until Maggie appeared at his office door, holding some papers, watching him. She'd been overseeing the final signing of the last papers making their company the proud owners of Cooper publishing. Cindy had been covering her desk, and normally there was at least one thing the younger woman would do, which would irritate him during the course of the day, but with all he'd been doing he'd hardly noticed her.

Brad had left the office and gone straight to a dinner meeting with Anderson, a celebration of sorts for the man's retirement and the acquisition. He had no worthy heirs to continue the business which his own grandfather had started, and to him, having Brad take the company was as good as any heir.

Friday his load was lighter but not by much. He had a mountain of correspondence to have typed up which Maggie delegated to Cindy, so that she could help Brad with the calls and notes for other interests. By noon he was so ready to leave for the weekend and never come back, at least for a week anyway.

"Your mother called while you were on with Ricardo. She wanted to know if dinner could be at your place; something about the ovens on the fritz again or something. She said she ordered from Sal's and you can eat around seven."
"Let her know that's fine with me."

"Also, your friend from San Diego called again."

"Coop?"

"Wanted to have me remind you that just because you head some fancy family business, you still have a duty to appear at special occasions. He said if me telling you that didn't work, then he would just find a way to pull some strings and have you officially recalled to active duty." Maggie noted, even though he was looking down at papers before him, the smile on his face got much wider.

"I'll call him when I get home."

"So, yes to your mother, and I should call and tell Coop to recall you?"

"Just the call to my mother Maggie."

"Yes boss." She turned to make those calls from her desk.

"Maggie." He stopped her by saying her name. "When you've returned my mother's call could you come back in I have something I'd like to ask you."

"Sounds intriguing, I'll be right back."

Maggie appeared at his doorway a few minutes later and he'd heard the one-sided conversation. So when the call had ended he had signed the last file and closed it, knowing unless Maggie was a sadist then he was done for the week. "So, what did you want to ask me?"

"I've been trying to find someone I trust to step into Anderson's seat on Monday; he's so excited about being officially retired. I'm having each of our department heads go over there next week and start looking through their files, to see if we can make any needed changes. Then we must decide where we go from there. But I need someone to head the operation until I can find a permanent face for Cooper publishing."

"Who do you have in mind?"

"You."

"Me?" Maggie was shocked.

"I trust you immensely Maggie. I know you stayed with my father out of loyalty and you passed up a great number of jobs much better and higher up because of that. I also understand you feel this need to be by my side to ensure no one picks a fight over any mistakes I make. But, dear Maggie." He smiled at her. "You deserve more; you deserve to finish out your working career in a job whose title will impress those neighbors of yours over in Brooklyn."

"I don't know what to say."

"Just say yes."

"But who will be your assistant? Stand in front of you when the bullets start flying?"

"Cindy, she is less than a quarter of you, but we'll survive. You can take the position as a month deal if you want. Come back anytime if you hate it, but I doubt you will, seeing as really I'll still be your boss."

"Are you sure Brad?" The shock was still written all over her face, and it kept Brad smiling. "More sure than anything Maggie."

"Then I accept." She stood up and held her hand out to him across the desk, as a shake the gentleman way.

"Then Monday we'll meet over at Cooper's office and get you started with the team. Do me a favor before you leave today, ensure the team knows via e-mail eight a.m. sharp."

"This means a lot to me Brad."

"Good, it means a lot that you took it too."

"And I'll still stand in front of you at the board of directors' meeting next week and take all those bullets."

"That means even more." He laughed to her back hearing her laugh as well.

A little while later he left. Charlie as always waiting at the main door, and they drove up-town and for the first time since the night of the gala he was able to relax and let his mind go back to seeing Danni. He wondered where she was, what she was doing, and if he should call to talk about the past and explain why he had never gone to see her.

But she led a different life, three thousand miles away, and there was also she could call him anytime if she really wanted to talk.

Once alone in his house he was out of his suit and in a hot shower before anything else. He dressed in track-pants, black with the white side seam stripe. They were good for the gym wearing shorts underneath, and being able to rip them off with ease with the snappers on the side. But today it was all about relaxability and comfort. He threw on a black t-shirt and with his hair still wet and uncombed he went downstairs taking a beer from his fridge, and finding his cell before taking a well-deserved break on the overstuffed couch in the living room.

He dialed a number without really paying attention, knowing the number by heart. He'd known the number for the last thirteen years and probably wouldn't forget it anytime soon. "Cooper." He heard his bud say when the call connected.

"Hey Coop," he said.

"Johnson, how are you?"

"Finally taking a moment to breathe, you?"

"Just hanging out in the air-conditioned confines of my office."

"So both of our days pretty much suck then, huh?" He joked.

"Only as much as we let it." Coop returned the joke.

"So, I only called because we're having a retirement party next weekend for the Senior Chief. I know he'd love to see you, so would the team."

"I'll have to ask Maggie to check. Is it on a Saturday?"

"As long as the team aren't called up, sure."

"On base?"

"At Max's."

"He still in the same place off Terra Nova drive?"

"Same place."

"Then I'll try and get out."

"Good, so tell me about the woman whose face shares a column space with you in the New York Times buddy." Brad knew which picture he meant; the day after the gala Maggie had placed the open society column on his desk. Someone had taken a picture of Danni and him dancing together. The caption was a basic who he was, who she was. He'd smiled seeing it but at the same time it held way too much in meaning; if they'd stayed together, if the accident had never happened then their picture could have been in there announcing something more important.

"That was Danielle Morgan."
"The Danni?" Coop asked having known him since Annapolis. They'd gone through the four years at the academy together and then to the training station in San Diego for the Navy's most elite of positions and teams. They'd endured Hell week together and later, after becoming the most coveted Naval warriors, had served on the same team before Brad had been transferred to a different team on base, and then later, especially after nine-eleven, he had been working with different teams, different fractions of the US militaries and sometimes doing missions alone.

"Yeah, the Danni."
"You looked pretty happy to see her in the picture."
"Oh, I was, probably more than I should have."
"What does that mean?" Letting out a sigh he rested the open bottle of beer on his leg, his feet up on the coffee table. "It was really good to see her, therapeutic almost."
"You always talked about her in the past like she was always with you man."
"I think I always carried a part of her with me."
"Have you seen her outside of this gala?"
"Nah, she didn't stay long either thanks to her brother's cruelty, and it wasn't a good time to suggest we hang out and catch up."
"How long she staying in New York?"

"I couldn't tell you."

"She still living in LA?"

"Supposedly."

"What does she do?"

"I have no idea."

"And why haven't you just called and asked her out to dinner or something?"

"Because she probably has a life that has grown past me."

"You never know until you ask." There was noise from Coop's end of the line. "I'll have to catch up later. PT is just about to start."

"I'll let you know if I can make it Coop."

"Good enough for me, later."

Hanging up he knew he had a few hours until his mother would arrive. With the dinner arriving at seven meant his mother would arrive probably around five to spend a few hours with him. He had nowhere else to be and after Peter's scathing words about his reputation for bedding women without a need for a second date, he wasn't heading anywhere to continue that cycle of disaster.

Downing his beer, he decided on an hour on the streets through Central Park, and then an hour of cardio in the basement, he didn't get enough time to keep as in shape as he had been at twenty-two, but he hadn't let himself go just yet.

Grabbing his fleece vest, and gloves, he tied his sneakers and grabbed his iPhone before leaving, knowing if he were running late it wouldn't matter; it was only his mother coming, and she wouldn't care if he was wearing sweats or if he'd even showered.

CHAPTER EIGHT

Waking up from a peaceful nap after a morning of seeing the sights, Danni went downstairs ready to go only to see her father leaving his office carrying his keys, and a jacket over his arm.

"Where are you going?" She asked.
"I have to run to the office to sign something, could you meet me at Louise's?"
"If you give me the address."
"Sorry, I forgot." He returned to his office scribbling on a pad as she watched him. He carried over the address. "It's just you used to well, you know."
"Don't apologize. None of this is your fault dad."
"I know but I still forget."
"So do I sometimes, but not since coming back to New York."

"Would you like me to cancel dinner with Peter tomorrow night?"
"Wouldn't that be rude?"
"No." He said bluntly.
"Are you sure?"
"I doubt very much after what I said to Peter and Felicity at the Gala that they are in a rush to dine with us either."
"I'll leave the decision up to you. In some ways, maybe Peter just needs to see I'm not a drooling vegetable, to stop whatever it is going on with him."
"We'll decide tomorrow then."
"Okay, well, get going and I'll meet you there."

"Oh, take the wine on the counter in the kitchen, and the cheesecake is in the fridge."

"I know dad." She laughed as he left, kissing her cheek on his way past.

Making sure she had her purse and then putting on her leather jacket, she got the dessert and wine and made her way out the door, only to see an envelope on the floor in the hall. She thought it odd her dad missing it, he'd been gone mere minutes. She picked it up while balancing her packages, and saw her name printed on the front. Frowning to herself, she left the house, locking the door behind her, and down the steps to the street, where a constant stream of cabs always went by. It took only a raised hand to hail the familiar yellow cab. Once inside, she told the driver the address, and relaxed, taking the envelope and opening it.

'You should have stayed away'.

The sentence made the hair on the back of her neck stand on end.

Shaking it off she pushed the card and envelope into her purse and tried to ignore the nauseous feeling now churning in her stomach. Leaning back and looking out the window as the street numbers climbed, and they traveled east more, the driver was skilled in the art of New York City streets and the one way uptown, downtown, across town layout.

Danni was in another world when the cab stopped.

Paying the fare, she ensured all the packages were secure in her hands, and climbed out on to the curb. She double-checked the door number and made her way up the steps to a house which looked only slightly different from her father's. Another brownstone in a city of apartments, skyscrapers and hundreds upon hundreds of houses all called brownstones.

Ringing the bell, she could see the light coming from inside. The sun had started to set when she left, and by now it was almost completely hidden by the surrounding buildings. She could see the shadow of a figure coming to the door, and it never occurred to her that the figure was masculine and not the one she should have expected after meeting Daisy and Mrs. Johnson a couple of nights before.

The door swung open and she wanted to say something but couldn't.

"Danni." Brad said seeing the woman he had been thinking about for most of the afternoon. He was running behind like he knew he would be, and he'd just come up from the gym when the doorbell had chimed. "I'm suddenly getting the feeling neither my father nor your mother will be joining us."
"Where's your dad?" He folded his arms across his chest, and she gulped silently at how strong that chest had become. "Told me he had to go sign papers and to come on without him."

"And my mother asked to have dinner here at my place instead of hers because her oven broke."

"Sneaky bastards."

"Very sneaky."

"Well, if this is too weird."

"What's in the box?"

"Cheesecake."

"Very sneaky." He gave her a wink.

"You should have it."

"Not that I want to abuse whatever reason they tried to get us to have dinner together but how about you come in, dinner will be here soon and you can help me eat that."

"Are you sure?"

"We're friends, right?" He asked, relaxing his arms and stepping back to allow her to move in the hall.

"Are we friends?" She stopped inside taking in the richness of the wood on the floor, the obviously sculptured railing on the stairs and the black iron chandelier casting light in the entryway. "I like to think we are." He took the box and the bottle of wine from her so she could remove her jacket and in a split instant he wished she hadn't. Underneath was a low cut black tank top covered by a thin white shirt. There were things about her body he would never forget, but she'd never had a chest so well developed the last time he'd seen her naked, and it seemed to strain against the dark fabric.

Once she handed over her jacket and he hung it on a hook next to his own, he led her towards the kitchen. "You have a nice place." She commented, playing with the short straps of her purse. "Thanks, my dad had it renovated while I was stationed out west. When I came home when he got sick, I lived with them for a while before I moved in and took over the business." "You don't miss the Navy?" She waited for him to put the dessert into the fridge, and his head popped back to look at her while the door remained open, letting the cool air out. "Beer?"

"Sure." She put her purse on the marble counter. He opened the two beers as the door closed on its own. "Here." He held it out, and as she wrapped her fingers around one their skin made contact and she almost jumped. Silly, seeing as he had held her as they danced two nights before.

"And yes, I do."
"Sorry what?" She tried to recover.
"I do miss the Navy."
"Where were you stationed?"
"San Diego was the first base after Annapolis and then I've lived all over the world pretty much."
"San Diego isn't far from me, closer than from here." Brad knew she was fishing to that question she had asked while they danced. "I know."
"Would you explain everything to me then Brad?"
"About me not seeing you before now, when we were friends?" He repeated her question, his thought in hopes he could stall but even he was smart enough to know he couldn't get out of this with her right there before him.

"You know, I should take a shower." He put his beer beside her purse; he was standing four feet before her.

73

"Smooth." She looked down at the beer in her hands. "There's a reason you won't explain it to me isn't there."

"Yes, there is."

"Whatever it is I want to know Brad."

"Then make yourself comfortable in the living room while I go shower, and when I come back I promise I'll tell you."

"Fine." She looked up at him. "But just remember my temporal lobe may have been damaged and erased my childhood memories, but my short-term memory is super strong now."

"Noted." He gave her a grin, and an eyebrow rose as he walked past.

While she waited, she walked around the living room, looking at the pictures in the frames on the floating shelves and mantel. It was clear to see that he loved his parents as much as they loved him. Seeing his father made something connect in her mind, until she came to a picture that she had to pick up to get a closer look; both of their families together, the ocean in the background and the sun on the horizon. She had to be around sixteen, and she was sitting beside Brad who looked how she remembered him.

XXX   XXX

While in the shower he had tried hard to phrase in his own head how he was going to tell her what had happened the week leading up to the accident, and why he had seen her that one time in the hospital, and never gone back.

Throwing on a pair of blue jeans and a sweater, he pushed his fingers through his hair, and padded down in bare feet to the first floor where he found Danni on the couch in the living room, looking up at the ceiling, her neck comfortably held by the back of the cushions. "Sorry if you were bored." He apologized. "It's okay." She kept her head resting back but those blue eyes connected with his. "I saw the picture over there from when we were young."

"That was taken the summer before the accident."

"I know."

"Need a new beer?" He asked, noting it was almost six; the food would be there in an hour. "I'm good."

A quick trip to the kitchen and he returned with his cold bottle and sat comfortable a body's width from her on the couch. He watched as she moved to sit sideways and the look on her face. He knew he'd promised, but he had avoided this for seventeen years.

"So, I'm guessing this recollection either has me being some sort of snotty brat, or you as a male pig, because there has to be a reason you are trying hard to not tell me anything."

"I've felt guilty since you woke up, I've known I should see you, but to begin with I let the coma then your rehab keep me away, and after that I ran out of excuses and I'm sorry." He started.

"I'm told the prognosis was grim the day after the accident. Seeing a potential future wife or girlfriend like that can't be easy."

"It wasn't."

"Tell me Brad." She reached out and touched the hand on the arm he had resting along the back of the couch between their two bodies.

"The weekend before the accident we had an argument."
"About?"
"I had my first cadet orientation. It was from Thursday to Tuesday, and both my parents intended to go down with me, except you got really pissed off about me going."
"I think I know why."
"You remember?"
"No, the weekend before the accident was my birthday."
"You were having this huge party; your parents were staying in the city over night with your brother, and letting you have run of the house and beach. You wanted me there, and we argued about it, I felt bad and the Wednesday night I climbed through your window to give you your gift in person, early. You didn't want to see me and we argued a little, but you couldn't stay mad at me for long."
"Why?"
"I know where you're ticklish."
"Do you?"
"Want me to demonstrate?" He leaned to put his beer on the coffee table but her words stopped him.
"Maybe after you finish, keep going."

"We, uh." He took a sip of beer.
"We what?"
"Before I left that night we...." Again, he stopped.

"Had sex?" She asked trying to help.

"Yeah, it wasn't like it was the first time or that our parents didn't know; your dad told me once he knew I used to sneak in your room at night and you in mine."

"And our parents didn't mind?"

"We were in love."

"So you tell me." She laughed a little.

"What?"

"Just keep going."

"Okay, so that Thursday I left for Annapolis, I called Friday morning, and you sounded pissed and too busy to speak. So I didn't call Saturday, which I would have had a hard time doing anyway, because we had drills to learn."

"And I'm guessing I had my party still?"

"Of course, it had been the talk of all our summer friends, most of which we went to school with. Thanks to our friendship there had been nearly a hundred kids there, some from your year, some from mine. I came back Tuesday lunchtime and I knew you were still pissed at me."

"How did you know that?"

"You didn't come over, call, or do what you normally did, which was leave me something in my room."

"Dare I ask what I would leave?"

"A little note or a shell on my bed.

"Sounds cheesy and sweet."

"I guess a little but I liked it."

"Did we talk before I left for Hyannis?"

"I snuck over to see you that Tuesday night."

"And?"

"I found you in your room in tears."

Engrossed in his words she felt her forehead crease with his words. "I was crying over?"

"Your party."

"You said people showed up so what was so bad?"

"Well, there had been some seniors who had managed to get some kegs and you got drunk."

"Drunk?"

"You were never able to hold your alcohol."

"We drank underage a lot?"

"A few times; when you were fifteen we stole a bottle of tequila from my house and did shots on the beach. You swore you wouldn't ever touch liquor again, but you did a few times."

"And at my party?"

"You told me you drank more because you wanted me there."

"Please don't tell me I did something stupid while drunk, if that's where you're going with this."

"Okay I won't." Brad swallowed some more of his beer and of course not speaking because what more could he say, she herself had said 'don't tell me'.

"I did, didn't I?"

"You sure did." He didn't want to tell her, see that look on her face like he'd seen before. "Do you remember the name Colin Jenkins?"

"No why?"

"Well, if you meet him while you're here in New York, and he acts odd with you, then don't freak out."

"What?" She wanted to shout but kept her voice level. "What does some guy have to do with a drunken night when...." She stopped mid-sentence. "Please don't tell me what I just imagined is true."

"Now that depends on whether your imagination is as good as it used to be."

"I have a wonderful imagination." She had meant the now 'her' did.

"Then yeah, it's true."

"I had sex with this Colin?"

"You sure did." He took the last swallow of his beer, glad for the break in eye contact because he couldn't do it, looking at the same eyes that had told him years ago.

"I'm so sorry Brad." He felt her touch his arm.

"That's why you were in tears when I found you. You didn't want to see me because you felt guilty and bad, and I gave you credit, you told me to dump you, get on with my life with someone who deserved me and could love me without acting like a brat when she didn't get her way, and honestly, I was mad, hurt, pissed off because of all the people in my life you were the one, the only one I trusted with more than my heart."

"I would have hated me."

"I couldn't."

"Why?"

"Because Danni, you were the center of my universe and well, I could forgive you."

"You are a better man than some."

"Is that speaking from experience? Did you cheat on some other boyfriend?" He tried to joke but his voice hadn't changed from that tight sound he made when his lips moved. "No." Danni shook her head, feeling sick with herself. "While we're on the subject, is there a boyfriend now?"

"No."

"You're kidding?" That changed the tightness in his vocal chords.

"No, I'm so busy working, still trying to find my footing in the world. What about you, girlfriends?"

"None either, same reason as you, this job keeps me tied to it."

"So, you forgave me?"

"Yes, I did and the following Friday you left with your parents and Peter to sail up to Hyannis."

"When did you hear about the accident?"

"I was just coming in from a run, Daisy was cooking dinner and my mother was playing the piano in the sun room. Dad had just pulled in to the driveway that Saturday after eighteen holes, and the house phone rang. I got it and it was your uncle Teddy. I knew from his voice there was something, and he wasted no time on small talk, asking for my dad. He was coming in through the mud room and I gave him the call. He stood there talking, words that stuck me to the spot, when he looked at me I knew something bad had happened."

"That must have been horrid."

"I don't remember how but we got to the Gabreski airport, took our old private jet up to Boston and went straight to the hospital. Your Dad was there, and Peter with his arm in a sling." Brad stopped speaking and pushed himself up off the couch. "I need another." He began walking to the kitchen, and once there he leant his hands on the counter and lowered his head. He felt sick, he felt every single emotion from that Saturday night tumbling around his gut and seeping north towards his throat.

"Brad." He kept his head down, hearing her behind him. "No one's ever told me much about the time I was unconscious, and though I want to know if it's too hard, then...." The words died before she could continue, from the look on that strong face. "The moment that call came, and then being inside the hospital, is surreal still; your dad using big words and terms and nothing sounded even close to good. You were in a coma; your doctors didn't think you'd survive because of your brain swelling so much. If you did make it, you'd never be the same girl I'd known." He stood up, but closed his eyes. "Your dad said I could go in to the intensive care room you were in. Say goodbye or whatever. My mind couldn't believe it was you lying in that bed. Your entire head, apart from your eyes, which were taped shut, was covered by bandages. Your eyelids were bruised and purple. The only thing that made me know it was you in there was your hand. I stayed a while, not sure what I said, if anything, and then we came back to New York. I had a hard time focusing: the news each day just didn't get better, and then we heard you were in an indefinite coma.

I had to leave for the academy. Being in the Hampton's and that house without you sucked so bad. I was in my second year when you woke up and my mom was the one who called. She told me Ethan had arranged for you to go for treatment at the rehab out in LA and no one answered me with a straight answer when I asked how you were. All I knew was you didn't know anyone you'd known, not one person from your past. When I was stationed at San Diego a few times I thought about driving up, seeing for myself how you were but I was gutless because I knew if you weren't my Danni I would lose it completely."

"And did you lose it when you saw me Wednesday night?" She moved closer to stand beside him. "No, because if it's possible you are more beautiful than you were at seventeen and it no longer matters to me if you are spontaneous, and crazy like the first Danni, none of it matters."

"Which Danni is better?" She hadn't missed the beauty part which had made her cheeks flush. "I'd like to spend some time with this you, and I'll let you know." He pushed off the counter, moving over to get that beer but her hand stopped him, making him turn to see her only a hair's distance between them. "Thank you Brad." She reached up circling his neck with her arms and it was the same feeling that grew inside him as when the old Danni had hugged him.

CHAPTER NINE

The doorbell ringing stopped the innocent embrace they were sharing.

Reluctantly Brad let her go, giving her nose a poke on the way past; he used to do that a lot, and it seemed natural and she still got that cute, almost quick cross-eyed look, when his finger touched her.

He opened the door to the night's darkness and there under the outside light stood Sal and Tony, the traveling chef and his nephew. "Hey Sal, Tony." Brad shook their spare hands as they came in and then closed the door behind them. They had all they needed with them and Sal was a very sought-after chef in a city where eating out was a way of life.

"So, where's this young lady your mother was telling me about?" Chef Sal asked as he followed Brad to a kitchen he had cooked inside of before. "Danni, this is Sal and Tony."
"Oh, hi." Danni shook both their hands while Brad noted the usual comment either would make over a beautiful woman, was stuck somewhere between throat and lips. "Sal here is a traveling chef." Brad explained when neither man moved or said anything. "Well I love food so what are you making for us tonight?" Danni beamed as she took a seat at the counter, watching the two of them move around to the other side, Brad not far and her nostrils were now looking for the scent she had caught while in their

embrace, that manly musk sort of deodorant faint fresh smell.

"Only the best for Brad and you miss Danni." Sal smiled wide and Brad knew the man's hormones were unfrozen now. "Did my mother have any say in what you're making?" Brad queried. "A little." Tony grinned, putting items inside the fridge, while his uncle took out some pans and a large Tupperware container holding smaller containers, and then his knife set. "How do you know our Brad? Do you two do business together?"
"Actually Sal, Danni and I grew up together." Brad settled next to Danni on a stool. "What a lucky man you are Brad." The older man shook his head.
"We haven't seen each other in almost two decades." Brad continued.
"Good thing we have food then, it brings everyone together now, I would love to have you both watch, but you're supposed to go in and sit at that expensive dining table while I make you the best meal you ever tasted. Two decades is a long time and you should be catching up with each other."

They both knew just by a look to each other that they should listen and move to the dining room, but as Danni slid down and moved towards the doorway she knew he wasn't behind. When she turned she saw the younger man step in front of Brad as she knew Brad was going for that beer, the one he'd needed to finish his earlier explanation. It was then she could tell just how impressively strong and solid Brad was compared with the other man, and wondered to herself what that chest would be like to rest on in bed but sent that thought flying before it went too far.

"Tony's going to serve wine inside." Brad led her to the dining room which his house-keeper had set with fresh linens and the place-settings before he even came home. He hadn't paid much attention to there being only two sets because he'd thought it was just he his mom, but now it made a whole lot more sense.

Danni took in the room, the soft sage colored walls, the furniture in aged walnut, and the linens brightening up the windowless room with the white shining through. The light above the table was set to dim, but as they sat Tony appeared, carrying a bottle of red wine which wasn't the one she'd brought but a more expensive one; she recognized the label. Tony lit the two candles in the setting, and then returned to turn the light off above them. There was more light, more of a mood to the air. and then the young man served their wine as if they were in a first-class restaurant.

"To old friendships." Brad held up his glass to her.
"How about to new friendships?" She countered with her own up in the air. "I like that better."
"Of course, I'm only here until Tuesday so we'll have to start small."
"No such thing Danielle Morgan." He took a sip of wine as he let his gaze linger a long time on her. She was modest and blushed, knowing his actions, and he kinda liked the Danni who was sitting there. He'd wondered over the years if they would have remained

together or friends and if they had been just friends, would they have still hung out having the occasional meal here and there, or would there have been nothing just like there had been?

"So, you're going back to LA on Tuesday." He ended the sentence with a look of thought and a quick hum. "Why do you say it like that?"
"I'm just working out how many hours that is, how many are needed for sleep and."
"Work, me spending time with my dad." Danni couldn't help but laugh.
"Work can be put on hold; I can call Maggie and have the entire two days wiped clear, and as for your dad." He laughed too. "There's a reason Ethan and Louise set this up, you really think you have to worry about spending time with your dad?"
"Maybe I want to spend time with my dad." He watched those eyes sparkle. "Now I know there's no big difference between the two Danni's."
"Why?"
"You know, you say that word a lot." He kidded.
"What isn't different?" She asked again.
"You always loved your dad; totally a daddy's girl, except whenever I was concerned and I could get you to do pretty much anything."
"I hate to disagree with you Brad but you can't make me do anything."
"Your mouth says the words but your eyes tell me something very different." Danni swallowed her wine hating how he knew her; she wished she could remember more than his face from the past.

Hearing footsteps they both turned and there was Tony carrying in two plates. As he put them down they were given a view of the starter course. A bowl of ice was on one plate, and it held ten open oysters in their shells; the other plate held two small gravy styled metal boats. "Here we have oysters on a half shell with lemon juice and hot sauce." He filled their glasses and Brad noticed Danni looking at the food with a wider smile. "You better share the joke."

"I was thinking how typical this is."

"This?"

"We're set up and then the first course is oysters, a natural aphrodisiac."

"Well, I'm game if you are." Brad helped himself to one of the shells holding it to his mouth and letting the slippery sucker slide in his mouth. "Me too." Danni took one also and it wasn't as gross as she thought it might be, seeing as she couldn't remember ever having one before.

They were pretty quiet while they each ate five, and Brad couldn't help watching her. He'd been feeling drawn to her the moment he saw her on the doorstep, and probably since the gala if he were thinking it through properly. Selfishly he wanted to be near her for as long as she was in the city and even longer if only their lives allowed it. "Tell me what keeps you in LA; I know it isn't a boyfriend."

"Maybe it's a girlfriend." She countered straight-faced with eyebrows up, but once she saw the surprise on his face she had to laugh. "No boyfriend, no girlfriend, no pets, no lovers if that's anything you wanted to know, just my job and my close friends."

"And your job is?"

"Not what I wanted at seventeen."

"Nothing wrong with being an actress and you are in LA."

"I never thought about it since I woke up. I own a restaurant in Santa Monica with a view of the beach."

"You own a restaurant?" That hadn't been on any lists he'd mentally made since he'd thought up the question.

"I own, run and cook for it."

"You cook?"

"I got my degree in culinary arts with a minor in business."

"So, I should tell Sal?"

"Even a chef likes to be cooked for."

"What cuisine do you serve?"

"Organic."

"Organic?" he repeated with a shrug.

"Nothing we use is processed; all of our inventory comes from either local farmers and growers or other companies, like the bread company; all follow organic rules and guidelines."

"So, who's covering while you're here'?

"Sam, my partner, and also a chef."

"Sam is?" Danni bit the inside of her mouth knowing what he was asking.

"A woman." She finally replied after enough time was taken to answer.

"Oh."

"So, you're happy in LA?"

"It feels like a home; it gets lonely when you go home alone every night."

"There has to be a man or there must have been some men."

"A couple, no one special." She wanted to say something like 'no one like you' from what he had told her earlier, but that wasn't fair to either of them because she didn't know if he had been the one unlike all the others. "I've been all about my work."

"I know the feeling." He was fiddling with the stem of his wine glass. "I have an idea." He picked up his glass and then hers nodding to her to follow him towards the kitchen. "Where are we going?"

"The kitchen."

"But Sal said."

"I know, but he'll enjoy talking about your restaurant and the organic thing."

Sure enough, as they arrived in the kitchen they were greeted by a frown from Sal, but once Brad explained, Sal had loosened up, and sitting at the counter facing him cooking at the stove top on the kitchen's island, the two of them talked on and on about the cooking world as Brad absorbed Danni and this strength and knowledge she had. Their main course, a filet of mahi, mahi pan seared and then drizzled with a pomegranate and basil reduction, roasted sweet potatoes and garlic and almond steamed asparagus he enjoyed the food almost as much as seeing the two of them dissect the food and styles.

"I can see exactly what inspired this dish." Danni told Sal who was relaxing as Tony finished cleaning the pans and utensils used for cooking. A second bottle of red wine had been opened and this was the one her dad had told her to bring. "Which is?"

"I would call everything so far the perfect aphrodisiac."

"Smart girl." Sal chuckled heartily.

"Was that your idea or our parents?"

"Louise gave me a place to start."

"Other than the oysters what else is on that list?" Brad joined in.

"Garlic, almonds, pomegranate, basil and the sweet potato." Danni turned to him giving him her attention.

"So pretty much everything?" Brad shook his own head.

"You forgot the wine." Tony who had been quiet said from where he was drying a skillet. "We're practically glowing from all the hormones." Danni kidded to Brad.

"And that would be our queue to leave." Sal rolled up the knife holder.

"I would make coffee but that could put you over the top so you know where the dessert is and we'll see ourselves out."

It had been Danni who had gone to the fridge to retrieve the cheesecake, taking it out of the box and placing it on the counter, while he got up to get a couple of plates, two from the dining room as well as the dessert forks. The kitchen was so bright compared to the candlelit dining room and he wasn't sure but he liked the feelings the soft light evoked; maybe that food was kicking in more? Once back in the kitchen he put the lights on that illuminated under the cabinets on to the counters, and switched off the main one casting the kitchen in to soft UV and not blinding.

"Mmm, looks cozy now." Danni was standing with a knife ready to cut the cheesecake when she felt Brad move up behind her, a hand either side of her and his face next to hers, but he must have been bending because she didn't feel his entire length down her back. "Make mine a double slice."
"Double?" As her head turned slightly she could see right in to his dark eyes so close beside her and trying to remain composed when she accidentally looked down to his mouth, she knew the moment he saw because his face got that much closer and softly their lips touched, Danni's body tingled.

It was just that moment of invading the space between them, and then it was over. Brad moved his head back to see her facial reaction, and it certainly didn't scream hatred.

"A double slice huh?" Danni continued what she was about to start, cutting in to the soft goodness of the dessert. He didn't reply but he didn't argue as he watched her movements. She placed the piece on one of the plates and then, instead of cutting another, she moved inside his arms until their bodies faced, and then pulled herself up on the counter. Once comfortable, she picked up the plate, took a small fork and held the fork out for him to try it. He did, letting her hold the fork for him. "That's good cheesecake."

"Is it?" Danni leaned in to him, her free hand now on the back of his neck, and pulled him in, but this time the kiss was hotter, deeper, and she could taste the flavor of the creamy goodness on his mouth. "I guess it's good but there's something better overpowering the flavor." Her voice was husky and slightly breathless as her mouth touched his wet lips, warming them. "Damn aphrodisiacs," Brad whispered, the last syllable dying in her mouth as this time he started the kiss.

"Spend the weekend with me."

CHAPTER TEN

"The weekend?" Danni's heart was beating so much she thought it would burst through her skin. His intensity while he waited his eyes catching everything as he watched her.

"Does the idea gross you out or something?" He stayed leaning against the counter between her legs which were still clutching him from when they had been kissing. "Far from it."
"Then that's worry in your face."
"It's not really worry."
"Then what?" He stole the fork from which she had fed him a piece of the cake, and moved to stand beside where she sat on the counter. His body was relaxed, and leaning on one elbow as he took another bite.

"I wish I could remember the 'before' us."
"Ah, so there's that, thing."
"That thing?" She shifted slightly, wishing he would look at her.
"The 'he knows something about me I may not know' thing."
"Close, I wish I could tell you that kiss was better now than before, that you've grown in to more of a man, that I knew personally the differences between who you call the two Danni's." She paused as he did make eye contact. "I want all the memories of the past between us back."
"Hey." He put the fork down and moved over taking her face inside his strong hands, she leant her head to

the side. "You are a different woman; your body has changed, you've changed and I'm not that kid anymore. Really we're both as good as strangers to each other and I'm up for exploring this Danni."
"Why?"
"There you go with that 'why' again." He kidded going back to the cheesecake.

"Okay, so what are your intentions for this weekend?"
"You need me to write down a list?" He winked.
"Just sum it up."
"In five words, get to know you again."
"Because?"
"I'm attracted to you, I'd like to think you find me attractive and from the past few hours we know we still get along well with each other and can have fun."
"You really are attracted to me, aren't you?" There was a frown he caught as she played with her fingers in her lap. "Why the surprise?"
"I'm." She slid down of the counter feeling very self-conscious. "Damaged." It came out as a whisper.
"No, you're not."
"Even my brother can see it Brad."
"The only thing wrong is not remembering the past. It's not like you drool and stutter and can't move certain appendages."
"You know, aside from my dad you're the only other person in this city who knew me, who sees through the rumors."
"I think you cleared those rumors up at the gala." He had finished the dessert and placed the dirty plate in the sink.

"It's almost eleven, how about I take you back to your dad's?"

"I thought." She stopped.

"The weekend starts tomorrow." He laughed. "You'd need to get a bag together anyway, and I think tonight you should decide whether you want to start something again between us or not." He cornered her against the counter top. "Because Danni, if we start something we're gonna have to figure out how to keep it going from different coasts. If you aren't sure you want to even try you have to tell me before we start, because I don't think I could lose you twice and survive."

"Okay."

"I'll grab my keys."

Inside his black Escalade, he took her hand as he drove comfortably one handed. She was talking about the few things she and her dad had done since her arrival and he was paying more attention to her soft little hand he held. The drive downtown was quick and he was mentally kicking himself seeing as he probably could have had her in his bed at that moment. But he understood her worries and concerns. He wasn't that selfish. He didn't want to hurt her either but a large part of him didn't want her being inside the city without him being at her side.

So, okay, he was a little selfish.

He wanted to make love to her, not like the sex with the women he hardly remembered since being back in

New York or even those from when he was stationed all over. He wanted to put his name on her and make her want him as much as his body burned for her at that moment.

A cold shower was certainly in his near future.

"I'll come in with you." He said as he found a parking spot out front of the place he knew Ethan lived in but had never been inside of. "My dad might be asleep." "The lights are on and I'll bet you anything he's waiting up to either apologize or find out how the night went."
"Maybe he assumes you're pleasuring me back at your place."
"Maybe." Reluctantly he let her go so they could both get out, and once together on the curb he took her hand again. "Tonight was wonderful." Danni said, as they started ascending the steps. "I thought so too." "And I don't think I'll decide not to spend the weekend with you, I'm sort of disappointed we aren't starting now."
"All good things."
"Come to those who wait." She finished pulling him to stop in front of the large wooden and glass double doors, the sheers didn't hide them from anyone watching from inside, but she didn't care as she kissed him hoping she could relay just how much she meant those words.

"Morning will come soon enough and you were slightly right earlier about spending time with your dad. I think its proper etiquette to ask Ethan's permission to steal his daughter."

"How very gentlemanly of you."

"I try." He stole one last heat raising kiss before he knew he had to let her go or he'd throw her over his shoulder and back to the car. "Shall we?" He let her open the door first, and as he closed the door behind them he heard her say. "Hi dad, I'm home."

"Danielle." He heard Ethan's surprise, and smiled to himself as he came to the wide entryway to the living room with Danni, where Ethan sat in the middle of the antique couch with a book on his lap. Ironic how now that his daughter was all grown up, he waited up for her; when she'd been seventeen there had rarely been anyone around when they'd snuck in after a party or a night on the beach.

"Brad." Ethan added getting up, and Brad moved further into the room and shook her father's hand like many times before in his life. "Shocked to see me home dad?" God bless Danni he thought keeping the smile on his face as Ethan had enough manners to look caught in a spot light. "Well we did hope." Ethan stopped. "We just wanted the two of you to have a chance to talk."

"I'm presuming you mean my mother in that 'we'?" Brad crossed his arms over his chest. "Louise and I meant no harm."

"No harm caused." Danni dropped her purse on one of the arm chairs which matched the couch. "Did you have a fun evening?"

"We talked."

"And yes, I am shocked to see you home." Ethan looked at the two of them. How he'd hoped, as Louise had, when they'd planned this little trick, that these two would be reunited in whatever it was they had shared years ago. He wanted to see the light in the eyes of his daughter she used to get from the man before him, see that full-of-life look fill her face. He also would love to see her settle down with someone who could love and care for her, and one day maybe some grandchildren.

"Well, I wanted Danni to get some rest and for me to be able to ask your permission on something." Brad slightly lied about the reason for bringing her home. "Which is?"
"I'd like to spend the next couple of days with her but I didn't want to interrupt anything you already had planned."
"Nothing more important than Danni having fun." Ethan let his grin show. "I think it's a great idea."
"Me too." Danni came to stand between the two men one she had learned in seventeen years was the best father ever and the other a man she was drawn to like a magnet and with just a simple flash of a younger version's face.

"How about I pick you up around eight-thirty?" He turned asking Danni.
"I'll be packed and ready."
"Good seeing you Ethan." Brad shook the man's hand again, before this time leaning down and kissing Danni on the lips gently. "Sleep well and thanks for tonight."

"No, thank you."

"I'll let myself out." Brad left and Danni stood there waiting for her dad to say something, ask something, but he didn't. He just stood there. "I can't believe you tricked me." She couldn't wait; the sound of the door closing it felt like hours.

"I just wanted you to have fun and it looks like you did." He could see that glint in her blue eyes he'd hoped would come back, not as strong as when she'd been a teen but if this was after a few hours with Brad then forty-eight hours would bring out their full luminescence.

"Do you think even with me not having the memories of the past, the ones with Brad that my mind or body still remembers him, maybe like a severed connection?"

"That makes sense with your brain injury."

"I did love him, right dad?"

"Without question, maybe more than you completely let anyone know."

"Then this isn't some huge mistake and what I feel is real?"

"Danielle, sweetheart, I gain nothing from not telling you the truth, but you have so much to enjoy if you go, so much you'll regret if you don't."

"Yes Yoda." She kissed her father's cheek. "I'm going to pack and then get to bed."

"If I don't see you before you leave, have a great time."

"I have a feeling I will."

"So do I."

"Brad." He heard the hushed voice behind him as he closed his mother's front door. "Hey Daisy." His mother's nurse and assistant was wearing her pajamas with a robe over the top and looked close to mortified that she had been caught looking that way. "It's late."
"Is my mother up?"
"She's in bed reading."
"What a popular pastime tonight." He joked as he saw Daisy's confusion.

Walking down the hallway only illuminated by the single hall lamp which was always on overnight like a night light, the stained Tiffany glass design was a little less bright than something you plugged in to the wall and could buy for a couple of dollars, but it went with the antiques and furniture owned or made by family members through the generations. He knew from his father's old stories that most of the study's furniture had belonged to a great, great, great uncle or something back when New York was known as New Amsterdam.

Pushing the door to his mother's bedroom wide enough to see her as he leant against the frame with his arms crossed over his chest and a leg crossed over the one holding him up. She was, as Daisy said, reading, sitting up in bed wearing her little reading glasses, and her white hair looked immaculately done even after a full day.

"Are you just going to stand there all night, or is there a reason you're here at almost midnight Bradford?" his mother said without her raising her eyes from the hard back she was reading. "I knew I smelt a set-up in my near future."

"Was it so bad?"

"On the contrary, I think you deserve a kiss." He moved, in sitting on the side of her bed next to the legs he never saw working, and leaned close enough to kiss her cheek, smelling the expensive Saks of Fifth avenue night cream she wore. "My, someone had a good night."

"A very good night."

"Then why are you sitting on my bed?"

"I dropped her off at Ethan's; we're going to spend the weekend together."

"Good for you."

"I came over to ask if there was anyone using the house this weekend?"

"You mean the Hampton house?" He knew she was surprised seeing as he hadn't been inside in years. "Getting out of the city should be good for both of us."

"It's about time you went back."

"So, is it free?"

"It's been empty since the New Year. You'll have to remove the dust cloths and buy groceries."

"Figured that."

"Are you driving out or taking a copter?"

"Driving."

"Good. So, tell me, is she still your Danni?"

"Close enough." He nodded getting up. "I'll call you when I get back."

"Have a marvelous time and enjoy her as much as you can dear."

"Trust me, that's all I'm planning on."

CHAPTER ELEVEN

Waiting on the bottom step of the staircase she had a prime view of the front door and would see the moment his black SUV pulled up.

So much for getting plenty of sleep: her stomach had been doing flips since the night before and her mind hadn't been able to stop playing those kisses over and over again.

"You're like the little Danielle waiting for everyone to get up Christmas morning." Her father stopped next to her, he had been up a while; and after having coffee together she had gone to finish packing her overnight bag which was now over by the front door. "Was I like this whenever Brad used to come over?"
"At the beginning of the summer." He sat beside her. "We usually arrived earlier by a few days to the house. You were bored always until the morning they were arriving, and you'd perk right up. You watched out of the sun room window until you saw movement from their house next door. Then you'd shout in delight and before we knew it Brad was racing across the yards, and you were flying out the door to meet him."
"That must have been wonderful."
"For everyone who saw. You two were close from the first moment you met at the age of five and six."

"He has your vote then." She nudged him with her shoulder.

"If it were up to me then yes, you and he would have been married."

"Talk about pressure."

"No pressure, not now. All I want is you happy and healthy."

"The only thing I worry about is the fact we both live in different cities with busy lives."

"I doubt Brad will stay with his family's company much longer, he doesn't enjoy it like John did. He promised his father he would step in but Brad is a natural sailor, John was proud of his son's military career. I think he might return to that before he's too old and he was stationed in San Diego for a while. Meanwhile you and Sam have been talking about taking your restaurant to different locations. You know it would work in any metropolitan city these days, with people's concern over healthier un screwed with ingredients. Who's to say you couldn't do that in whatever city works for the two of you?"

"I should probably enjoy this weekend first; see if we're compatible anymore."

"I have no doubt you will and you will be."

The movement of something dark from the corner of her eye made her look towards the door. She could see the SUV clearly on the road and felt her entire body begin to tingle with anticipation. Her palms started to sweat, and her mouth was drying up.

"Have a good time honey." He got up from beside her, patting her arm. "I'll see you when you get back."

"Don't have too much fun without me."

"Hardly." He laughed as he retreated to the kitchen while she pulled herself up and made it to the door as Brad came to the top of the steps. "Morning." Brad's voice sounded like a growl as he lifted her up in his arms and kissed her with more intensity than any kiss she'd ever experienced in her life.

"Are you ready?"
"I've been ready for what feels like forever." She felt breathless as she looked at his lips while her feet were off the floor. "Keep saying things like that and I may never let you leave." Brad put her down and picked up the brown leather bag he presumed was hers. "We should get going."
"What do you have planned?" She grabbed her coat and had it on before the front door closed behind them. "We are going on a road trip."
"To where?"
"Southampton."
"Why?" She stopped, making him stop too as he had already taken her hand.
"I'm instituting only one rule for the next two days."
"Which is?"
"No more asking why."
"I'm just naturally curious."

"I thought it would be therapeutic for both of us."
"I'm guessing we're staying at your family's place?" Brad opened the door to the SUV and waited, holding it as she got in. "Is that okay?"
"I'd love to see the place."
"You know I've only been back once since your accident."

"Because?" She looked at him and the corners of his mouth lifted.

"At least you didn't use why." With his free hand, he poked her nose gently. "Like I said last night, it wasn't the same without you."

Holding her door open for her, he waited until she was settled and then threw the bag in the back, along with his own, and got in. "How long a drive is it?"

"Two hours, maybe less or more depending on the traffic."

"So, we have plenty of time to talk now, so we don't have to waste time down there which should be filled with hot sex and activities done only behind closed doors."

"Wicked mind you have there Danni." Actually, hearing that turned him on a little. Though he would love to have non-stop sex he also wanted to know everything about her and he knew two hours down wouldn't be enough.

As they headed towards the midtown tunnel Danni was a little quiet as she took in the city, where it seemed only tourists were out so early on a Saturday morning. "Did you work on big ships?" She asked and Brad frowned for a moment. "You mean when I was in the Navy?"

"Aha."

"I did a few months while in the academy, but I've served on dry land more than afloat."

"What does a sailor do on land?"

"There are plenty of things to do on land," laughing at the tone in her voice. "The only time I was aboard a ship or submarine was when we were being transported somewhere."

"We?"

"My team and I."

"Oh, were you like a pilot?"

"Nope."

"So, what did you do?"

"I was on a SEAL team."

"Seal?"

"Let see, how do I explain this?" Brad said aloud, as the end of the tunnel almost blinded them with the sunlight from the eastern sky. "Ever heard of the world war two frogmen?"

"No."

"Um, ever see the Charlie Sheen movie called SEALs?"

"No."

"How about a Demi Moore movie, there was another actor, a guy in it." He thought for a moment. "Viggo Mortenson."

"Is that the movie where Demi shaves her head, and there's some woman senator from Texas or something who screws her over something?"

"That's the one."

"I watched it a while back; my friend Sara had a thing for Viggo after the three Lord of the Ring movies."

"Well, those men Demi trained with are what I did and passed in becoming a SEAL."

"I don't remember the movie that well."

"Basically, we train in elite warfare; the name SEAL comes from Sea Air and Land because we can move unnoticed, and we basically go in where no one else can to do things we are rarely able to talk about."

"So, you use guns?"

"Guns, knives, explosives." He turned quickly from the road looking at her. "We also have special skills which make up the team. There's always someone who can rewire any sort of engine, can fly any vehicle, sharpshooters, we can all do the physical stuff, long distance running; languages are a big one and I don't think there's a gun made I don't know how to assemble and disassemble."

"Guns scare me."

"Well I don't have one on me right now."

"So, your job is dangerous? Was your team like the ones who rescued those army guys stuck inside Afghanistan?"

"Yeah, that was done by a team like mine, and yes the job is dangerous."

"But you liked it?"

"Pure adrenaline rush."

"And you miss it?"

"Every day I wake up and I remember I'm in New York."

"So, you'd go back one day?"

"Maybe, I have obligations here."

"But if you had a choice?"

"I'd be back in San Diego in a heartbeat."

"How do the families handle you guys having such a dangerous job? Do you get shipped out for long times?"

"Tours can be overnight or weeks, we never know and rarely are able to call home to tell anyone."

"Is that part of the reason you were single?"

"A lot of the guys are married, in fact some for a very long time. Even the girlfriends who are worth anything last a long time too, except in our circles very few couples stay in the dating phase long."

"How come?"

"You have to cherish each and every day you have together, and it's a different world."

"Sounds intense."

"The teams are close, families too. If something good or bad happens it affects all of us."

"Has anything bad ever happened?"

"We've lost some men, I actually was on solo assignments for the last few years so I didn't have the team to see all the time, but my old team lost three men on a mission they were on after I left. It was hard on all of them like you'd imagine but everyone comes together in a way I can't explain and do justice."

"So even the families of the men are friends?"

"Yep." Brad settled in to the drive on the LIE as the traffic thinned out after they got past the Shelter Rock Road exit.

"One of the guys we lost, his wife had been pregnant. Now she moved back to Louisiana to be with her parents, but after the baby was born she moved back because she missed the friends she and her husband had. The wives and girlfriends are great helping her out and there's never a function that she isn't invited to, and probably there never will be."

"Sounds wonderful for her, do the wives get together outside of the men?"

"They do, whenever they want. Of course, the husbands' being gone does bring them a lot closer during those times too."

"Then being here away from that huge family has to be hard."

"Yeah, it is."

"Is there anyone you're especially close to?"

"Coop." He said without thinking.

"Coop?" She repeated loving to hear all this from him.

"Cooper Lee, he and I were in the academy together and then went to join the SEAL program together."

"And you both made it?"

"We're closer than any brothers could be. See, the instructor's pair up the men using their different strengths to create an amazing combination. Coop is extraordinary when it comes to explosives and strategic changes."

"And your strength?"

"Languages, and there isn't a vehicle made that I can't operate."

"A tank?"

"Yep."

"Submarine?"

"If need be but you need a few more hands to operate that properly."

"Helicopter?"

"Yep."

"Seven-forty-seven?"

"Yep."

"Um, space shuttle." She joked but when he didn't respond she looked at him waiting until he said. "Yep."

"Get out of here."

"No really, we were all trained on the space shuttle down in Florida just in case."

"In case what?"

"A terrorist situation happened."

"Are you serious?"

"Very serious."

Danni was quiet a moment and Brad let everything settle in her mind. It was obvious it was a lot to take in. The guy sitting next to her was able to fly the space shuttle, not something everyone could boast about. "So, is Coop married?"

"No."

"He has a girlfriend?"

"No."

"He's a monk as well?"

"As well as what?"

"You aren't dating anyone either"

"Coop's never admitted it to me, I've never pushed the subject but I think he's gay." He kept off the subject of himself. "Ooh, isn't there 'a don't ask don't tell' policy in the military?"

"You got it."

"Would it make a difference to anyone if he were?"

"No. Coop was the team's XO, executive officer." He explained his abbreviation. "Everyone respects him and after they lost the team leader on a mission, another officer came in and took over, and he went along, figuring if they wanted him to have the team they would have given it to him. About six months later the admiral asked him if he wanted to lead the team, and he wasn't sure he wanted to. But the rest of the guys who had found out about the offer persuaded him it would be good for the team."

"Because everyone likes him?"
"Mainly, but a huge part is acclimatizing a new member. There's a saying we live by. 'We are only as strong as our weakest link'. It takes more than a handshake to trust a man beside you with your life."
"You trust Coop with your life?"
"Yes."
"Wow, I'm surprised you stayed in New York so long, you speak about being a SEAL as if you are still in the team."
"Theoretically I still am, except I'm taking a little leave."
"For almost two years?"
"I can go back whenever I want."
"I have a feeling you will."
"You better believe it." That earned her a smile.

CHAPTER TWELVE

"Tell me about you, I know you're a chef but I don't know much more." Brad had the SUV on cruise control as the road opened up with little traffic before them. "What do you want to know?" Danni had turned sideways in her seat so she could watch him as he talked.

"It must have been hard waking up, you didn't recognize anyone, right?"
"Not a single person." Danni closed her eyes, putting the back of her head against the cool glass. "It was all nurses and doctors before my dad arrived, and I didn't know him or Peter who was with him. Everything seems surreal now, but after countless tests the doctor explained my memory loss to all of us in the room. My dad looked deflated."
"There was nothing that internally told you he was your dad?"
"There was something, I don't know if I could describe it but my head was still freaking out."
"Must have been scary."
"Everything back then was frustrating."
"Why?"
"Aside from knowing nothing I was supposed to, I also couldn't move much, not even get up and walk around, because my muscles had weakened from the coma. I had to learn everything some people take for granted, but since then I always wake up in the morning and wiggle my toes just to make sure."

"How long were you in the hospital?"

"After I woke up?" She saw him nod a yes. "A couple of days, then the doctor suggested to my dad that he think about sending me to a rehabilitation center. The one in LA is the best money could buy and Dad knew it was what I needed. I guess going didn't bother me as much as the memory thing. I went; my dad came for the first week while I got settled, and before he left I took my first steps with a cane. You'd think he just saw a baby walk for the first time, he was so happy. He returned to New York and a week or so later I got this huge box of stuff. A scrap book someone had put together of everything I didn't know. There was a picture of you in there, but not much jogged a memory."

"You've had no memories?"

"No, it's like seeing pictures in my head. Sporadic things. Nothing that makes much sense."

"But you remember we kissed, had sex?"

"I have this weird snap-shot of both times."

"How long were you in the rehab?"

"A year, I got my GED while there, then moved to a sort of halfway house and went to culinary school. Dad moved out for a while so we got to spend time with each other, and it was he who helped Sam and myself with the restaurant. Sam was a class-mate and we both veered towards the organic field, so it seemed natural."

"When you were talking to Sal you mentioned your menu is based on whatever is fresh from the growers that day: doesn't that make it hard to plan around?"

"Sometimes, but we have the basics all the time, mainly the protein side, the meat, fish etcetera. We take turns each day on our way in to work, stopping to get what we need. We call the other person at the restaurant to tell them and together, by the time we meet around ten, we have an idea of what we're going to serve."

"And you enjoy it?"

"I love seeing people experience fresh foods for the first time, the looks of enjoyment on their faces. I'm telling you, fresh free-range beef is so tender."

"Free range?"

"It only ate whatever was in the fields, like they would a hundred years ago, grass and stuff."

"You have my mouth watering."

Seeing they were not far from leaving the LIE for the Riverhead exit, Brad decided to take a short cut his father would sometimes take on high traffic days. It cut from the LIE on route forty-six south until you hit the sunrise highway, but he knew there were a lot of farms off the other highway, and seeing as they had to get groceries anyway, he should let her get the ones she loved more.

For two hours and at three different farm stands, one of which was like a small country farm store that had a larger selection of everything, including their own homemade fruit and meat pies, and fresh cut flowers. Brad liked seeing this vibrant Danni as she looked as if right at home for her as she asked to speak to the one farmer's wife, who was in her forties and made every single pie they sold.

That had been Danni, able to talk to anyone, as she didn't see social status like a lot of their teen friends had.

Around noon they finally pulled in to the oval driveway on Meadow Lane, Southampton. There was water either side of the house, on one the Atlantic, on the other Shinnecock Bay, splitting the one-street slip of land from the mainland. At the turn of the last century, the slip was actually longer, Dune Road, another section similar to Meadow Lane, had been connected before a hurricane had washed away a few houses and the road away.

Parking in the driveway he watched as he carried their two bags and a couple of the brown bags containing some of the food, while Danni carried two others and was also taking in the houses on either side of them. Both were about a hundred yards away separated by manicured lawns and shrubbery, and he was waiting to see if she knew which had once been owned by her father, who had sold almost as quickly as their family had been torn apart.

"Which house was my father's?" She asked as he pressed the button to lock the car behind them, as they were halfway to the front door. "That one." Brad pointed East.
"It doesn't look familiar."
"The new owners painted it that pale grey and added the faux shutters as well as the new sun room on the south side." He began unlocking the front door, telling her what his mother had told him, because just

looking at the changes made his stomach twist. "I don't know what I was expecting." She followed him inside and stopped in the entryway. Brad almost ran in to her as he turned around. "Was there ever an antique table over there?" She was pointing to the space beside the staircase. "It got broken a long time ago." He laughed remembering how. "What?" She looked up at him.

"You and I were sliding down the stairs, you were fourteen, I was almost sixteen, and I fell off the side, breaking my arm and that table."

"For real?"

"Honest to God." He let both of their bags slip from his shoulder at the bottom of the stairs as he continued further in to the house.

Danni's mind was searching within itself again while she followed him towards the back of the house; the kitchen was large, open, with more windows than south facing walls held plaster. The center island was a pure butcher's block which looked old and well cared for. She placed her own packages beside the ones Brad had put down. "The view is amazing." Danni looked out to the vast ocean before them.

"Daisy loved working in this kitchen because of the view. She misses it now she and my mother are in the city most of the time."

"Does your mother get out here much?" She was leaning at the sink looking in each direction as she heard the door to the refrigerator open and light reflect on the glass she was looking through. "Not much, she doesn't find the beauty in it now Dad's gone."

"Must be hard, so this place goes empty?"

"No, she lets friends come out and use it. There's a lady who keeps it in shape all year round."

"Still, it's such a beautiful place."

"Up for a walk?" he asked, letting the door close now all the perishable items were safe inside the cold interior. "Where?"

"Down on to the beach."

"Sure."

"Who lives in the house over there now?" She hooked a thumb in that direction as Brad unlocked the back door from the kitchen. "I don't know, I've never met them."

"It's beautiful," Danni said again as they made it off the partial wooden deck without a railing, and onto the short strip of grass before the sand. The tide rarely changed the look of the strip about twenty feet deep to the water.

"Whatever you want to do this weekend we can." Brad was holding her from behind as he spoke in to her ear; his lips traced the contours of the delicate flesh. "Anything?"

"Within reason." He loved holding her in his arms and wanted to bring to life an old memory of the two of them having sex right there on the sand as they had when they'd been teenagers and all the parents had been gone for the day. "So aside from the kiss I'm dying to get from you, I can do whatever I want."

"Starting with a kiss is good." Obligingly the intensity from the night before returned and the swirling wind picking up around them was unnoticeable until he felt Danni shiver in his arms. "Maybe we should go inside." He rubbed her arms. "How about a short walk first?"

After walking a fair way East, they were heading back to the house when Brad noticed there was a car now at the house Danni's family had once lived in. "You know if you wanted to go over and see the inside...."
"That would probably be too weird." She stopped his words.
"Well if you change your mind."
"The only thing I have on my mind right now is you."
"Me?"
"Yes, you."
"What exactly is your mind thinking?"
"That I want to see what is under those clothes of yours."
"I've never had a woman say that to me; actually, I've only ever heard a man say those words."
"A man said them to you?"
"No." He laughed.
"Am I too forward?"
"I wouldn't expect you any other way."
"Was I always this forward?"
"Trust me when I say we probably would never have gotten in to some of the trouble we did, if it hadn't been for your forwardness."

"We got in to trouble?" Her cheeks were flushed pink from the wind which was coming and going catching them like a wave. "Nothing serious."
"What did we do?"

"There was the time we got caught in your bedroom naked by your brother."

"Peter?"

"He bugged out and of course had to go and run and tell your parents I think it infuriated him we didn't get in to serious trouble"

"What did our parents do?"

"Sat us down and made sure we were using protection."

"Huh, what else did I do which got you in to trouble?"

"Got us."

"So?"

"There was one time you encouraged me to skip class with you."

"Big deal." She laughed as they reached the back deck.

"Fine, you were an angel." He laughed.

"See, I knew I was an angel."

"My angel." He whispered in her ear.

"Okay, there was the first week we met." He said feeling his chest warm at the memory, something so long ago which he hadn't thought about in so many years. "I was five. What on earth could I do to get us in trouble?"

"Well." He took her hand, knowing she was cold from her breathing, and headed them towards the house. "You had been given an Easy-Bake oven for your birthday, and we were over in your house, and you wanted to make me a cup cake, except your parents forgot to pack the cake mixes that came with the toy. You made me sit in your room and wait while you went and got all the things you thought you needed to make one yourself."

"I get the feeling this doesn't end well." She squeezed his hand.

"It doesn't." He started laughing slightly at the image in his head. "I can't remember what you put in the bowl you had taken from the kitchen; the cake wasn't the problem. It was the candle you had snuck out of a drawer as well as a box of matches."

"How much damage did I cause?"

"You set fire to the rug, bed cover, and half your stuffed bears and dolls."

"Dad and Theresa must have flipped."

"I think they were too freaked over you and I being okay, but I remember my father giving me the lecture once I went home. They knew everything that happened, hard to miss three fire trucks and two police cars in your driveway."

"What did he lecture you about?"

"I was older, should have known better, that I should look after you like a big brother."

"And did you?"

"Look after you?"

"Yeah."

"We were inseparable."

"And then when we were older you fell in love with me? How old were you then?"

"Ten."

"You were ten?" She scoffed as they entered the house.

"The moment my hormones kicked in I couldn't stop thinking about you."

"But the accident got in the way, and you did."
Thankful for being inside she took her jacket off,
forcing them to release each other's hands. "I never
for one minute forgot about you Danni."
"Come on Brad."
"I carried you with me for longer than you'll ever
know." Danni saw his movements, his inability to
make his eyes leave the spot on the ground. She knew
he was telling the truth, this man, this wonderfully
strong man had thought about her for so long.

CHAPTER THIRTEEN

"There's something I want more than anything," Brad heard her say as he took their jackets to the mud room off the front hall, where there were coat pegs. "Lunch?" He asked. "No." He heard a slight thud behind him and turned as his arm was halfway to the peg for the second jacket.

Danni stood there in the hall wearing just her bra and panties; the noise had to have been the buckle on her jeans hitting the wooden floor.
The look on her face was pure seduction and lust.

There was nothing he could say because he knew his eyes were glued to her as he moved smoothly to her. Taking her in his arms he kissed her with a deeper intensity which she matched. His hands roamed down her smooth skin of her back until he reached the lacy material holding in the firm but wonderfully full and round butt. It felt good in each of his hands and he lifted her up, her legs closing around his waist.

"Hold on." He whispered as he started for the stairs. "I'm not going anywhere without you." She held on tight and he carried her as far as the bottom of the stairs, and then was momentarily distracted from feeling her chest through his shirt as his body bent at the knees. "I had to get my bag." He'd actually retrieved both as he then started making it up the one flight of stairs as if holding a female in his arms while carrying luggage was like carrying a feather in his palm. He felt no strain aside from the one in his pants as her body gently caressed him without her knowingly doing it.

Because of his mother's disability, his father had built an extra room off the downstairs which had become the master bedroom, leaving the upstairs floor for his and the guest quarters, as well as a nice room with an ensuite bathroom for Daisy.

His room; little had changed. The bed was a king and not a full one, all personal items he'd had in there were gone. He knew they were either gone for good or inside the apartment in New York. The walls had been painted over the years but the white walls and blue fabrics were still there, along with a view he had loved his entire life of the Atlantic Ocean; miles and miles of nothing but water and sky; a never-ending horizon. Just like the kitchen, the back of the room was all glass, it was like looking out of a greenhouse when you were in bed, and when it rained. Rain had been something both he and Danni had laid there and watched on days when there was little to do, usually after she had snuck inside using the side stairs outside to his little balcony.

Dropping the bags on the floor without care for where they landed, he went back to using both of his hands, and lowered her on to the bed, kneeling himself as he came down atop her using one hand to hold him from crushing her, allowing her to roam her hands wherever she wanted.

"Oh, wow." He had just begun kissing her neck again.

"Huh?"

"What amazing architecture." Her voice was even but her back arched towards his own body. "I was thinking the same thing." Though his focus was on the shape and contours of her body. "It would be more believable if you were looking the same direction." She made that laughter that lit up his chest. "My view is better." He pulled himself back getting in between her line of sight to the bright afternoon sky as he peeled off the sweater he was wearing. "No, I still think this side is way better." Her voice was catching in her throat as she took in that wide strong chest, his dark hair covering slightly the peck area and the trail down the center of his stomach, her hands splayed out across the tanned skin and she hoped he knew it was him she really meant.

Sitting up slightly she just had to feel that chest, her hands, lips, even her tongue lightly licked the skin as her teeth grazed his flesh slightly. He might smell good and manly with whatever it was he used in the shower or as deodorant but he might as well be made of the purest chocolate; he was delectable.

Without asking if it was okay Brad reached around her body and deftly unhooked the two hooks on her bra which were holding her breasts from his eyes. There had always been something about her breasts which he'd compared other women's to over the years, and he had been dying inside wanting to see what they were like now they were fuller. Would he even compare the same two sets to one another?

Danni couldn't wait to get the material off her chest hoping he would start making her feel the next level of intense intimate feelings. She couldn't miss the unmistakable bulge against her thigh. She flung the lace uncaring where it would land and took great pleasure in how his eyes looked deep in to her as if his look was an actual deep tissue massage and she felt her nipples harden from not only the coolness of the air but those dark eyes.

"Danni." He said as he kissed her again melding their chests together and he had to close his eyes, pretend he was doing something else because he was so worked up already. He rolled them over, making him on the bottom as they still kissed. When he felt her sit up he took her breasts in as they hung naturally and suckled on one while his fingers gently teased the other.

There was no way even with the difference in size that these were any different from the ones from the past.

With her fingers in his hair holding him to her chest as she enjoyed the feelings coursing through her, she wished he had removed his pants so she could get a glimpse, a feel of the one thing she truly wanted and soon, he was the first man who with just a mere touch had her hotter than anything.

"Okay." Again, Brad rolled them over and she again was on her back, the afternoon sky was so steely grey behind him as she looked up, and it was as if a storm was coming in. Something made her close her eyes as she felt him move off her slightly, and for the briefest of moments she remembered something, saw a flash in her mind of something she didn't know, except she saw rain, heard the sound of it hitting glass. Male laughter beside her and it was darker than now, like nighttime.

The feel of his hands at her hips, the movement of the material being slid down her legs made her mind refocus, and she took in Brad as he eased her panties down her legs leaving her bare. He himself was naked and she took in his lean hips and everything in that area; what she saw made her blush. There was no doubt he was a man, a very lucky man when it came to how very well he was built.

"Still with me?" He whispered, as he lay beside her letting his hand move down her stomach swirling slightly around her belly button and then dipping low to where her body held the warmth and cover he was waiting to experience. "Yeah." Rolling on to her side as she lifted her leg over his hip giving him unspoken permission to do what he was doing, she used her upper arm to touch him, the first time yet so familiar. She liked how he sucked in a sigh at her fingers touching him intimately; his own fingers were skilled and she felt her hips move involuntarily.

"Hold on." He disconnected his fingers from being inside her. He didn't want to screw anything up and looked around the floor near the door where he remembered throwing his bag. "What?" Danni sat up on her elbows watching. "I need." He took two steps on the cold wood floor and found quickly in the outside pouch what he had been looking for. "These." He held up the largest box of condoms that Duane Read had on their shelves. He'd anticipated this and bought them on the way home from dropping her off the night before.

"I hate to tell you this because you probably spent a couple of bucks on that economy super-sized box." She joked. "But we can't use them."
"Can't?" He asked as he climbed back on to the bed.
"I am very allergic to latex."
"How allergic?"
"If latex touches me I blow up like a balloon or get this rash."
"We never had a problem before."
"I hear I used to suffer from the strangest rash which only appeared in the summer months."
"Yes, you did." He smiled wide.
"Yeah, the doctors figured it out after the accident; let's just say my father was only slightly mortified when he connected the dots. I suppose us having sex when we were young is a lot different when it's unspoken and under their roof."

"It's been a long time since I didn't use these." He threw them behind his back; they hit something but nothing breakable. "I take the pill so aside from say diseases we don't have to worry."
"Nice thought." He frowned while watching her. "Do you have any diseases?"
"No."

"Neither do I, okay, where were we?" Leaning in as they remained on their sides he kissed her again pulling her in with his arms. He was smiling and knew she was too, again her leg lifted and sat on his hip as her foot gently ran up and down his skin tickling it and feeling that softness women's legs have compared to his own.

"You were about to show me some moves, maybe ones from the past I used to like." She whispered in his ear as she let his wandering mouth slip lower down her neck. "Honestly, my moves sucked back then, if I was to show you them then you may just run screaming back to New York." His head came up and with the hand his head wasn't resting on, he removed a strand of hair from her cheek. "Then trust me when I say you don't need any fancy moves to impress me."
"Now I have to pull out all the stops." She felt something brush against her folds and it wasn't until there was something waiting entry down there, something hard and forceful, that she knew it was finally time.

Brad didn't want her to tense or even for that matter know when his teasing was over. With his hand holding that leg which had been resting on his thigh his hips delved deeply and quickly all the way in and he watched her for responses, shock or euphoria, he wasn't sure what he expected; she'd regain lost memories of the two of them from that split second?

Mainly he just wanted her to enjoy it as much as he knew he would.

With the rhythm set to slow Brad pulled Danni up to straddle his body using her leg muscles to keep the pace. It allowed him to watch her breasts move in gravity-defying motion. He daren't close his eyes, he didn't want to miss anything, because only one thing was the same, Danni's face was magnificently telling.

It was killing Danni, this slow, steady rhythm. She wanted the man inside her to brand her, make her his and dominate to his heart's content, so she squeezed her internal muscles with a pulse she knew would drive him to have to take over, and as she flung her head back feeling a first wave of pleasure wash over her she was grateful he got the message.

Feeling her going over the edge, it took everything in him to not nose dive and follow her. He was ready, his body wanted to badly, but he was determined to not let it happen.

Holding her hands above her head he waited, looking down into her eyes as she regained her equilibrium, and with his own hardness still deep within her, feeling each and every quiver, he went through the starting launch sequence for the space shuttle to regain the footing he needed to take her there at least once more.

"You didn't." Danni panted, knowing for a fact he hadn't finished, he'd unselfishly let her go over the edge, but he was holding back, the vein in his neck was pumping showing only there the effort he was using to keep himself together.

"No." As her muscles relaxed, he started that rhythm again, but this time, now that the pleasantries were over he took her like he'd tried to as a teen. She'd been forthcoming yet silent when they'd had sex, not wanting him to know she liked to be over-powered and dominated, but he'd figured it out, and even now he knew she liked that too without words. "I'm trying to impress you."
"You don't have to try, you impress me without this."
"Hold on." He moved them, joined still, to the edge of the bed, the bottom where he was facing the window wall to the ocean. Reluctantly he allowed her to slide from him and then turned her once she stood so her back was to him. Guiding her back to sit on his lap he impaled her again as he kissed her neck, and while one of her hands held his head gently to her skin, his own hands were raising her up and down him.

CHAPTER FOURTEEN

"I had a different experience." Danni was lying with her head on his chest while he held her at his side. One of his hands was gently running up and down her bare back. "Good or bad?" He hadn't been able to stop smiling since the moment of euphoria.

"Oh, Brad the sex was...." She stopped, unable to find a word to do justice to what he'd made her feel.
"What?" He locked eyes with her.
"I don't want to pick a word because I don't think there's one to tell you about how you made me feel."
"I was having the same problem." He rested his head back wanting this time in bed to never end. "But I didn't mean the sex was the experience which was different though the sex so definitely was." She started rambling with nerves. "Then what did you mean?"
"Did we ever lie here at night and lookup at the stars? Rain and stuff hitting the glass?"
"We did." He moved to look at her closely, lying on his side like she was. "Did you remember that?"
"So, it happened?"
"We did that more than once, but there was one special time."
"Would you fill in the gaps?"

"You were thirteen, the summer was a wash-out and we spent a lot of time inside." He began. "My dad and I had been at a game at Yankee stadium during the afternoon, and we had party plans for a friend of mine who was having a BBQ for his birthday that

132

night. Except it was cancelled. So, when I came back here you ran over, wearing your bright red slicker. You were all dressed for the party and were so bummed because you'd wanted to wear your new dress from Paris to show it off. My mom adored you, the little girl she had always wanted, and suggested you and I go to dinner at the country club so you still could. She had Charlie drive us over, and after, we came back here. We'd planned on watching a movie. But the power had gone out because a tree had fallen somewhere on the main-land. So instead, we lit a few candles and laid up here watching the rain, and laughing about stupid stuff." Brad touched her cheek so delicately she almost didn't feel it. "It was the first time I was brave enough to kiss you, we made out for hours."

"I remember that night."
"Another snap shot of an image?"
"No, like a mini movie."
"But I thought...." His frown returned.
"I've not had anything like that until the moment I was lying here for the first time again looking up at the sky."
"So that was the first one ever."
"Completely unique."
"So you not only remembered that but the hall table earlier too."
"It's a little unsettling and I'm not sure what to make of it."
"For some reason, something is triggering these recollections."
"You."

"Me?" He scoffed.

"My dad told me there was a lot of my past entwined with yours."

"Maybe it's a fluke."

"Don't sell yourself short." Pulling herself so the skin of her chest rested on his chest she kissed him, partly to stop him from dissecting whatever it was she was experiencing and partly because she yearned to feel him inside her again.

"How about something to eat." Danni asked as she rolled off Brad, who had lain there, letting her use his body for the last thirty minutes. "Depends what you're offering." He smiled at her from where he lay on his back, content to stay there forever and never leave for anything. "Something fresh and delicious and maybe one of those bottles of wine." Moving around she looked for her bag she knew he had carried up, and spotted it before she moved over to open it, feeling the coolness of the air on her naked skin.

"I like this image a lot." Brad watched as she crouched down looking inside her bag. Her backside not only filled each of his hands perfectly, but from where he was lying enticed him to want to get up too; they were perfectly pear shaped and his eyes were glued to them. "How about we stay like this?"

"I'm afraid my knees would get tired." Finding her silk robe which hung to her mid-thigh she pulled it on, as she stood, and fastened it as she turned back to face him. He sighed with his attention cut now that her smooth skin was covered. "Fine." He groaned jokingly. "My ego is bruised when a female would prefer to cook than let me make love to her."

"Trust me when I say you'll be right back where you want in no time."

"Promise?"

"Yeah." She laughed as she went in to the bathroom to freshen up a little.

He was wearing only a pair of Navy sweats, the two white stripes on the outside of each leg making his lower half seem so thin Danni thought as she watched as him make the journey to and from the garage carrying logs of cut wood for the fireplace, in the large living room where he had told her they would be eating dinner-no formal, or proper table etiquette, simple and easy, leaning against the sofa while using the coffee table to hold anything.

Having bought some fresh range chicken breasts, Danni cleaned and floured them, then she chopped some Prosciutto and sage and halved a lemon. She made a salad and in ten minutes the chicken was cooking and Brad was now in the kitchen looking inside the small wine fridge below the counter for a white wine. "Something smells wonderful," he said coming to stand behind her as she cooked the chicken in the skillet, the three other ingredients already infusing flavors into the white meat. "It's one of my favorites."

"You always did have good taste."

"Was I a snobby brat?" She turned off the heat and turned to look at his face, searching for a sign he was lying or stretching the truth, but she saw nothing as he said. "No, I actually admired you for how caring and gentle you were."

"Was I?"

"Social class never mattered to you like it did to our friends. Sure, you loved the clothes Theresa brought back from her shopping sprees, but there was once a pair of pink."

"Sneakers." She finished off seeing something in her mind.

"Yeah, you wore them until they were worn through." He watched her turn back to serve the meal on the two white plates waiting on the counter. "You always seemed to have more fun talking to someone outside of our world than anything. There was a guy who used to do our yard work. A Mexican immigrant who spoke little English and looked as if he saved every penny he made. People we knew joked about the holes in Miguel's shirts, his pants held up by string and the truck that I'm sure was duct-taped together, yet every week he was here for the day. You always brought over your lunch with more than you could eat, and shared it with him."

"Did you eat with us too?"

"Always, you asked him lots of questions, as if you were trying to get to know him. You found out he had a wife and four young children, that he drove out here almost an hour from where he lived to work on the yards of the rich; it was guaranteed work."

"Did he mind?"

"Never, he liked you a great deal."

"What did the parental units think of that?"

"Absolutely nothing, your father encouraged you to do things like that."

"Does Miguel still do the yards? They look very well cared for."

"Oh." Brad took the plate she held out for him. "No, he doesn't."

"Why do you say it like that?" Danni followed him to the living room where a fire crackled in the fireplace. "God, I don't want to see your face again."

"What?" She sat beside him uncaring that her thighs were barely covered and she could feel the shag rug on her behind. "Miguel was killed."

"Oh-my-God how?"

"His neighborhood wasn't so safe. A stray bullet if I remember."

"How senseless."

"You pretty much said the same thing then too, aside from being in tears when you told me." He took a bite of the chicken and felt his taste buds dance. "This is good."

"Isn't it? Poor Miguel, I'm glad I had feelings and cried then."

"You did more than cry."

"Meaning?"

"First you worked out how much money he made during the summer, you knew his route and the people on this stretch who used him, and you dragged me to each house after dinner that night and you explained to each adult what had happened and that you weren't asking for much, but you were putting together a collection. You had figured an amount like he would have made forty thousand or something."

"Did I raise even a fraction of that?"

"You raised every single cent with checks written to you." Brad smiled; she hadn't touched her food because she was so intrigued with the story. "Both our parents were so touched, they thought I had a bigger role than escorting you that they both matched the checks. Your dad drove you to the bank first thing the next morning, and you cashed the checks and got a cashier's check."

"Wow, I feel like a saint almost."

"Oh, there's more to the story."

"There is?"

"One of the neighbors, he was unmarried and had no children. He lived at the end of the stretch; he was at your house when you got back, as I was."

"And?"

"Well, he too had been good friends with Miguel, had been the first in the area to hire him, asking the neighbors to as well. He was a Supreme Court Judge in the city; he died in nine-eleven. Anyway, he told you how wonderful you were thinking of the family, and asked you to give something to Miguel's wife."

"What?"

"A house."

"A house?" She repeated.

"A place in Brooklyn he had grown up in and had been renting out. He knew that Miguel's family had little and though he'd given you a check he also wanted to do this because he didn't have a family of his own to leave it to."

"Wow."

"And then there was the last part."

"The last part?"

"You had me doing some running around and making calls while you were at the bank."

"And?"

"You were fourteen, had known Miguel for years since you were six and his children were between eight and twelve by then. You had me calling all our friends, explaining what we were looking for and within the time it took for you to get to and from the mainland most of our friends had come through too."

"With what?"

"Clothes and toys, amazingly we got four bikes as I remember and then as the judge was leaving my mother and Daisy arrived. Theresa had come downstairs and they too had gone through their things and there were more designer clothes for the wife than what we would be giving to the children. Sad thing was, most of the items brought to us were barely used because your father had worried the family may get offended but you told him no one would ever know and you roped both Peter and I into helping you sort through things to make sure."

"How did we get all of that stuff and the money to the family?"

"Your dad and my dad left while we were busy and came back with a U-Haul truck."

"Man, I did all that?"

"You sure did. Your dad and I went with you and we drove to Miguel's house. The boarded-up window in the front the proof of what had happened. You got out, walked up to the front door as it opened and

introduced yourself to Rosa. Her eyes had looked red but she smiled when she realized who you were."
"Miguel told her about me?" It sounded incredulous.
"Of course he did. Then you told her how sad you were, it made her tear up but when you handed her first the check I thought she would keel over. She was shaking her head; more tears ran down her face as you gave her the deed telling her she could move immediately if they wanted and your dad had to hold her up. Then you explained about the truck apologizing if she was offended and she took you and hugged you for so long I didn't think she would ever let you go."
"Did they move?"
"That afternoon, they had little possessions and your dad and mine used the room left inside the truck to help them, while the judge sent his personal car over to drive the family there."
"That's wonderful."
"That's one of the bigger reasons I loved you."
"I think I would love me too."
"And that's also why you weren't a brat."

Danni let that sit for a moment, she had been sipping her white wine while he had been talking, and seeing the glass almost empty he refilled it while she picked up her fork and started eating. "Isn't that cold?" He knew his wasn't so hot but it still tasted decadent.
"I like cold chicken."
"I know you do." He laughed slightly as he chewed.
"I'd never eaten cold chicken till I met you and now it doesn't bother me at all."

"Hey, as long as it's cooked through there's nothing wrong with that."

"If you'd eaten the food I have since being in the Navy you wouldn't ever worry about cold food again."

"Was it gross?"

"Chow on base wasn't bad. Most bases have Macdonald's these days which is great, but when we were on missions the team always had MRE's to eat which, believe me, are only good for keeping away malnutrition."

"MRE's?" She asked.

"Meals ready to eat."

He put his fork down now, he was done. Washing it down with a mouthful of wine, he was refilling his own glass when he said. "Think little plastic rip top baggies filled with culinary dishes like meatloaf, country captain chicken, and my absolute worst choice, beef ravioli."

"In a baggie? How do you cook them?"

"You don't have to; they come with a flameless heater. Of course, warm is better than room temperature, they come complete with the entrée, side dish, crackers, peanut butter or cheese spread, a dessert and instant coffee or tea. There's also some matches, toilet paper and a spoon, but don't imagine something huge; the package fits inside a combat vest."

"Not that I ever want to try one but that must be only slightly better than starving."

"You got it." He chuckled.

"Did you eat them a lot?"

"I lived on nothing else for a few months once." He looked down to the liquid in his glass, watching the flicker from the flames play on the glass and its contents. "A mission?"

"Yeah." He downed a long swallow. "I can't talk about it; I would tell you, but, you know...."

"Can you tell me anything?"

"It wasn't a very nice place." He made eye contact as she put the last piece of food in to her mouth.

"Iraq?" Danni asked.

"Yep."

"You can't tell me what you and the team were doing?"

"This was after, I did solo missions a lot. This mission was with a couple of guys from different agencies."

"FBI, CIA, Army, Marines?" She threw out there.

"Possibly."

"What's the worst thing you've ever seen?"

"You wouldn't want me to tell you." He put his glass on the coffee table. "I don't know about you, but I am dying for something filling for dessert."

"You want to go back to bed with a full stomach?" She moved to straddle his lap her fingers beginning to play with his hair. "Who said anything about going back to a bed?" He carefully and slowly ran his fingers just under the edge of the silk rob hanging down from her neck covering her breasts without hiding what was underneath; he watched her nipples harden through the fabric as her body shivered.

CHAPTER FIFTEEN

Waking up suddenly he could have sworn he was inside his dream.

Hadn't he been spending the day with Danni? His Danni and not back inside Iraq that day which he would never clear from his mind.

"What was that?" He heard Danni ask sleepily beside him and he knew then the load bang was not from his head but from somewhere close by.

"Stay here." He fumbled around the floor for his sweats, after a few hours of being down in the living room he had finally brought her back up to bed. His eyes briefly caught sight of the bedside clock; the red letters telling him it was almost two am. She was insatiable, and he couldn't get enough. "Okay." He saw her in the slight illumination allowed by the night sky; the sound of rain was hitting the glass.

Yawning and scratching his shoulder he got as far as the stairs when his gut twisted as if someone had stabbed him hard. There was no mistaking the glow coming from the front side of the house. Something in the driveway was in flames, and he would bet his entire trust-fund it was his SUV. His feet picked up their movements, taking two of the steps at a time, and he was alert in seconds. Unlocking the door he felt the heat instantly as it pushed him back. He knew without some assistance from the fire department it would burn for a while with the full tank he'd had, after filling it on the mainland before they'd arrived. The rain would do little to extinguish it.

Knowing his cell was in the kitchen he ran and got it, forgetting to close the door, and looked up the stairs hoping Danni was asleep while he took care of this. No need to freak her out until he had to.

From the illumination of the red and blue lights of the emergency crews from the mainland across the water, he knew someone on the stretch had called, so instead he pushed the buttons of a friend in the city he needed, and wanted in charge of whatever was going to be investigated. "It's Johnson, I need you ASAP. I'm at the family house in Southampton and my car was just blown up," he said, once he heard the man's greeting.

"Is everyone okay?" A male voice asked, and a man not much older than himself came from the side of the house wearing a robe over his silk pajamas. "Yeah, thanks." Brad didn't know who this man was, but he doubted whoever put the bomb there would do it wearing sleepwear; he didn't let it trouble his mind. "I'm Gene, my wife and I live next door, you must be Louise's son."
"I'm Brad." He held out his hand and took the formal handshake from the neighbor. "Any idea what happened?" Even standing twenty feet from the flames it warmed Brad, who was unaware of the rain. "We were in bed," Brad replied, as the first emergency response team pulled up with a hiss of hydraulic brakes. Firemen began running around

144

doing their job while one man, the one Brad figured in charge of the team, came to them avoiding the flames by walking in an arc.

"Lieutenant Meadows." The man said.
"Brad Johnson, this is my family's house. We arrived this afternoon and were asleep when I heard an explosion and came down to find this."
"We'll get the flames out and figure out what happened." As Meadows walked away, talking into his radio, Brad suddenly felt a soft hand on the middle of his back and he turned his head to see Danni wide mouthed looking at the carnage. "What the hell happened?"
"Danni, this is Gene, he lives next door," he said trying to avoid responding, and Danni gave the man a wave before her eyes went straight back to the flames.
"Brad."
"Somehow the car exploded."
"How would that happen?"
"I don't know." He responded, but beside him Gene said.
"Probably a bomb of some sort; who'd you piss off?"
Brad gave the man a quick look of thanks and took Danni's hand inside his own.

"Is that true?" He could feel her skin get cold, the slight trembling.
"A bomb would make sense." In some ways, he hoped she didn't hear his reply. "Who would do something so evil?"
"How about we go inside?" He suggested and Danni was slow to move as it seemed she was mesmerized

by the glowing embers as the hoses started dowsing the flames. "If you two need anything." He heard Gene say behind him. "Thanks, nice to meet you."

Inside the house, the front door still open to the outside world working in the night, Danni stopped inside the living room, cleaned up from dinner and their activities-just looking at the couch she could see the two of them there enjoying each other-but a shiver ran through her and in just her silk robe she crossed her arms around herself and rubbed the tops of her own arms.

"I should call your dad, let him know. He can come and get you."
"I know I promised not to say it but why."
"Someone just blew my truck up Danni."
"I don't want to go." She turned to him putting her arms around his bare shoulders. "This probably has something to do with my old job Dan' this might get dangerous."
"But here in America? What bad guys would go to so much trouble, and why wait until you weren't in the car?"
"It's some sort of message." He let Danni slip from his arms as his mind raced through possible people; wishing they were closer to the city: it was going to be late when the person he called would arrive. "I have a friend, he's in the FBI now, I called him and he'll be here as soon as he can."
"You really think that was some sort of message?" Danni had gone white and when there was a knock at

the door she physically jumped making Brad determined to get her back to the city and her father.

"Mr. Johnson." A new male voice said, and looking towards the front door he saw two new men, both in police uniforms. "Officers." He moved from Danni, who he watched from the corner of his eye, as both of them went in different directions. She was going upstairs and he sighed inwardly; this was the last thing he wanted or expected to happen while they were spending this time together.

"Bradford Johnson?" The older of the two cops asked, as tall as Brad but wider, a definite beer gut hanging over his thick leather belt holding so much in. He narrowed his attention on the man's face realizing he knew him. "Officer." Brad stopped unable to place him.
"William Daily, we used to play ball together when we were teens." He nodded as the man came back to him. "It's been a long time." Brad held out his hand to the old friend. "How have you been, Sergeant?" He noticed the strips on his sleeves. "Been good until tonight when I get a call about an explosion from one of the upper crust houses." The man fixed his pants, heaving them up slightly. "This is my partner Nick Fox." Brad shook the younger man's hand too. "Brad and I know each other from summers playing football over on the mainland." He began explaining to his partner. "But Brad left at eighteen for bigger and better things. I hear from your mom you made Commander."
"I did."

"Navy?" Nick asked.

"Yeah, I should tell you I called a friend in a federal agency. If this is connected to anything I may have been involved in, with my military service, then you won't have clearance to see the files."

"Huh." Will nodded. "You think this could be connected to your work? I thought I heard from your mom you had left that and started running the family business." The man frowned but he seemed like the same mellow guy and the information a fed was due didn't seem to either register or bother him. "I am except what else would it be? Unless of course the youth of Southampton have switched from mailbox baseball to rigging cars with bombs," Brad joked.

"You've got a point there." Will found the humor and was about to say something else when Danni reappeared now wearing jeans and a hooded sweater which looked so big on her.

"Will, I'm sure you remember Danielle Morgan." Brad introduced the men to her, but Danni was only looking at him. "I do, how are you Danni?"

"Shaken." She said.

"Excuse me." A male voice cut in, and it was Lieutenant Meadows. "I think you should see this." He handed Will a clear evidence bag holding what looked like a piece of paper, duct tape stuck to the top and bottom. "You been getting any threats?" Will frowned deeper as the two of them looked at the piece of paper; Nick leaning over his shoulder. "No." Brad could say with ease, not unless Maggie had intercepted a call or message, and passed it to security or dismissed it but he doubted that very much, he'd have to call and ask her. "Can I see?" He was handed the plastic baggie and the words were written in thick black marker. *'I warned you'*.

"Can I speak to you in the kitchen?" Danni's voice cracked. Handing back the evidence bag, he followed in to the space where she had cooked a great meal, but was now dark and empty; only the light above the stove was lit. "I should call Ethan; the sooner I do the sooner you can get out of here." He was scrolling through the numbers on his phone, when he felt her hand touch his arm. "I got a shirt out of your bag for you." She held the soft black cotton and he noticed her hands were still shaking affirming his resolve to get her to safety. "You were really, really good at your job, right?" Her question confused him as he pulled it over his head. "As a SEAL?" The fabric hid his frown.
"Yeah, you protected people, right? Kept them safe." Her eyes were watering up and his gut wrenched. "That's why you need to get back to the city." He pulled her in to his arms, her face resting on his chest. "No, I need to stay right here next to you."
"Danni."
"Will you protect me?" She pulled back looking up in to his eyes.
"Of course Danni."
"Then I should tell you, I think that bomb was meant for me."

"What?" He let her go but his hands slid down her arms until he could hold her hands. He moved over to the kitchen table and sat her down. "Why would you say that?"

"This." He watched her as she reached for something in her back pocket. "I didn't pay it much attention the other night, I was preoccupied." Danni passed him the note that she remembered in her purse when he'd said it was some sort of message. She'd thought of this upstairs. "When did you get this?" He took in the words *'you should have stayed away'*. "Friday night, I was leaving dad's place for your house, and it had been pushed under the door."

"I need a beer, you?" He got up placing the letter on the table, and walked to the fridge. "Sure." She got up to follow, but her knees felt so weak. "You'll protect me, right?" She repeated her plea. With a beer in each hand he walked to her wrapping her, back up in an embrace. "No one's going to harm you Danni."

"I don't want to interrupt." Will's deep voice disturbed them. "The Fire boys are done and getting out of here."

"Thanks Will."

"If you don't mind, I'd like to stick around until your friend gets here, I have no problem handing a case over which is probably above my ability to investigate, but you're in my town, and I want to keep an eye on the two of you."

"I'd appreciate that." Brad let Danni go again; she walked back to her seat at the table. "You and your partner want a coffee?"

"If it's no trouble?"

"None at all." Seeing Danni looking off in to the darkness of the night outside, he knew he had to get her mind off thinking too much and until he had all the facts he wouldn't completely agree that the bomb was meant for her.

"Did you two have a dinner break yet?" Brad asked Will as Nick came in after closing the front door. "We were about to when the call came in." Nick spoke up. "You know we have plenty of food." Danni also spoke up; glad her eyes lit a little as she got up and went over to the fridge letting the light out, as she took in what was there. "You don't have to go to any trouble." Will began.
"Nonsense, cooking will take my mind off that car blowing up."

While Danni began pulling things out on to the counter behind her, Brad pulled Will in to the living room. "I think the bomb was a message to Danni."
"Why?"
"She got a threat Friday night in the city." He passed Will the note.
"What do you make of it?" Will mussed.
"Someone didn't want her in the city."
"From what I remember she's been gone a long time, why would her returning after all that time be such a problem?"
"That's a good question. The last time she was here she was seventeen and a kid."
"And then the boating accident." That frown was there again.
"Yeah, the boating accident." Brad turned his head to look back at Danni talking to Nick, as she was

preparing whatever it was she was cooking up for their late-night visitors.

CHAPTER SIXTEEN

Until another knock at the front door came Danni had literally forgotten anything was wrong.

Even cooking at three in the morning for two officers in uniform had become normal in her little bubble, as she prepared them each a steak with baked potatoes and asparagus.

She was just sitting down talking with the two men while Brad was putting away the skillet and pan she had used, when the knock came; she kept her eyes on Brad's back as he retreated and was wondering what to expect.

Brad let a sigh he'd been holding in, escape him as he opened the door and saw Ted standing there, a hand on the door frame as he leaned there. "Man, thanks for coming out." Brad held out his right hand which Ted took and shook without pause. From where Danni was standing she had a prime view of the new man. She blinked a few times because she couldn't believe what she was seeing, a man who looked almost like Brad's twin, except this man was blonde and deeply tanned, and when he smiled at Brad there was a very noticeable cleft in the strong chin which Brad certainly didn't have.

"I brought a forensic team." Ted told Brad. "Hopefully the fire department didn't screw up any evidence." Brad looked past him to see the men and women doing their job with what was left of the vehicle. "I appreciate this."

"Any ideas about who is twisted enough to do this to you?"

"I don't think this was focused on me."

"Am I going to get a headache over this one Johnson?" Ted shook his head.

"Possibly."

"Better have some cold beers in here then."

"Follow me." The front door was left open again as Brad led the way back to the kitchen.

"Sergeant Daily, and Officer Fox this is special Agent Turner."

"Ah, the big boys are here Nick." Will pulled himself off a stool, but with civility shook the agent's hand. "We'll get going; I'll have a patrol car sitting on the main bridge, keeping an eye on who's coming and going." He turned his weight towards Danni. "Thanks for a very appreciated meal Danni, it was good to see you again." While Will verbally thanked her Danni returned the smile Nick gave her, and both men left while Brad said. "Ted, this is Danni Morgan. Danni this is an old friend of mine, Ted Turner."

"Pleasure." Ted held on to her hand a little longer than he had the officer's, and Danni could tell this guy was used to being the GQ man, a man women drooled over; but all she could do was see the hardness in his features, and a scar on his left cheek told her he lived on the dangerous side of life.

"Want to fill me in now the Leos are gone?" Ted took a seat where the older cop had sat. "This was found outside." Brad handed the evidence bag and then went to the fridge and took out a beer, putting it before Ted. "I warned you, who warned you?" Ted asked Brad.

"No one warned me but Danni got a note on Friday night." He handed over the other, which he had put inside an evidence bag Will had given him. "You should have stayed away." Again, he read aloud. "What should you have stayed away from?" He directed at Danni. "I wish I knew." She looked from Ted to Brad. "I live in LA, I arrived in New York City Tuesday morning, and this was delivered to my father's home. I have absolutely no idea what it's referring to."

"You live in LA but your family lives in New York?"

"I've lived on the West Coast since I was nineteen; this is the first time back."

"No threats out there?"

"None."

"Someone might have you mixed up with someone else." Ted concluded, putting the papers down and picking up his beer, downing half the bottle in one swig. "Or it was aimed at you Johnson."

"I don't think so." Brad leant his elbows and forearms on the counter, with his back bent over. "I think the person who sent this to Danni did it knowing who she was."

"I do too, except I don't know anyone crazy enough." Danni agreed. The more she thought about it, the more it made sense, and for some reason her mind kept nagging at her that it was aimed at her.

"I get the feeling I'm missing something important."
Ted put the almost empty bottle down. "When Danni
was seventeen her family were in a boating accident.
Her step-mother was killed, her younger brother and
father survived."

"I suffered severe brain trauma, was in a coma for
two years and I was sent to LA days after I woke up. I
have about three seconds of memories from before
the accident; everything was wiped like a magnet to a
hard drive." Danni finished.

"What kind of boating accident?"

"It blew up, I was eighteen at the time, I don't
remember the specifics." Brad answered. "Then
maybe the boat and your car were blown up by the
same person." Ted took out his blackberry. "Have any
of the rest of your family received threats Danni?"

"My father probably wouldn't tell me if he did, and I
don't speak to my brother."

"What's your last name again?"

"Morgan."

Hearing the name Morgan made Ted's fingers freeze.
He looked up at both Brad and this woman, and
paused for a moment. "Is Ethan Morgan your father?"

"Yes, why?" Danni almost physically jumped at his
words.

"A month ago, the bureau was called in to help with a
home invasion. Your father came home from work
and the house had been literally pulled apart. Because
of his friendship with most of the judges in the city
they wanted us to look in to it but your father couldn't
see anything missing, nothing out of the ordinary and

our print search only revealed his and your brother's prints in the house."

"Well Peter used to live with him and I'm sure goes there to visit."

"Did anything happen?" Brad asked.

"Aside from finding dirt on your brother's past, no." Ted aimed at Danni.

"Dirt?"

"DUI's and a few assault charges, mainly minor drunken bar fights."

"That explains why Peter doesn't drive." Danni suddenly felt as though she hadn't been told everything by her whole family. "Ever figure out who did it?"

"Nothing, we canvassed the neighbors, the housekeepers and nannies-nothing. Ethan's business practices are clean, no whispers of anything dirty."

"Could this be connected closer to the boating accident?" Brad said aloud what he hadn't wanted to, but since seeing a connection to Danni it's all his mind though about. "Where did it happen?" Ted started typing again.

"Halfway between here and Nantucket, Danni's second cousins are the Kennedy's."

"I read that in the file we have on your family." Ted looked up and saw Danni's look of horror, that he knew something which might embarrass her. "I have to say I knew your father had a daughter but I merely figured you were estranged from him. I didn't look in to any of your background or any further back than ten years in your father's and brother's lives. I don't remember any information on this boating accident either; the Coast Guard'll probably have it. I'll put in a request." He started typing in to his blackberry.

"What are we going to do?" Danni asked Brad.

"We're going to get back to the city."

"This person found me there, found me here. Maybe I should go back to LA?"

"No." That stopped Ted's fingers as he looked at her. "Until we know what we're working with you stay in New York."

"Why?" She asked.

"That's her favorite word." Brad tried and failed at humor from the look she gave him. "Simple." Ted said. "Brad and I can't protect you in LA."

XXX   XXX

Danni had been quiet after the conversation in the kitchen; Ted had left to see how the crime scene team was handling the carnage outside. Danni had walked off upstairs and he stayed in the kitchen tidying up trying to gain some sort of strength, because, to be honest to himself, that explosion had rattled him.

Rattled him more than he'd ever admit, and he wondered if it would have had he still had a weapon and flack vest tucked in his closet.

He'd hoped when he got upstairs that she would be asleep, but she was sat on the edge of the bed, her legs pulled up to her chest as she looked out to the night sky. "Hey." He sat beside her putting an arm across her shoulders and pulling her closer. "That feels nice."

158

"Hmm, what does?"

"Being held, having you here."

"I'm not going anywhere Danni."

"I've been trying to figure out why someone would want to hurt me."

"And?"

"Did I once know something I shouldn't?"

"I don't know."

"Well isn't that usually why someone tries to hurt someone else?"

"I guess that's one reason."

"So once the team is finished we're leaving then?"

"Yeah, Ted will drive us back to the city."

"And you'll stay with me?"

"Of course." He kissed the top of her head.

"But not at my dad's house right, with it having been a place someone's already broken in to."

"Your worry about knowing something; not being able to go to a place which was a crime scene a while ago; where's this coming from?" He easily pulled her back and on to his lap to sit sideways, and he loved holding her, feeling her as close as two people could get while dressed. Once comfortable Danni said. "I have an addiction to reading."

"Don't tell me, suspense thrillers."

"Suspense dramas." She fixed him with a smile which he knew was as big as he would find from her for a while.

"To answer your question, we shouldn't stay at your dads because you're right, and my place, although it has a sophisticated alarm system, wouldn't stop another explosion, and this person knows we're together so it's an obvious choice."

"There is no way I'm staying with Peter." She said firmly.

"You might not like the idea but...."

"I'll be on the first flight back to LAX if that's the plan."

"Then I know where we can go."

"Where?"

"Somewhere no one would expect, and a place so secure I should have thought of it sooner."

"Police station, FBI holding cell, Fort Knox?"

"Funny." He felt her get up, and he could tell from the lightening horizon and the obvious clock next to him, that it was almost four-thirty. "I'll go see how long Ted and the team are going to be, you should make sure everything's together."

"I should shower, the entire time Will and Nick were here I wondered if they could tell you'd been enjoying my body."

"And I certainly had been." He got a wicked gleam in his eyes as he watched her intently.

"Why'd this have to happen? Last night I felt so happy and content, a new feeling for me in the last fifteen years," She admitted.

"I don't know."

"Well it sucks."

"Someone may have interrupted our night Danni, but I promise you where we're going we'll still be able to enjoy ourselves, and aside from making sure you're safe I am going to make sure you are content."

"Make love to me again and I will be Brad." She stood on her tip toes and kissed his lips softly. "I'm getting in the shower."

"I'll tell Ted we're getting our stuff together. Just don't finish before I get back, I want to feel your skin all slippery under my fingers."

"Bradford Johnson, is there something kinky I should know?"

"I wouldn't go as far as to call it kinky." He kissed her quick and left the room as he heard her laugh, and smiled knowing he was taking her mind if not his own off this cloud which was starting to get dark above their heads.

CHAPTER SEVENTEEN

Sitting in the back of the unmarked dark car Danni had been able to stretch out and sleep on and off during the drive back to the city. She wasn't sure how Brad knew this Agent Ted Turner, but they spoke like old friends who had spent time together, and knowing what Brad used to do she wondered if it was a military connection.

She smiled to no one but herself as her body tingled from her replaying the evening she had spent with Brad. He was a man, no arguments there, he knew how to please a woman, absolutely without a doubt and even while her body silently yearned for those strong hands to touch her intimately again, she also had to silently wonder who some of the women he had mastered his sexual craft on had been. Were they beautiful, rich, strangers?

She had absolutely no idea where their destination was, outside of the obvious, they were almost back in the city; she could tell from the dreary grays and blacks the city seemed to hold. Compared to LA, this town in rainy days seemed out of a movie, a black and white one.

"Hey Danni." She felt his hand on her knee and she opened just one eye to peek at Brad leaning around the seat to see her. "We're gonna stop quickly at my place. I want to get some things. I'm not sure how long I'll be."
"What about my stuff?"

"Once we're settled we'll call your dad and have him come over, and we'll explain everything."

"I need to talk to him as well." Ted joined in.

"Is this turning into a threesome?" Danni sat up with her body forward between the two of them. "Is that what turns you on?" Brad asked almost shocked.

"Hey, I meant like the three musketeers." She laughed. "And I would have thought after." She looked quickly to Ted who seemed occupied on driving and paying little attention. "Last night you understood what turned me on." She whispered the last part.

"I'm intrigued." Ted turned briefly to face her before looking back on the road. Danni blushed and Brad cupped her left cheek in her hand. "Enough of that kind of talk or I'll be watching you hanging from Ted's shoulder as he carry's you away."

"I've never liked the caveman approach." She knew Brad was kidding, trying to keep things light. "Hasn't failed me yet." Ted mumbled loud enough to be heard.

While Brad had gone inside his place to get his things she had stayed in the car with Ted. This man exuded sexuality in the raw Neanderthal way and it was a very intimidating thing to her.

"So, you're the one huh?" His voice cut in to her thoughts of him.

"What?" She met his steely eyes in the rear-view mirror as she rested back in the middle of the backseat. "I knew there was a girl, sorry-woman, in Johnson's past."

"Aren't there in most men's?" She tried to kid.

"True but there's always one, the one you regret hurting, letting go or even never having the balls to make a move on."

"Speaking from experience?"

"Possibly." He nodded his head and without seeing she could only guess there was a certain someone in his mind making him smile as he remembered. "So, which did you do to her?"

"I let her go." His voice softer and filled with emotion.

"Oh."

"She and I were married but life happened." He turned in his seat to be able to speak directly to her. "It took me a while to heal, and I still have the mental scars mentally to prove it.

"How long have you known Brad?"

"Not as long as you."

"Were you in the military too?"

"Possibly."

"How'd you meet?"

"Brad probably wouldn't want me to tell you, you should ask him later."

"Is it embarrassing or something?"

"Or something." He coughed to clear his throat pointing towards the sidewalk behind her. "Here your boy comes."

She felt the trunk of the car open as he threw in two bags, and then as he came around getting into the car. "I'm all good," he told Ted who had kept the engine running and now put the gear shift into drive on the steering wheel. "So where is this safe place?" She asked as she saw Brad using his cell and said. "Sorry."

"It's okay. I was just checking to see if I got any e-mail." He put the iPhone in to his sweater pocket.

"We're going to my mother's apartment."

"Your mother's?" She repeated.

"Doorman; security system; only one possible way to gain access."

"Unless you're a GI Joe like this one." Ted interrupted.

"And no one would think to look for you there," Brad finished.

"But they thought to look for us at your mother's place in the Hampton's."

"Someone has probably been watching you since you arrived."

"Comforting thought, thanks Ted." She let her body shiver involuntarily as she watched the streets they passed, and then Central Park on their right.

Brad knew what had caused Danni's silence. He let her be with her own thoughts because there was little to say or do while in the car, and with Ted right there. They were minutes from their destination and once alone he could hold her and reassure her and whatever else it was she needed.

With there being a lot of stuff they had to take inside Ted had parked in the 'no stopping' zone and Brad had run in to get one of the baggage carts from the bellman. Apart from their things, he hadn't wanted to leave the food at the house to spoil.

Ted left them with just a handshake in the lobby and then was walking away to go and see what he could find about the boat accident and any other items connected to Danni's family. Once the elevator door closed and they were alone traveling the seven floors to the penthouse Brad pulled her in to his arms as he leant on the mirrored wall. Her length aligned with his and the soft moan which escaped her from his roaming hands or the hardness in his jeans telling her how turned on he was, told him she felt it too. When the door opened too soon he was about to pull the emergency shut off, but Danni was already beginning to push herself off him.

"Is your mother going to mind?" Danni whispered as Brad dug in his pocket for his keys, and to adjust himself so no one saw how hard he was. "I doubt it."
"But it's like six in the morning and on a Sunday."
"The way I see it, they want us to spend time together so this is what they get." With the door unlocked he stepped inside, and for the second time in not so many days there was Daisy with a look of fright on her face. "Bradford, Miss Morgan."
"We need to stay a few days."
"Should I ask?" The lady raised her eyebrows.
"Not until we get settled."
"Your Mom just woke up."
"If I take my old room I'll get Danni settled in the spare bedroom."
"But...." Daisy stopped herself from saying anything and nodded, moving in the direction of the kitchen.

The bedrooms were down the hall; his father's old office separated the hall. His parent's bedroom one end, an ostentatious affair which used a quarter of the apartment's floor space, and then after the guest bathroom the other side of the office was the spare bedroom. Brad opened the door wide, smelling the floral scent of pot pouri, and took both of her bags inside as Danni followed. He placed his two handfuls on the bench at the foot of the king-sized bed, and turned to see Danni frowning as she looked at a painting on the wall. It was something he hadn't thought about and he was interested to see what she would say or ask about it.

"My mother." she whispered, looking up at the blonde woman painted delicately on the canvas before her. The countryside surrounded the familiar woman as she smiled at you, her eyes blue and inviting, and it was as if she were looking in a mirror. "I forgot about this." Coming up beside her he looked sideways taking in her reaction. She looked as though she had never seen a picture of the woman before. "She was beautiful."
"Your mother had that made for your dad as a wedding present. It hung in his office, my dad said, but you know, when she died he couldn't bear to look at it anymore."
"It must have torn him apart." Her eyes seemed to be capturing each brush stroke and color to memory.
"He had you which I'm sure helped, but like my parents, yours were high school sweethearts too."
"Dad explained that when I woke up."

"Mom was best friends with Natasha, she says she was there for most of the painting being done, so when Ethan said he couldn't bring himself to have it around as a reminder of what he had lost, she asked if she could have it, to care for it in case either of you ever wanted it back."

"Do you think I look like her?"

"I always have, you have her eyes, cheeks, pretty much everything facial wise except maybe your lips are a little fuller."

"She's beautiful."

"And so are you." He touched her back. "Let me go drop my stuff off, my rooms across the hall, and then I should go tell mom we're here, so take a few minutes to breath, because once she knows you're here God help you."

"Why?" She giggled. "Oops."

"I'll forgive you that one." He kissed her cheek. "As long as you still love being a girlie then you'll survive."

"Should I call my dad?"

"I'll do it; I have to make some calls anyway."

"Sure."

Once his few bags were inside his room he left the more familiar and still decorated like his old room seeing Danni sitting in the arm chair inside the open door to the guest room, was curled up and looked as if she had fallen asleep and he was glad she was getting some rest.

"Daisy just told me you and Danni were here." He was about to knock on his mother's door when it opened and there she was in her wheelchair, about to open it. Her hair in curlers and her cream silk pajamas covered by her dark blue robe. "Yeah, change of plans."

"Something wrong with your place?" She was looking up at her son, knowing there was something he wasn't saying. Being evasive had been worthless when his father had done it, she could see through both men, mainly because of how caring they both were. "I'll explain in a little while, Ethan's going to be coming over."

"If you had a smile on your face I may have believed there was a reason to celebrate suddenly but I get the feeling there isn't."

"I'll explain everything. Can I use Dad's office for a while, there are some calls I need to make."

"Sure honey, you know it's nice to see you behind that desk in there."

"It'll always be dad's and intimidating to be in there."

"Go on in. Where's Danni?"

"In the spare bedroom."

"Why in there?"

"Because." He started and his mother's face lit up. "Whatever you think is right dear, but I would have thought you'd share your room with a woman you like an awful lot."

Nodding with a smile he didn't respond as he walked away, knowing his mother was still in full-on push mode. He could swear she wouldn't be totally satisfied until he and Danni were married.

Marriage, God, for the first in a long time that word didn't sound like pure torture.

Shaking off his thoughts, he entered the office he could still see his father in from when he was a kid, and closed the door behind him. For a brief second, he closed his eyes and asked his father's spirit for the strength to do whatever had to be done. The fact Danni meant so much to him scared him more because if he couldn't stop some sick person who sent her those messages, then he may lose her again and with it the rest of himself.

His first call as he settled in to his father's desk was to Maggie. he had to change the plans for Monday morning and he needed her help, Anderson publishing would have to wait. His second call was to Charlie, the trusted chauffer would be a prime target after his private car was destroyed, and he wasn't going to risk the older man's life. He would get a rental or possibly just stay inside as much as possible. There were also cabs which could be used if needed.

Man switching his head back to combat mode was giving him a headache.

Finally, he dialed Ethan's number. This wasn't a call he wanted to make and he'd have to play it cool so as not to get him as suspicious as he knew his mother was.

CHAPTER EIGHTEEN

"Hey Dad." Danni had showered and dressed in a pair of loose black pants and a white shirt she was tucking inside her pants when she heard her father's familiar cough as he cleared his throat. "So what's going on honey?" The sound of his footsteps made her turn from the mirror on the dresser. The even tread stopped and she watched as a sorrowful expression filled his face as he looked up at the painting she herself had spent the last hour on and off gazing at.

"Didn't Brad tell you?" She moved closer to stand beside him.
"He just asked me to stop by. I was on the way to have brunch with your brother and Felicity." He took his eyes off the painting but looking at his daughter had the same effect. She was so much like Natasha, more than he could ever voice without breaking down. There was never a day he didn't miss his first wife. Theresa, the woman had been a good step-mother to Danni and had given him Peter, but she could never replace Natasha, and Theresa had known that, something that had been between them their entire relationship.

"It sounds like being called here saved you from the brunch from hell."
"Something like that, I wish Peter was more understanding with you."
"Dad, I'm not an invalid."
"I know that, Peter I'm sure is just jealous of all the attention you get."

"I think it's more than that dad."

"If only the two of you would spend some time together, get to know one another."

"Dad." She put her hand on his arm. "One day, but it's got to be something he wants. I want him to be my brother because it's his choice, not because he's concerned you'll cut his trust fund off."

"A father can still wish, right." He kissed the top of her head.

"Daisy told me she had let you in." Louise's voice made them both look towards the doorway. "How are you Ethan?" She held out her hands to which she watched her father walk towards and take. You could see they were dear friends, that in their interwoven pasts they had both loved and lost their best friends. "You look wonderful Louise."

"I wish I was as young as our children again, but I can't complain." Was there really a blush on Brad's mother's face? Danni smiled to herself. "We're going to have brunch in the dining room. Bradford said we're waiting for someone but could go ahead and start." Louise maneuvered her wheelchair in the hall with ease, and Danni walked with her father to where Brad stood, talking on his cell still at the end of the long dining table where he could look out of the large window which filled the room with the morning light.

Hanging up from Ted who had found files and left to meet them and was closer to his mother's place than the federal building downtown, he saw the three of them coming in. Brad took in Danni more than their parents; it looked as if she had maybe grabbed a few

172

winks of sleep. He was jealous; all he wanted was some shut-eye; all he'd been able to get was maybe a few hours before the explosion.

"Now can we know the big news?" Louise had never had patience and Brad took Danni's hand, she was sitting beside him on one side of the table, his mother at the head where there was never a permanent chair, and Ethan was getting comfortable opposite them. "We had some trouble down in Southampton; I decided it was best we come back," Brad began, unsure how this would freak out their parents. "What kind?" Ethan asked as Daisy poured him a cup of coffee. "Someone blew my SUV up." Brad said watching both of them, while Danni squeezed his hand.

"Excuse me?" Louise put down the cup she had just picked up.

"You didn't hear me wrong, the SUV was blown up."

"By who?" Ethan asked, his face covered in shock just like his mother's, and Brad said, "We aren't sure."

"We were asleep when it happened." Danni felt impelled to say.

"Thank God neither of you were hurt."

"I second that." Louise agreed with Ethan.

"Who the hell would do something like that and why?" Ethan asked. "Is it something from your past?" He aimed at Brad.

"Oh dear, I feared something." His mother grabbed his arm.

"It's got nothing to do with my past." Okay so they weren't a hundred percent certain on that, but with the two notes. "It has to do with mine." Danni spoke up making both adults look at her agape. "But...." Ethan said and stopped. "I got a threatening note Friday night delivered to your house dad. I didn't think anything of it, and then after the car exploded last night the fire department found another note, which made me think more about the first."
"What did the notes say?"

The sound of the chimes for the doorbell made the conversation pause a moment.

"The first said 'you should have stayed away', and the second was 'I warned you'. They're both in the custody of a federal agent." Brad pushed his seat out, letting go of Danni's hand as he heard the front door open and then hushed words before Ted appeared following Daisy. "Ethan, this is Ted Turner, a friend of mine I called when I thought it was me this had been aimed at, Mom, Ted."
"Sir, Louise." Ted was polite enough as he moved around to shake both of their hands, as he held a briefcase in his left hand.

"I can't believe this." Ethan got up to pace while everyone had taken a seat, Ted had taken a chair beside the man while Danni wished there was something she could say to her dad so that pain she knew he was now experiencing would go away. "You told them already," Ted stated without asking Brad, who took the opportunity to drink some of his coffee.

"Teddy, are you sure?" Louise asked, and Danni realized she had to know the man to refer to him in such a way. "I got the old report faxed to me." Opening his briefcase, he took out a thick manila file. "Thank you," He said to Daisy who set a cup of the coffee before him.

"Which old report?" Brad knew Ethan would ask. "The boat accident Dad."
"What would you need that for?"
"Well Mr. Morgan, we decided while waiting in Southampton that, seeing as Danni has been in Los Angeles until last week and the catalyst for that was the accident, then it's a good bet whatever happened that day on your boat is somehow related to this person now fixing their attention on her because as a seventeen-year-old, what could she know?"
"The boating accident was just that, an accident." Ethan's voice was tight. "How about you go through that day, I read the report but I'd like to hear it from you."

Danni watched her father, hearing the sigh escape him as he sat down again, and braced himself for the memories from that day. "I had been in the city the night before. A meeting was going to run late which it did, so I stayed at the apartment we had back then and planned on going out to meet Theresa, Peter and Danni at the dock where our boat was moored during the summer, except when Danni was little and we had the boat towed down to Florida for a while.

Anyway, I must have arrived at the boat club around noon, the three of you were there already, you didn't want to go. You and Brad had some falling out right before, and you were begging me to let you stay, that the trip to Nantucket would be boring, but I wanted all four of us to be together." Ethan paused rolling his head to ease some tension in his neck. "You were pissed beyond belief, but then you were the typical teenager. You went down to your cabin while Peter was helping me get the deck set, and Theresa was making sure everything was unpacked in the kitchen. The day was bright blue and warm, there was little breeze, so we kept the sails closed and set course for my cousin's.

We had stopped and anchored halfway, Theresa wanted to relax and get some sun, and while she and Peter were topside I went down to your cabin where you were reading something. We talked about the entire situation between you and Brad."

"You know what I did at the party?" Danni was red-faced as her eyes opened wide, looking between the two adults. "I'm afraid so honey."

"Well this is embarrassing for some reason I can't word."

"Brad told you?"

"I did." Brad answered realizing he hadn't thought about how some things had come back to Danni and that maybe she hadn't told her father yet, but he would let her say something.

"So you were downstairs with Danni?" Ted brought the conversation back.

"I think we spent an hour down there talking, until Theresa knocked on the door and told us it was dinner time, and could I start the small grill we had on board. We left her with Danni while I went up and got it going. We had dinner and then as planned we all hung out below deck playing cards. We were going to sleep on board and set sail again in the morning. It was a long weekend and we hadn't spent much time together during that summer because of my work. Usually I would work three days and relax at the house the other four, but we were in the middle of an acquisition, both John and I were tied to our offices." "The Brewster merger." Louise remembered how lonely that summer had been, even Theresa had been gone doing things, and she had stayed at the house watching over the children.

"I couldn't sleep, Peter was adamant he wanted to sleep under the stars and you disappeared to your room. I decided to wake Peter to watch the sunrise and I had woken Theresa in the process. She liked the idea and said she would see if you were interested. She couldn't wake you, you mumbled something about 'go away' to her, and she was making coffee when the sun came over the horizon. I went back down to see if I could persuade you to join us. You grumbled a lot Danni, hated being woken, but you said you would come up; you wanted to brush your hair and teeth first. I went back up on deck and it was moments before there was a weird noise and then...." Ethan closed his eyes and rested his head in his hands.

"Dad." Danni had never heard any of this, nothing sounded familiar, it was easy to know what would come next but she so desperately wanted the rest to be described and explained. "The boat exploded. Peter and I were at the bow and when the boat shook we slid off unable to catch the railing. After that first load bang there were a few others, and whatever was left of the boat ended up in small pieces. Peter and I were floating for a few seconds before I spotted the yellow bag the life boat was in, I swam to get it and easily pulled the toggle that inflated it, and then helped Peter climb in before I did. There was some fire on pieces of wood floating around, lots of smoke, and as we floated around those moments Peter spotted you face down in the water." Ethan wiped a few tears from his eyes and Danni noticed Louise was holding one of his hands.

"I had to do CPR, once I felt a pulse I thought you would wake up. But Peter pointed out what I had missed, you had a bad laceration on the side of your head. There was no one around but the life raft comes with a waterproof bag on the side, holding flares and a small radio. I called in the Mayday, and not long after a helicopter came. The coast guard lowered a diver and he assessed the situation. You hadn't woken up and with a special gurney contraption they airlifted you while we watched one of their boats getting closer. Once we were taken aboard the ship, we heard you had been taken straight to Boston, and when we got in to Mystic, Connecticut the police helicopter flew us to join you."

"And Theresa?" Danni knew the ending but wanted to know. "She was never found, honey."

CHAPTER NINETEEN

"The file says that the Mystic Coast Guard collected as much of the wreckage as possible and the NTSB concluded after your statement and your son's as well as what was recovered, that it had to have been an onboard malfunction." Ted said as they all knew that was where Ethan's story ended. "They believed there had to have been some faulty wiring or something which caused the explosion." Ethan leant back in his seat.

"Are we to assume that someone purposely sabotaged that boat to kill all of you?" Louise felt a cold shiver pass through her entire body. "I still can't see a connection to anyone of us to someone crazy enough to try and kill us." Ethan shook his head. "I mean; there's a possibility this could be related to your military career?" He looked at Brad who in turn looked to Ted. "I already put a call in to the Pentagon and Homeland security. They'll let us know in a few hours if any missions Brad was involved in may have come state side." Ted was playing with his cell typing something as he spoke. "Honestly Mr. Morgan. We aren't grasping here."
"How about maybe a husband or spouse you may have pissed off?" Ethan again looked at Brad who, as Danni held his hand, felt him physically flinch which made her wonder again how many women were in his past.

"There's a lot less than you think." Brad said quietly. "I know this is hard Ethan."

"Hard?" There was a tight choked sounding laugh in his voice. "That would mean someone purposely tried to kill my entire family."

"I know this is hard Ethan." Louise touched his shoulder. "Teddy and Brad will do everything they can, okay."

"I'm going to need to ask some questions about that time: who you were in dealings with, anyone who had grudges against you. Anyone who Danni may have come in to contact with, who thinks she knows something."

"I kept Danni far from my work; she never even visited my office."

"How about people who could have come to the house in the Hampton's?"

"None, all business was conducted here in the city."

"Then how about we rebuild the days leading up to the accident?" Ted was getting slightly frustrated, he understood this was hard for the man but he would have figured, this being about his dear daughter, then he would be doing more talking and less arguing.

"Danni spent Wednesday and Thursday with me." Brad spoke up. "Aside from the couple of hours she and Theresa went shopping Friday morning, we were together from when I got back from Annapolis until they left."

"The entire time?" Ted was asking for clarification because there were twenty-four hours in a day, and the two of them had been teenagers. "We had no problem with Danni sleeping over or Brad sleeping at the Morgan house," Brad heard his mother say as she pushed her chair back from the table, and went over to the buffet, where Daisy had set up the carafe of coffee and other pieces. "It was a common thing." Ethan smiled slightly to his daughter who had said little, and that look in her eye was killing him.

"So something could have happened while you were with your step mother?"
"I suppose so but I couldn't tell you, remember."
"Sorry." Ted took out a legal pad from his case. "Where was Peter during this time?"
"He went shopping with the women." Louise, returning with the coffee cup two thirds filled, held it expertly in one hand while maneuvering herself with the other. "Theresa wanted to get him a new pair of water shoes."
"Do you remember anything, anyone hanging around that summer Louise?"
"Not really."
"What does that mean Mother?" Brad frowned.
"Well, most summers Theresa and I were pretty much always together, but that summer I saw very little of her. Between visiting Annapolis with you and her trips to the city; you remember Danni and Peter were often being watched by us." She aimed to her son.

"Are you sure it was that summer?" Ethan asked.
"Positive but hold on." She reached for the small two-way cell on the table. "Daisy, could you come in here a moment please." She asked her assistant and moments later, as she couldn't have been too far away, the woman appeared. "Sit and join us a moment, you should know what's going on and you'll probably know some things I may have forgotten."

She filled Daisy in, whose face showed little shock after the initial news about the explosion of the SUV. "You're right, it was that summer, Mrs. Morgan probably spent three nights in the city out of the week."

"Tell me what you're thinking." Ted turned to Ethan. "To my knowledge, Theresa wasn't at our apartment much at all after we made the trip down to the beach house."

Danni watched as she saw something cross her father's face. Her first conclusion, hearing Louise and Daisy, was that there was some secret her father either knew or had just found out, that look was one of pain and hurt.

"Care to elaborate on that?" Ted asked her father and Danni watched intently. "My wife was having an affair." He ended that with a cough.

"With who?" Louise was shocked.

"Do we really need to get in to that? The man isn't someone who would know how to set something up like the boating accident up."

"If he had money he could have paid someone to do it for him." Ted countered. "If he wanted to get rid of me so he could be with her, then a family trip would not have been it." Ethan fired back.

Brad sighed inwardly. They were getting nowhere, with Ethan refusing to believe there was more than a mechanical malfunction, and he hoped it didn't have to get more serious before Ted concluded that someone was intent on scaring Danni.

The sound of the doorbell chiming again made Brad move, releasing Danni's hand, Daisy was naturally getting up and he told her to remain; it was Maggie, and he needed a few minutes with his assistant in the office. He rolled his stress-filled shoulders as he walked down the hall and seeing Maggie dressed down on a Sunday was almost a relief. With all the craziness he knew she would keep his feet close to the floor, she had a soothing, calming way, and she'd been just the trick the first time he had been subjected to a board meeting.

"Maggie."
"Is this all for real?" She whispered as she watched Brad close the door behind her. "I'm afraid so."
"Poor Danielle, that girl needs this like a hole in the head."
"Tell me about it. Did you make those calls yet?" He asked as he led her towards that office she had been inside before, he knew that. "Actually, I haven't," she answered as he closed the door behind them, giving them some privacy. "I had a thought I wanted to share first."
"Which is?"
"Remember Ben Goodman, he was a year above you in school, and his father was on the board of directors before he passed away."
"Vaguely." Brad took the seat behind the desk and Maggie sat comfortably in the chair opposite.

"He was a location reporter for CBS after college and then after being captured while reporting in Iraq in two thousand and three, he moved to Boston, and started with the Boston Globe."

"Okay, you have my attention."

"He's been looking for something more to sink his teeth in to; he started writing a book on his ordeal overseas. I think you should offer him the job."

"But I offered it to you Maggie."

"And I will always feel honored, but right now my place is beside you."

"Is this an excuse not to leave?"

"No." She chuckled. "I just remember his father and how he feared for his son's life."

"How long was he captured?" It had been before his time, and in two thousand and three he himself had been inside the country doing things he'd been trained for. He still could have been in the man's position, he hadn't seen papers about it, but only the rumors from his mother's letters and calls after it happened and he knew his own father had mentioned it at the time.

"Four months and when he came back he was a mess but he's rebuilt his life piece by piece."

"How do you know he's looking for something more?"

"Your mother mentioned something a while back; she still speaks to his mother from time to time."

"Then you have my permission." Brad put his elbows on the desk, leaning forward and rubbing the back of his neck. "Why don't you get the ball rolling on that?" He watched her take the blackberry in her hands. "We'll have to cancel as many appointments for me as well; I want to work from here as much as I can."

"Sure."

"Want some coffee?" He offered.

"Are you going to get it?" Maggie joked.

"Of course, I should also make sure Ethan isn't giving Ted hell."

"Ted's here already?" His assistant had met his friend back when he'd first agreed to cover the job his father had loved. "He's trying to get Ethan to cooperate."

"Ethan can be stubborn, especially when it comes to family."

"Oh, how I know."

Leaving Maggie to her call, Brad heard a noise coming from the direction of the front door and saw Daisy walking back. Her face rarely showed anything in the way of emotion but you knew when she was a little miffed. The usually quiet day had been interrupted. "Did someone leave?" He asked Daisy.

"Ethan."

"Did it get bad in there?"

"Not at all, he wanted some time to think and offered to go and get Danielle's things."

"Ted's still here?"

"In with your mother, and Danielle went to her room."

"I'm just going to check on her."

"No need to tell me."

Glancing briefly as he walked by the dining room where Ted was busy speaking to his mom, he walked further down the hall and found Danni standing there looking up at the painting in her room again. "You okay?" He asked coming to stand beside her and she turned to face him. "I was just thinking how everything in Dad's life has been basically misery. Natasha died, his high school sweet heart and then he has to deal with not only Theresa being an adulterer, and then her death; but I haven't given him any rest either." Unsure what to say he just stood there listening. "Peter's a pain in the ass and I don't really like that Felicity."

"Felicity's just a spoiled brat." Brad stated.

"Do you know her well?" Danni looked up at him.

"I suppose."

"Did you ever date her?" He watched her eyes look away and he knew when her father had made that accusation about his 'conquests' in the other room, that she had taken an extreme notice to it.

"We went out for dinner once."

"Just dinner?"

"Yes, just dinner." He repeated. "You know your father was a little wrong in what he said back there."

"About?"

"You know." Brad moved further in to the room sitting on the small chaise at the end of the bed. "Me and all the women I've dated." He used air quotations on the last word. "Have there been?"

"Would that make a difference to you?" He took in her slow movements to stand before him, as if her legs were connected to the slow way her mind was trying to answer that. "It's something I thought about before this morning."

"When?" He frowned ever so slightly as he took her hips in his hands holding her there before him. "Last night when we were in bed."

"Care to explain why?"

"It's...." He took in the flushed cheeks and her soft words. "You just know the right places to touch, the perfect things I've never experienced before."

"So, you think there has to have been a phone directory thick list of women I practiced on?"

"There hasn't been? It sounds like you have a reputation."

Danni was almost reluctant to allow Brad to pull her down to sit sideways on his lap, but she let him. His fingers turned her chin so she had to look at him without straining her eyes. "I'm not going to lie and say there's been no one since you Danni because that's a waste of time. But there has been a lot less women I've bedded than I've been spotted out with."

"So basically you're trying to say people see you with someone and presume?" There was a little disbelief in her voice, she knew it.

"There are two social page headlines they use for me. One is this party hard bed a different woman each night of the weekend, and the other is the one my mother uses, the one which refers to my need for bachelordom."

"Neither one sounds very nice."

"The second one has been closer to what I've lived like. Believe it or not just because I've had dinner with a lot of women doesn't mean they've ended up in bed with me."

Brad sighed. "I've spent a lot of time since being back here working, learning what I need so I don't screw up as bad as I know I have; and there have been times when I had caved in to my mother's need to see me with someone, and then other times when I called women I knew to be a suitable companion to some function I was ordered to attend." He looked in to her beautifully astute eyes. "I want you to remember one thing more than anything you may hear, which I know you're going to scoff at before I even say the words. But any woman I took to bed never lived up to one person who has been inside my head for a very long time Danni."

"Who?"

"You." Danni held her breath as she bit the inside of her mouth trying to stop the scoffing he knew she would have. She didn't know how to respond to his admission, true or false she was willing to give him maybe forty percent in belief. "And I can see you're fighting to argue." He laughed slightly as his arms squeezed her slightly in his embrace. "I wish you knew what we had back years ago and maybe you'd be willing to believe me."

The shrill tone of his phone in the leg pocket of his cargo pants made him place his head on her shoulder as he reluctantly took the cell from his pocket and answered it without looking at the caller ID.

"Johnson." He said, feeling Danni move slightly and he removed his head from where it rested as she got up from his lap, the lack of her contact made his legs cold. "Johnson I'm not interrupting anything, am I?" It was Coop.

"Not really."

"Oooh, did you get to see your girl, or is it someone else?"

"Danni's here." Saying her name aloud made her turn to look at him as he stood up.

"So, are you working on reconnecting with her?"

"I think we've reconnected pretty well." Brad laughed. "You know maybe you can help me with something."

"Anything man. But I doubt there's anything I can tell you to help impress Danni."

"I think there is, I'm going to put you on speaker phone, hold on."

"Sure."

Pressing the button on the side and then holding it in his hand he said. "Danni, on the phone is my buddy Coop from San Diego; Coop say hello to Danni."

"Hi Danni." She heard the deep voice of a man who sounded as if he were smiling. "Hello Coop."

"Coop, I'm gonna ask some questions and I need you to answer with the first thing that comes in to your head."

"This sounds fun and slightly dangerous." Coop's laughter traveled out of the speaker and Danni was confused with what was going on; she could only stare at the phone. "What was pinned to the inside of my locker at Annapolis?"

"A picture of Danni."

"I had two letters in my vest when we went on missions, one was for my parents if I ever got injured, and who was the other one for?"

"Danni."

"Would you say I have a reputation for bedding women?"

"No."

"Why not?"

"Because back when we were young enough to enjoy such a night out you'd just get drunk and tell whoever was hitting on you that you were the property of Danielle Morgan."

"Okay I get it." Danni stepped in. "You made your point Brad." She gave him a smile. Brad disabled the speaker phone setting, putting the phone to his ear. "I appreciate your help old buddy." Brad was pleased with himself. "Glad I could oblige, now I need a favor from you."

"Which is?"

"Know anyone close to the New York Yankees?"

"Do you mean close as in distance or someone who works there?"

"Funny, someone who works there of course."

"Possibly, why?"

"I was hoping as a sure way to get you here for the party, if you could get something signed by Jeter or all of the team, it might be hard now Jeter retired; for the Senior Chief. You know I forgot he was a die-hard Yankee fan until I was over talking to Patti yesterday. I know the team would chip in for anything you have to buy."

"I can take care of it, don't worry about that. It can be for the team."

"Awesome, thanks Johnson."

"Don't mention it."

"So, I'm guessing things are working out okay with Danni?"

"We're enjoying time together." He snuck a look at her; she was looking for something from her bag. "Good."

"Except unfortunately my car blew up while we were asleep last night." Coop was quiet on the other end a moment, and Danni's moves stopped. "Mind repeating that?" Coop asked.

"You heard me." Brad began telling him as Danni having found her own cell left the room leaving him there. "Someone seems pissed at Danni."

"I agree." Brad was reluctant to admit that any more than he had to.

"And she has absolutely no memories?"

"She's been getting flashes of some stuff since." Brad trailed off.

"Since when?"

"We got together she said."

"Huh, there's something about you Johnson."

"I wish, right now we need more of her memories back."

"I would have to ask Jamie but if she's getting memories which didn't you say that area of her brain was damaged then maybe it's just like when one of your engines has a loose wire, maybe she needs something to connect them."

"Like what?"

"You remember Espinoza from Team two?"

"Jesus? Sure, I remember him."

"Well he had that TBI which kept him off duty for almost nine months. Jamie had read about some treatment a doctor was doing at Walter Reed and pulled some strings to send him out to D.C. I mean I don't know his deal or Danni's, but maybe there's some sort of treatment, maybe some procedure they haven't tried on her?"

"You know I never really got to know Jamie, but I've met her a few times for physical's and stuff."

"If you're curious give her a call."

"I don't suppose you know...." Brad started to ask but Coop cut in.

"Jamie's off base today but I'm sure if you called she wouldn't mind."

"You sure?"

"I'll tell you what; I'll call her first, make sure she's free, and if she's busy I'll text you."

"Sounds like a plan and unless anything comes up I'll see you next week."

"I'll be in touch buddy."

"Bye Coop."

CHAPTER TWENTY

Brad hung up and looked towards the door, not realizing Danni had come back and was watching him from where she stood leaning on the door frame. "I called Sam and told her I wouldn't be back Tuesday, because I have a feeling after Ted being adamant about keeping me in New York until this is over, I won't have a chance to get my flight." Danni moved further in and dropped her cell on her bag. Brad got up and for some reason he didn't completely understand he had an urgent need to take her, hold her tight and kiss her until his lips were sore.

Danni sighed, her lips tingled and his mouth was now kissing down her neck, hitting that crook where her knees would buckle from the sensation. Almost instinctively Brad picked her up, holding her length against his own and it was another one of those things he seemed to just know, like ESP that her legs would weaken.

Brad wondered if she could feel his erection, it had stirred to life with the first touch of his lips against hers. He knew there were things they should be doing and they should be in the other room, but he had something else he wanted to do more than anything.

"Why are we going this way?" Danni half sighed half whispered, as he walked holding her still backwards towards the door which led to his bedroom. "I was trying to be a gentleman but my mother reminded me you should be in my room not the guest room." He spoke quickly not really wanting to disconnect his lips and once the last syllable was out he took her lips again making any comment she was going to say disappear. His fingertips brushed the door handle to his room when he heard a distinct female cough off to his right.

Reluctantly he stopped kissing Danni but still held her there, her feet hovering above the floor about a foot. Maggie looked embarrassed as she stood there in the darkened hall, the lamp on the side table lighting her up from behind. "Your timing sucks." He told Maggie.
"I can tell. I just wanted to ask quickly if you want me to reschedule Thursday's board meeting?"
"No."
"Then I'll be in the office whenever you're done." Maggie paused. "Hello by the way Danielle."
"Hi." She replied quietly, and once Maggie had turned to walk back to the office he hastily opened the bedroom door and erring on the side of caution he locked it behind him.

He didn't let go of Danni until he lowered her on to the bed and even then, her arms were still around his neck holding tight and he knew he was smiling.

"What's with the cheesy grin?" Danni asked.
"I can't have a cheesy grin?"
"I've just never seen someone so happy." She watched as Brad peeled his shirt off, his legs were straddling her hips. He had such a great body that when she leant up to kiss that skin she felt his hands

at her own shirt, the buttons opening faster without being popped off, and whether it was a lot of female's or just one the man seemed to know how to get someone naked quickly.

"I've not smiled like this in a very long time." Once her shirt was undone he began moving it down her arms, her own hands seemed to be under the back of her own shirt, making his movements tricky, but once she relaxed her arms he reveled in the pleasure of being able to take both her shirt and bra off at once. "You should do it more often."
'That would mean you'd have to be here all the time'. He wanted to say but he let the moment pass as he gently pushed her down and kissed down her neck towards her breasts. Her fingers playing in his hair, holding him there and more than anything he wanted to be deep inside her again, feel that intense euphoria that had trapped him with its claws each time they'd made love the night before.

Made love, not sex; a statement he shocked his own mind with as he thought it.

He moved swiftly finishing their disrobing to gain the joining his body was aching for, and with his eyes closed he thrust deeply in to Danni, whose back arched in his hands and a moan escaped her lips. He knew this was going to be quick, not leisurely as those times the night before, but he could tell from the way her body was responding that he wouldn't feel guilty about not getting her there as he knew the moment she was close and it was his own doing that made her follow him down the rabbit hole.

Lying there, the darkened afternoon light cutting across the sheets barely covering them Brad kissed the top of her head as she remained asleep in his arms. He was making a mental note of everything, each breathe she took, the way her mouth was open slightly, and knew it was from being unable to sleep breathing through her nose. A small nasal problem he had found adorable, especially when she got a cold.

He wondered if she still had that problem, if she even ever got a cold being in LA.

Reluctantly he knew he had to return to Maggie, he was sure his mother and Ted had wondered where either of them were too.

With another look back, her body lay across the bed, the length of her spine on display. He was tempted to take all his clothes off again and go over there, but that would only have happened if they were at his place, and there was nothing as dire as threats going on.

He didn't see Ted or his mother in the dining room, but he found Ted with Maggie in the study. Maggie was laughing at something and looked up when she heard him close the door behind himself. "Your mother went to have one of her treatments," his assistant informed him, and he knew that was the semi-secret way to refer to the physical therapy on her legs with which Daisy tormented his unwilling mother each and every day. "So, what did I miss?" He retook his seat behind the old desk.

"Nothing as important as ensuring Miss. Morgan's completely safe." Ted gave him that look. "I know, I'm sorry." He could actually feel the heat in his face.

"Look! Our little Bradford is blushing," Maggie teased him.

"Okay, I deserve it."

"I'm waiting for Ethan to get back." Ted tried hard not to let them see his eyes rolling. "And I finished all of my calls." Maggie added.

"What do you think so far with all of this?" Brad asked his friend.

"Well, the lab got no useful prints off anything including the letters. The bomb was constructed with nothing that can't be bought at your local Home Depot, and as of ten minutes ago there's no way to trace anything to a specific store." He paused. "I have agents looking in to Ethan's business activities of seventeen years ago as well as a thorough investigation of the boating accident."

"Then we wait for those to come in."

"Be quicker if Ethan was a little more cooperative." Maggie said.

"Or we could get to whatever memories this perp thinks Danni knows." Ted had said it as he held the mug of his second coffee close to his mouth before he took a sip, but Brad remembered what it was he was going to do.

"I have a thought about that after speaking to a friend of mine." Brad took the cell from his thigh pocket and checked; no calls, no texts. "Give me a minute." He went through the entire phone book he'd had the last tech guy at the apple store put on there from the old cell he'd had before the switch to the iPhone. That had been back a few generations of phones ago. But this cell held the same numbers he'd had for the last fifteen plus years and there were close to more numbers than he needed in there and some he hadn't used in almost as long.

Finding the number that he was sure anyone who'd been in Team Seven or for that matter any Team on the Coronado Base knew, he pressed the green phone button on the screen and placed the phone comfortably at his ear. It rang three times and then an out of breath man answered the phone. "Hey Taylor it's Johnson," he said, seeing Maggie looking through some paper work and Ted texting someone. "Well, I've been waiting for you to call, Coop called Jamie an hour ago."
"Where is your lovely wife?"
"She's just gone inside to get something; we're out by the pool."
"I'm not interrupting anything am I?"
"No, just a quiet day home with the kids."
"Kids? You mean you have more than a daughter now?"
"We sure do, twin boys. They'll be three in a few months, and Izzy's eight."
"Jesus, the last time I saw her she was a baby."

"Time goes fast my friend. So, I'm guessing this has nothing to do with the party this weekend?"

"Afraid not, I needed a medical opinion on something and Coop mentioned something Jamie helped Espinoza with."

"TBI?"

"Yeah."

"Oh, I get it." Matt's small chuckle came down the line. "Does this have something to do with that woman you used to talk about when drunk back in the early days on the Team?"

"Your memory has no problems." Brad said dryly.

"Here's my wife, hold on. Will we see you next week?"

"I'm gonna try my best."

"Good, here she is." He heard the phone being rustled on the other end.

"Commander Johnson." A female voice which sounded happy came to him.

"Commander Buchanan."

"How are you, and how long did it take you to find the evil doc's number?" He remembered the time the doctor had overheard his comment about her being evil but it had been meant in a fun way which thankfully she knew. "Been better, I don't know if Coop spoke to you or Matt but there's something I need to ask your medical opinion on."

"Hey, that's what I'm here for but you know without a personal evaluation I can't give you anything solid."

Feeling like he told the basic story a million times he filled Jamie in. "So Coop mentioned I should call after you sending Espinoza to Walter Reed for treatment."

"I sure did. We had exhausted every possible avenue with Jesus and this was our last shot."

"What kind of treatment was it?"

"You'll not believe me even if I told you."

"A head transplant?"

"Nothing so evasive." Jamie laughed. "Hypnosis."

"Get out."

"Seriously. There was absolutely no medical reason for what Jesus suffered except he had the injury, he never had any open skull trauma but did have severe swelling from being knocked back hard by an explosion. His head hit a wall and snapped sharply, shaking the brain. As a result he lost mobility to certain motor functions, but like I said, there was nothing we could do because there was nothing physically to operate on or treat."

"And that worked?"

"Nine months later he returned back to active duty and today you'd never know."

"Think that could work for retrieving memories?"

"What could it hurt Brad? I mean, it's without invasive measures, and I would certainly suggest this now as a first course of treatment."

"Is this something new?"

"Using it for TBI's I don't think so, with how skeptical people are over hypnotism unless it's to lose weight or quit smoking I can see why it isn't used more. There is still a great deal of debate within the medical community about whether hypnosis can even be called medicine. The older docs think it's crazy medicine."

"Would you have the number for the doctor who performed this?"
"I don't have the number on me here at home but the doctor's name is Major Lewis Cole. He works weird hours so if you call Walter Reed you might catch him today."
"This is great. Thanks Jamie."
"Anytime. Matt said you were coming for the retirement party next week."
"I'm gonna try."
"Will you be bringing this lucky woman?"
"Let's see how the week goes first."
"Well, just don't take any risks. I know Coop is still holding out you will return for good soon."
"I definitely plan on returning Jamie."
"Good, call Coles and let me know how it goes."
"I will, thanks again and say bye to your husband for me."
"Will do, bye Brad."
"Bye Jamie."

Placing the phone on the desk he could see the two of them had been paying some attention to the call. "Did you guys get any of that?"
"Kind of one sided." Ted joked.
"That was a friend and doctor in San Diego, she had a sailor with a TBI, he lost his mobility, and like Danni there was nothing surgically or with medicine they could do to treat him. But she sent him to a doctor in

DC who in nine months got Espinoza back on his feet."

"Voodoo?" Maggie took her turn to joke.

"No, hypnosis."

"Hypnosis?" Ted shook his head. "First isn't that unconventional, secondly we don't have nine months."

"Who said it would take nine months for Danni, and I think it's worth a try." The sound of Louise wheeling herself in to the room made him pause a moment. "Not only can it answer whether she knew something, but also it would give her the life back that she lost."

"Are you really considering this?" Ted asked.

"What else can I do?"

"Are you sure there have been absolutely no memories?"

"Well." Brad looked at Ted. "Supposedly there were a few things that she recalled since meeting me."

"Are you sure?" Louise came closer to them.

"I can only take Danni's word and I always have."

"Then let me try something first."

"What?" Brad watched his mother intently as she took a large leather photo album off the bookshelf. "I always wondered if you had been around, if you had been strong enough to deal with everything, if maybe her recovery would have been better."

"You aren't blaming me, are you?" Brad got defensive.

"Certainly not and Ethan never asked for our help, if I'd pushed maybe I could have made it happen sooner." With the book on her lap securely she was about to turn to leave when Brad said. "I think she's sleeping."

"Actually, she's in the kitchen with Daisy; I guess you didn't spend all of her energy behind that locked door of yours."

Both Ted and Maggie looked at one another and held laughing in seeing Brad, this strong man who neither had ever seen or known in a real relationship in years, being different, smiling and more relaxed in his demeanor.

CHAPTER TWENTY-ONE

"What are the two of you doing?" Louise came in to the kitchen to see Daisy, who normally had no one around as she prepared dinner, looking excited that there was someone to talk to. Daisy rarely spoke to strangers but then Louise had to keep telling herself that Danni was far from a stranger in their house. As a teen Danni had been to this apartment, slept over inside her son's room many times, and like then it was lovely to have her inside the walls.

"I was getting under Daisy's feet." Danni took in Louise. There was so much love in her face when she looked at you, but then she knew from those old eyes that if you pissed her off God help you. "She was certainly not," Daisy protested.
"Well, either way, I wondered if I could steal her for a few minutes."
"Fine with me." Daisy went back to what she was doing and Danni followed Louise carefully as they went through the archway in to the living room just off from where the front door was. While she chose the antique armchair, which felt familiar to her, Louise had parked herself beside the low arm-rest.

"Brad mentioned you may have remembered a few things since the two of you have spent some time together the last few days."
"A couple of things, nothing big."
"Would you tell me?"
"When I walked in to the house at the beach, I knew there was a table missing below your stairs."

"I'm sure my quick temper over it being broken wasn't something you recall."

"Were you mad?"

"That table had been hand built by my grandfather, but when I realized Bradford was hurt I calmed down." Louise paused. "You were in tears because it had been your idea."

"I seem to have gotten your son in to some predicaments back then, the first being the fire from my Easy Bake oven"

"That came back to you too?"

"No, Brad told me."

"Anything else." Louise was trying hard not to push but this would mean so much if Danni could just remember what Brad had meant to her, maybe her dreams could come true and her son would get the woman he had always loved.

"Some personal things." Danni blushed.

"I'll ask no more." Louise patted the top of her hand that rested on the armrest. "After Brad left for Annapolis we cleaned out his room at the beach house. We knew, John and I, that our son would never go back to the house."

"Because of me?"

"Yes." It wasn't blunt Danni knew, that answer was just honest.

"I knew it from the moment he returned from Boston; he was so withdrawn and quiet. He did hardly anything but sit in his room until I suppose the memory of everything in there which reminded him of you became too much, and he noisily threw everything in his closet." Louise picked up the heavy leather album. "I saved as many of those memories as possible. I knew one day he would regret his sadness and anger over being so helpless. I put this together." She tenderly passed it to Danni who took it with the same amount of care.

It was one of those older fashioned photo albums where there was no plastic cover to protect the contents but rather the sheets of the almost translucent tissue paper, each picture held in securely by the small corner anchors she hadn't seen before on anything but movies. The first picture was of the two of them as children sitting apart on a retaining wall, the ocean behind them. She wasn't sure how old they were but they were young, probably around five or six. Brad seemed to not care for the little blonde girl just feet beside him, as he looked at some comic book, and she had a look on her face like he smelt. The picture made the corners of her mouth rise, these were the moments she wished she could bring to her own mind, be able to know what she had been thinking.

Louise sat there quietly as Danni seemed to take a few minutes with each of the pictures. She knew the young woman was processing everything she saw and hoped the biggest thing to stick out would be how by the time you got a few pages in that distance, that unfamiliarity of one another was gone, and the knowledge of friendship was held in each set of eyes.

The pictures from when they were teens interested Danni much more, like the one of the two of them dancing, she in a pretty pastel pink dress while Brad wore a shirt and tie. "That was at a family friend's wedding reception," Louise told her. There were a lot with the beach and other local backgrounds she had seen while down in Southampton. In each one she could almost feel what the old her was thinking, how she felt as Brad chased her with a bucket filled with something while she wore her bikini, sitting on their bikes while the person took the picture, her eyes not looking at the camera but rather Brad beside her. One of her laughing as she tried to cover her face; she was lying down somewhere and if not for the strings of her halter top she would have thought she'd been naked. "He took that of you on one of the nights you stayed over, I believe." She was told when Louise caught her touching the photo.

The last picture completely took her breath away.

They were laughing with their eyes to one another, smiles on both of their faces as he cupped her cheek so tenderly, her ponytail doing little to secure the few loose tendrils of hair flying in to her face.

She couldn't doubt now that there had been something very special between them. As nonchalant as Brad had made it seem, as if their paths weren't entwined to always be together before the accident.

That girl in the picture loved the boy looking at her with the same love in his face, a kind of love which would have grown more, followed him wherever he went because that's what you did when you felt like that. It seemed like Paris, college in New York may never have happened anyway if the feelings this moment captured on film evoked in her was even a fraction of what she had felt that day.

"I always get choked up when I look at that last one." The soft voice beside her pulled her from her thoughts. "I can understand why."
"Whether you can recall it or not, there is no doubt in my heart Danielle that you cared very much for Brad and he of you."
"I think you are very right." Danni had to close the book. "Thank you for sharing it with me." She held it to pass it back.
"No dear, those are your memories whether you know it or not. I'm sure your heart knows." Louise gave her a soft, motherly smile. "Brad hasn't seen those in a very long time, maybe the two of you could look at them together later."
"I think the past still haunts him." She wasn't sure where that had come from, but it did sum up a lot about the way Brad was to her in the past few days.
"It haunts him terribly." The words were said back to her and she had to try hard to keep the tears welling in her eyes to stay where they were. She avoided Louise's gaze and smoothed her fingers along the soft leather cover.

XXX   XXX

"Major Cole?" Brad asked when a man answered the number he had finally gotten after a few calls to Walter Reed Medical Center.

"I'm sorry to bother you Major. My name is Commander Johnson and I got your number from a friend, Commander Buchanan."

"Ah, Jamie, yes."

"She was telling me about some work you did with a fellow team mate of mine and I have a personal issue I was wondering if I could speak to you about?"

"Certainly, you're familiar with my work in TBI's then?"

"Only slightly I'm afraid, but that is why I need to ask your opinion on something."

"I'm afraid you caught me at a bad time; I'm about to go in to a group session. I can take your number and call you later tonight if that's okay?"

"That would be more than okay." Brad gave the man his number and once repeated back to him he said, "Yes that's it."

"Give me a few hours and I will call you after dinner."

"Thank you very much."

"Speak to you soon Commander."

"He's going to call me back." He was now just in there with Maggie; Ted had gone off in search of even more caffeine. "I got a call from Ben Goodman, he is going to fly down tonight and I said he could meet with you tomorrow morning."

"Sounds like a plan. Thanks for everything today Maggie." Brad, for the first time that afternoon, sat back in the chair closing his eyes. "I'll call Cindy in the morning, have her keep the office running so I can be here for calls she puts through, and any work we have to do."

"Are you going to stay for dinner Maggie?" He could feel sleep tugging him further in to the chair.

Maggie knew when Brad had fallen asleep and she wasn't offended. She knew since being here he had been on autopilot and now with this added stress when it should be filled with rekindling his lost love, he was beyond tired. The board of directors should see this side of the financial figures, but she knew as she silently got her things together and left him there resting, that the crusty old men on the board were only interested in seeing progress and numbers.

She caught Danni walking back down the hall towards her, looking like a lot was on her mind. "Are you okay Danielle?"

"Oh, yeah; are you guys done?"

"For today. I'll be back tomorrow." Maggie looked back towards the study. "He's sleeping, give him twenty minutes or so, he has this weird short nap thing he learnt as an officer, unnerving but works." She gave the young girl a warm smile. "I wanted to look through this again in private anyway." Danni said.

"Louise's album of you two, huh?"

"You've seen this?"

"No, but I know she put that together with a great deal of care a very long time ago."

"It's amazing what something so inanimate means to me."

"It holds your past dear, of course it means something." She paused. "Tell Brad I'll see him in the morning and have a good night Danielle."

"I think I will." Maggie heard her say softly as she left her to walk down towards the bedrooms, and went looking for Louise to let her know she was leaving.

CHAPTER TWENTY-TWO

He woke up with a start.

His heart was beating so rapidly he thought it would lurch out of his chest.

No one was in the office with him, and as his mind cleared from the place it had been, he noticed the grandfather clock built in to the bookcases ticking loudly as it always had. If he was right he'd been asleep for thirty minutes.

Stretching, Brad moved from the desk and out to the hall. The kitchen's light lit up the hall and there was a vague sense of voices coming from that direction.

Inside was Daisy cooking while his mother was speaking with Ted. "Hey sleepy head," Ted joked: he held his case, and his jacket was folded over his arm, so Brad figured his friend was leaving. "You leaving?"
"I have dinner plans with a certain woman in my life, who, if I don't get going is only going, to make my life hell." He bent down and kissed Louise's cheek, shook hands with Brad and waved bye to Daisy who blushed from the attention. "I'll call if anything happens, but I'll be here in the morning." His words followed him as he left.

"Where's Danni?" Brad asked his mother and Daisy.
"I think she went to your room."
"Everything okay?"

"We looked through the photo album."

"Oh." Brad had never been able to lift the cover off the book which held pain for him, and when he had seen her taking the book from the shelf, knowing she was going to try and jog something out of Danni, he had felt sick. He was sure it had been an emotional journey for her. "I'll go check."

"Make sure you have all of her things in your room Bradford, we don't want there to be any confusion about where she's sleeping tonight."

"Yes mother."

The first thing he saw was Danni sitting on his bed, the sheets and comforter were back the way they had been before they had messed them up earlier. Before saying anything, he did as his mother said and went to collect the two bags, but they weren't in the spare room. Turning back in the doorway of his own room he saw them sitting beside his dresser.

"How was your afternoon?" He sat behind her and kissed her neck softly.

"Brad." She turned her head and softly captured his lips. "Your mother showed me this." She had it open to the last page and when he looked down at that picture, all words caught in his throat. "I think I'm starting to understand your pain."

"My pain?" He lay back, gazing at her with his eyes half closed.

"It's a lot harder to be in this place remembering, Brad. I didn't realize how lucky I was having no memories."

"How do you feel about the photos now? Anything seem familiar, help you to get anything back?" He didn't want to talk about his 'pain'.

"This picture keeps drawing me back."

"That was taken the week before I went down to Annapolis."

"Those two kids loved each other so much Brad." Something in her voice made him move his arm, and he saw tears silently falling down her cheeks. Those tears were almost worse than the gut wrenching feeling from seeing that picture.

"Yes, they did."

"Not that I ever doubted you, but I suppose I never knew exactly what I lost."

"Hey." Sitting up, he used both hands, his fingers taking away the tears. "You didn't lose me, I'm right here."

"You are now, for fifteen years I've been going through life thinking no one loved me, not like a man should love a woman, and all this time you were out there."

"I should have visited you when you woke up."

"But I get it now, I really understand Brad." She gently placed the album on the other side of them. "You were hurting so badly from losing what that picture shows me; if the roles were reversed, I don't know if I would be strong either to make that first step. You had no idea how bad or good my condition was."

Danni let that sit there in his mind. Since being told they had been an item in the past, a few days before, she had wondered why, not really grasping the intensity with which this man before her had faced life at such a young age.

"We could have had so much time together," Danni kissed his cheek.

"You forget our lives were going in opposite directions anyway."

"Were they really or is that something you made up in your mind to help with the pain? Because honestly, if I saw that look in my eyes as I have in that picture I know I would follow that man off the face of the earth."

"Danni."

"I wish I knew the past Brad. I have all these emotions, I don't understand when it comes to you. Until that ball Tuesday, you and I were practically strangers. I lost fifteen years of being with you."

"Danni." He repeated once he could get a word in.

"I mean, I could have married someone else, had children and never known about you." She got up and started pacing.

"Danni." He jumped up too and took her upper arms gently in his hands.

"What?" Her eyes focused on him.

"We can't play the coulda, shoulda, woulda game. Let's take some solace in the fact that fate or our parents brought us together again."

"Why'd they wait so long?"

"Danni." He had to laugh, letting her go. "Please, let's just deal with the now."

216

"Okay." He watched the fight over the subject leave her face as she walked closer and put her arms around his neck, standing on tip-toes and gently kissing his chin.

"Are you done working? I saw Maggie leave, she told me to tell you she'll be back in the morning."
"All done, Ted left a while ago too."
"Ted, he's an enigma of a character, how do you two know each other and how does he know your mom?"
"Ted and I worked together."
"And?"
"And what?"
"Why so secretive?"
"We worked overseas together in a joint force effort about seven years ago."
"When you were GI Joe?"
"SEAL, please, there's a difference." Dannie relished in his deep throaty laughter as his hands held her close to him. "Fine, you won't tell me, I won't ask anymore."
"I'll tell you one day, not today though, okay?" He let her go, but she couldn't be disappointed as he took her hand and led her to the bed, pulling her down to lie atop him lengthways.

"I have some work I need to take care of the next few days; I can do it from here so we can spend as much time together as possible."
"I like the sound of that." Danni's fingers were underneath his shirt touching his abdomen. "Good."

"I told Sam I'd let her know when I'd be back but I get the feeling you'll have to entertain me for a little longer than we thought."

"That I can definitely enjoy." He kissed her fiercely as the sound of the house phone ringing in the distance down the hall interrupted the indecent thoughts he wanted to play out.

"I don't mean to interrupt anything." His mother's voice filled the room from the intercom on the extension of the phone, beside the bed. He'd had his own line for as long as he could remember. "What is it mother?" He knew he only had to speak and she would hear him now the intercom had been turned on. "Danielle, your father called, he's on his way back, he'll be joining us for dinner." There was a pause and both of them were about to respond when Louise continued. "I'm afraid your brother and Felicity will be joining us also."

"Thanks Mom." He hit the button on the phone and rolled back to Danni who sighed very loudly. "Great, I have to deal with the devil and his fiancé."

"They'll be the minority of people who think bad things about you." He said. "Hmm, except sometimes I think my father thinks the same as he does."

"Ethan loves you sweetheart."

"But to them, even you. I'm not their Danni."

"Then they have to learn to love this you, like I have, and that can only happen with time spent in the same room."

Danni bit her tongue before using his lips to silence her own. Man! Did she want to comment on his use of 'learn to love this you like I have'. Was he meaning he was in love with her? She knew he had once, could he be again, because she knew in her entire being she had never felt like this for any man since waking up at nineteen.

CHAPTER TWENTY-THREE

Brad was sure each person sitting around the table felt the same tension hanging over the air. He could tell Danni wasn't playing with her food because she wasn't hungry with a stalker after her, but because since arriving with Ethan, both Felicity and her brother had said nothing to her, and only gave her looks across the table. This only made Brad want to take Peter outside and beat some sense in to him.

"Have you set a date yet?" Louise tried to get a conversation going with everyone, but with little luck. It was frustrating, she thought, as she looked at Felicity. "We were thinking June."
"So soon?" Ethan voiced.
"It's only two months!" Danni finally gave up on her food putting her fork down and picking up her wine glass instead. She hated wasted food; especially good food, and Daisy's chicken casserole had been flavorful and delicate.

"My mother is busy fluttering around; she's all over the place, trying to get things organized." Felicity never once looked at Danni.
"Who's catering?" Ethan asked, and Brad knew it was a common subject Danni could be brought in on.
"Mother asked Edmund over at Le Shay."
"Do you know Edmund?" Daisy asked Danni straight out.
"Unfortunately, I've not had the pleasure." She wished Brad could save her, and take her somewhere, just the two of them. Louise had told them before her

family arrived that Ethan didn't want Peter or Felicity to know anything about what had happened down in Southampton or that there had been threats, and Danni felt fine keeping them in the dark.

"Well he's a five-star chef in one of the most popular restaurants here in the city. He trained in Italy." Felicity paused slightly looking down her surgically fixed nose at her soon to be sister-in-law. "Where did you go to school again?"
"Felicity." Ethan thumped his clenched fist on the table.
"Dad, no." Danni spoke up. "I know what felicity thinks of me, Peter too, and quite honestly I don't give a flying fuck." Daisy who had been collecting the dinner plates paused in her movements, just like everyone else in the room momentarily stopped their actions. "Well put, my dear." Louise held her glass up to Danni while she felt Brad's hand squeeze her knee.

No more insults were flung, but then the conversation had another noticeable dip in flow after. Daisy was just serving the espresso when Brad heard his cell ringing. "Excuse me." He got up and made it to the study where it had been charging on the third ring. "Johnson." He gave the usual greeting. "Commander Johnson, this is Major Cole."
"Thanks for returning my call."
"I'm not interrupting anything am I?"
"Actually, I appreciate the distraction."
"So, what I can tell you, you mentioned earlier you had a personal reason to pick my medical mind about TBI's."

"Seventeen years ago, my best friend suffered a damaging brain injury resulting in a two-year coma, and upon waking all memories from birth through to the explosion which caused the injury were gone. There have been some threats made from someone who blew my car up last night. The FBI and I believe it's connected to what happened to cause the injuries decades ago. This perp thinks she knows something and until now there have been only a few flashes of memory."

"She?"

"Yes, I know what you did with Espinoza was to do with mobility, but I was wondering if you'd ever had experience with retrieving memories."

"What we do is still in what you would classify as experimental. We are gathering as much data and proof of success and failure to prove once and for all that hypnosis is a genuine therapeutic treatment. We've only worked with a hundred cases at Reed since we got funding, and yes, some of it has been more along the lines of PTSD which I'm sure you know is common for war time veterans, but nothing solid and proven, nothing the medical association would believe right now anyway." Brad heard something on the other end of the line. "Retrieving memories are hard; mainly it's used by psychologists for repressed traumatic memories where the person suffered abuse in early childhood. The one drawback is that the child's retrieved memories are sometimes not what actually happened so we try not to as psychologists to do those kinds of cases without someone who can cohobate the events."

"That wouldn't be a problem; I grew up with the woman."

"I see, and you said she was injured in an explosion which resulted in a traumatic brain injury and then a coma?"

"Yes."

"Would you know which regions of the brain were injured?"

"The temporal lobe I believe."

"And there have been just a few memories in the last seventeen years?"

"She said to begin with it was like a few snap shots inside her head, of people she didn't know. The last few days there have been memories she said are more like mini movies."

"Interesting; could there be a catalyst to this sudden occurrence after you said, what, fifteen years?"

"I suppose me."

"You?"

"I saw her up until the accident, when she was in the hospital but I was a teen, upset over what happened and was told she probably wouldn't ever wake up. Last Tuesday was the first time I'd seen her in all these years."

"I see." Brad was sure this doctor was writing everything down. "And someone has targeted her with threats including blowing up your car because they think she knows something about the first explosion, which took those memories away. Do I have this right?"

"So far."

"I don't suppose the young woman in question is there, if she is could I ask her some questions?" The doctor sounded slightly excited.

"Can you give me a moment? I didn't tell her about my call to you."

"I'll be right here; I wanted to get something anyway."

Leaving his cell on the desk he went back to the dining room, where the lack of chatter was noticeable. "I need to steal Danni a moment," he informed everyone and even though Brad knew Peter wasn't as loaded as the night of the ball, the kid was still not holding his liquor well. "A little after-dinner dessert before you move on to the next woman when my sister goes home?" Peter threw at Brad.

"Business." Brad forced himself to say. "But you ever refer to me as some player or anything derogatory again, and I'll take this downstairs," he warned. "And you ever treat Danni with anything less than respect again and I'll do it right here in front of everyone."

"Let's go." Danni whispered, appreciating the white knight thing, the flexing of his protective muscles.

Brad stopped her in the hall outside the study. "I'll explain more after but I'm on the phone with a doctor who does work with people who have brain injuries. Coop was telling me about a guy we worked with who was injured and this guy in nine months had him walking again." He touched a hand to her cheek. "It's up to you, but if you want those memories, if you want to know if there really is something you saw someone do, then we can go in there and speak to him."

"Does it involve surgery?"

"No, I'll let him explain."

"Sure."

"Major Cole." Brad holding Danni's hand led her around to where he had been sitting at his desk and pulled her down to sit on his lap. "Here is Danielle Morgan, Danni, this is Major Cole, he works down in DC at Walter Reed."

"Hello Major."

"Ms. Morgan." The major coughed to clear his throat. "The commander was just filling me in on some details, I'm sorry to hear your ordeal of seventeen years has been heightened by this new threat."

"Thanks."

"He said it was your temporal lobe which suffered damage?"

"A doctor explained it once as there being some sort of cauterization to that part of my brain."

"And you spent two years in a coma; you woke up knowing no one and nothing?"

"Absolutely nothing, I didn't know my name, the year, my family nothing about my childhood."

"And you never had any sort of brain surgery?"

"I believe the only thing they did was insert some tube in to my skull to release pressure but I'm not sure."

"We could find out easily enough from your medical file. Now over the last seventeen years, you have had some recollections, memories?"

"Silly flashes, but it was no different to me than seeing a face on the television, the images told me nothing."

"And recently you experienced different types of images?"

"Moving images, a few with sound; I walked in to a house knowing a table was missing, that I had been laughing in a room while watching the rain fall on the windows above me."

"Fascinating." Danni could picture the man frowning in thought on the other end of the call. "Can I ask a personal question?"

"Certainly Major."

"Is there any one place where these recollections have happened more, or maybe a person with you?"

"Brad was with me at all of them, I mean the commander."

"Interesting, I think you were right, Commander; and tell me, if we were to try to help Ms. Morgan then you know enough about her missing past to know truth from fiction?"

"Yes."

"Major, how do you intend to help me?"

"Have you ever had any hypnosis therapy?"

"No."

"Good, my colleagues and I are working with hypnosis in care of veterans down here, who have all suffered from TBI's with a varied range of physical problems and disabilities."

"Do you think you could help me?" Danni leaned further towards the phone which sat on speaker mode before both of them. Brad could hear the hope in her voice and rubbed her back, hoping he wasn't giving her false dreams. After seeing the album, he knew more than anything she wanted it all back, everything. "I would be willing to give it a go, there are no guarantees but like I explain it to all my patients, they have little to lose if it does fail."

"I'm willing to try."

"Good, just to make sure we can proceed then I'd like to take a look at your medical files, but I'll need permission from you, which hospital were you initially treated in after the explosion?"

"Boston Mass. General." Brad answered first.

"Wonderful. I know a few old fellow med students doing work there. I'll need you Ms. Morgan to complete a form I can fax you in the morning, so I can get a look at those files."

Danni listened as Brad gave the Major the number for the fax line, and then she said goodbye as did Brad. She was still on his lap and the overwhelming feeling going through her was making her a little bit numb. How many times had she prayed for everything back? How many times in just the last twenty-four hours?

"Is this for real?" Danni looked deep in to Brad's coffee colored eyes as she remained sitting there.

"Yeah."

"And your friend Coop knew about this?"

"One of my old team suffered a brain injury and for some reason couldn't move his body. Nine months later he's back on the team. I suppose Coop never thought about it until I was speaking to him earlier, and then I called my old team doctor who gave me Major Cole's name."

"Wow."

"Only Ted, Maggie and my mother know, maybe for now we shouldn't get anyone else's hopes up, just in case, you know."

"I agree." She didn't want to let her father down any further. "We'd have to go down to DC."

"That's not a problem."

He watched her as her face remained thoughtful. A few minutes and then he saw a smile creep across her lips. "What?"

"You know, hearing the Major call you Commander sounded really hot."

"Hot?"

"Hot and sexy." She was picturing him wearing white pants, a naval hat and his chest all baby-oiled up and looking bronzed. "I suppose that's a good thing?" He winked to her.

"Very good thing." With her hands, gently on his upper chest, she leant forward and whispered in his ear. "Very, very good." She would keep that image in her head for as long as she could.

CHAPTER TWENTY-FOUR

Having Peter and Felicity there was actually a good thing, because her dad didn't ask about the time she and Brad had disappeared, and once the guests were gone and Louise had said goodnight, she let Brad lead her back to the bedroom, and once that door was closed and locked they went right back to the intimate place they took each other.

Waking up with the sun coming through the window Danni was momentarily disorientated about where she was. Looking around, nothing jumped until the unmistakable manly scent on the sheets and the single red rose on the pillow beside the one beside hers registered. Then she remembered: she knew who had left it there and what had transpired during the hours inside the room alone with him.

Stretching the sleepy muscles in her body, she knew she was smiling, probably like a goofy kid. But even with there being some nutcase thinking she knew something she didn't, she hadn't ever felt like she did at that moment, at least she didn't remember ever feeling so content.

It was eight-thirty and Danni knew Brad was likely already getting to work in the study. She wondered if Maggie and Ted had arrived yet.

Thankfully this room had an ensuite bathroom unlike the guest room Louise had been sure to tell her was not the room she would be sleeping in. There had been no embarrassment, no blushing and maybe a deep recess of her mind knew the woman would say that, something natural she would have expected had she never lost her past.

Choosing a pair of low hip sitting jeans and a black t-shirt, fitted and cropped slightly, she was drying her hair when she noticed how young she looked, her skin was always tanned thanks to living near the beach and her blonde hair was almost platinum. She'd always wanted dark hair, at least since she woke up. Sam had dark chestnut hair always cut pixie short and Danni knew it would never work with her own hair but she could always dream.

Pulling her hair back in to a ponytail she slipped on her Crock flip-flops she'd worn on the plane to New York and which her father had repacked in her suitcase and delivered the night before. If this was LA this would be normal attire for going to work. Maybe it had been the sun outside or her demeanor but she felt content and at peace. A sense she normally only felt at home or work.

Another reminder, maybe her mind knew more than it let her know.

The sound of talking in the area of the kitchen drew her in that direction as she noted the study door was closed tight. She'd hoped to see him this morning, smile to him and make sure she hadn't made anything up.

"Morning dear." Louise said before she had time to figure out who was in there talking. She saw Maggie standing at the coffee maker, Ted sitting around the small breakfast table with Louise. Daisy was nowhere to be seen. "Morning." Danni told the three of them, and there must have been something in her eyes because Maggie said, "He's in the study; you should take this in to him." The older woman walked closer and held out the mug with the hot black liquid. "Oh, I don't want to disturb him if he's working."

"Trust me, he'll appreciate this distraction." Maggie laughed. "He said he wanted to see you the moment you were awake."

"You can't disappoint him dear." Louise joined in.

"But if he's working?"

"He's just looking over papers." Maggie told her, still holding out the mug for her to take.

"He has a meeting in twenty minutes, but until then he's in there all by himself."

"Don't let him not see you until after his meeting Danni please." Ted finally spoke. "Why?"

"I want him to be as happy as possible before I see him."

"Bad news?"

"No news."

"Has my dad helped anymore?"

"Nothing."

"Maybe I should call him?"

"Go see Brad first." Ted gently told her.

Leaving them in the kitchen she passed Daisy who was carrying some sheets from the bed she had shared with Brad. "Morning."

"Ms. Morgan, I'm just getting a jump on things."

"I would have done the sheets."

"No need, I change them every other day when they are being used, part of my routine."

"Oh, okay." Danni stopped outside the study door and wondered if she should knock or just go in. Choosing the first she waited until she heard his 'come in' and then slowly pushed the door open with her free hand. He was there behind the desk again, papers in his hands and a mountain of others before him. "I'm not interrupting anything am I?"

"You are a sight for sore eyes." She watched him put the papers down and turn in his seat as she came around the back of the desk. "Maggie said to give this to you."

"I need something else first." Once he had taken the mug and placed it on the blotter covering the main section of the desk, he took both her hands and pulled her down to him kissing her with such deep passion she thought her knees would buckle again.

'How could any woman give up such sensations for Paris and college in New York'? That voice inside her head asked.

"Thank you for the rose." Her voice was soft and partially out of breath as she naturally took a seat on his lap. It seemed she did it a lot and it was so comforting. "I felt bad leaving you there this morning."

"I understand you have work to do, will you be free for taking a break at lunchtime?"

"I shouldn't see why not." He poked her nose and along with her eyes getting crossed she frowned.

"You used to do that when we were younger."

"Yes I did." He smiled.

"It's not a memory just a feeling." She leant in to him resting her head on his chest and feeling his chin rub the top of her head.

"I have something here you need to sign and give back to Maggie." With the hand not stroking her arm he took the fax form the Major had sent over. He placed it next to his coffee which until she had come in he thought would be the only thing to really waken his body, but her being on his lap was doing that naturally. "I'll do it in a minute."

"How did you sleep?"

"Fine once you let me get some." She joked.

"Hold on, I think you have that around the wrong way." He felt her move and before he could blink she was straddling his legs in the chair. Her chest now aligned with his as she looked deep in to his eyes. "I don't think last night was just my doing."

"No, I'll admit I was there too."

"You don't like me keeping you awake?" She began kissing along his jaw line and her hands played with the back of his neck in his hair which was longer than he'd worn it in the Navy. "Trust me when I say if it bothered me I'd tell you."

"Oh, I do."

"Good, then kiss me until my meeting starts."

XXX   XXX

Ethan was coming in from an early morning meeting
down the hall from his office when his secretary
Norma greeted him as she had for the last forty some
years. "Here's your mail Mr. Morgan."
"Thanks Norma, I have some correspondence for you
to get to later. Did you call down to human resources
about the new medical benefits package?"
"Gina wanted me to tell you she's put it together and
she'll send it up the minute the first draft is complete
for you to look over."
"Good. What time is that meeting with the SEC
boys?"
"Eleven."
"Okay, bring those papers in and collect the work I
have for you in a while. Can you get Keith on the line
and put him through to my office?"
"Yes Mr. Morgan."

Leafing through the pile of mail he went on in to his
office closing the door between his and Norma's
office, giving him some privacy. He'd been at the
office since seven, and even with the meeting and
paper work he'd been going through, his mind was on
his daughter. Since leaving the Johnson apartment the
night before he had not been able to relax, even
knowing Brad would let nothing or no one hurt her.

He still didn't believe anyone would want to hurt her,
he just couldn't.

He sat in his plush leather desk chair a brown envelope caught his eye. It was an eight by ten size and was light, unlike the ones they got which held thick documents. There was only a computer printed sticker on the front and no return address or company name and there was also no postage stamp.

"Mr. Morgan." The intercom sounded on his desk. "Keith for you on line three."

"Thanks Norma." He picked up the handset, tucking it between his ear and shoulder as he looked across his cluttered desk for the letter opener. "Keith, how is it in London?" He asked the man who ran the European branch of his company. "Rainy as always." Keith's British accent laughed. "I e-mailed those numbers to Norma when I got in here this morning; you should have seen them or at least you'll get them soon."

"Good." Ethan, not able to find the gold-plated opener on his desk, he began going through the drawers. "I wanted to broach something with you, get your input."

"Fire away."

"I am thinking about sending Peter to London to learn the European half of the company."

"Didn't the poor bugger just get engaged?"

"His fiancé can go too." He'd thought up the idea while not sleeping and he had come to the conclusion he didn't like Felicity as much as he thought, his sons behavior had gotten worse since the two of them had started dating two years before and his drinking even worse. He knew Felicity would hate being away from her own family, and this would be a good test of their relationship.

He also didn't like the two of them ganging up on Danielle.

"Have you talked to him about this?" Keith asked as Ethan's hand came in to contact with the cold metal blade he had been searching for, "Not yet, I wanted to ask your opinion first."
"Well I'm flattered. How has he been doing there, and what position will he be filling here?"
"He's been handling the account department. I thought maybe you could put him to work on the FTSE accounts there, let him learn the ropes of the stock exchange floor."
"Starting him from the bottom then?"
"It will be good for him." Ethan began opening the brown envelope as he spoke, tearing the paper easily.

Inside felt like a piece of photo paper the same size as the envelope and his heart almost stopped when he turned it from the white untouched side to the image the other side held.

His daughter in all her naked glory, her most intimate places hidden by both Bradford's hands, and also luckily the window's cross sections, he knew they were intimately joined as Bradford kissed what looked like her ear.

A very intimate glance through the window of the house in Southampton.

His hands shook as he took his eyes from the sight to see another picture underneath, another night shot. But this time Danni's face washed with the glow of the flames of what must have been the SUV after it exploded. She w only her silk robe which came only as far as halfway down her thigh, and her face was shocked as she held Bradford's hand. He was wearing only pants in the night air, a few other figures he didn't recognize, and also the man he remembered meeting when he'd sold his beach house to him.

There was a Post-It note placed on the first picture. 'He can't save her'.

"Ethan, did you hear what I said?" Keith's voice pulled him out from the place his head had gone and made his heart slow down. "I'm sorry Keith, something came up. I'm going to have to call you back." Without waiting for the reply, he slammed the phone down, disconnecting the call, and went back to the first picture.

He wasn't blind, an idiot or delusional; he knew his daughter had been sexually active for more years than she could remember. Knew the man who knew her so well was a good man; but what should have been an extremely beautifully erotic-as well as someone else's daughter-picture was sickening with that note connected to it.

Putting them back inside the envelope he grabbed his suit jacket just as someone knocked at the door.

Norma walked in, a look of confusion on her face. No doubt Keith had called back asking if something was wrong. "Mr. Morgan?"

"I'm going out for a few hours. Cancel my meetings and unless it's an emergency you can't handle, don't forward any calls Norma."

"Certainly sir." She paused. "Is there anything else? Ethan?"

"Just something I have to do." He touched his loyal secretary's shoulder as he left, knowing if he had shown her, explained everything, she would have started worrying. She may be an employee, but over the years she had been the one he spent twelve hours a day with five days a week, business trips and probably more time with than his own family.

There was a familiar friendship between them and she knew more about the secrets in his life than anyone.

CHAPTER TWENTY-FIVE

"So, what do you say Ben?" Brad asked after going over the man's resume, asking questions and then explaining what he needed, wanted, was hoping to achieve by owning Anderson publishing. "I say you have me salivating to get to work."

"Typical journalist, slick with words." Brad grinned to the man he hadn't known since being on the football team in high school. "When can you start?"

"Today, tomorrow."

"Really?"

"I gave the globe my walking papers a few weeks ago."

"What were you planning on doing if you hadn't found a job?"

"I've got enough saved up, I was going to relax a little. Reluctantly of course, I probably would have free lanced some work."

"Well I need someone to step in as soon as possible. How long do you think it would take for you to get a place and move down here?"

"My dad's house is ready for me to move in, so a day or so to get my stuff down here."

"How about I call over there and tell them you and my team will be in on Thursday to look over everything. We need to make sure we can make a profit with this as well as make it as effective as possible. I can have their HR manager get you the information on those who work there, decide if it's a team you want to work with, or you and my guys can hire new staff."

"I have the job?" Ben sat up in his seat.

"Of course."

"Thursday works well for me, I'd actually like to meet the staff face to face. I've been a big believer of being able to read someone at first meeting knowing if we'll mesh."

"This is your show."

"How about I meet your team over there this afternoon?"

"I'll have Maggie call our boys and have them meet you today then."

"Thanks Brad." Ben stood holding his hand across the desk to shake.

"No, thank you." The sound of people in the hall made Brad stop anything else he was getting ready to say and before he had time to get back to his interrupted words, the studies door opened and in came a very angry heated looking Ethan, followed closely by Ted and Maggie. "Brad, I don't mean to barge in but we have to talk now."

"I'm sorry Ben, go with Maggie and call me if there's anything you need this afternoon; but do call me once you're done, and let me know what your plan to proceed is."

"Don't worry about it, thanks again Brad."

Waiting for Maggie and Ben to leave with the door closing behind them, Brad remained standing, Ted looked like he was ready to swing at Ethan if not jump in, if the man was there to pummel Brad; a look not too far from the one that looked like Ethan wanted blood, possibly his.

"Care to explain what brings you barging in to my office?" Brad said evenly, with his hands on his hips. "Yeah, this came in my mail." Ethan threw it across the desk and turned away, telling both Brad and Ted that whatever was inside was not something the man wanted to see again.

With the envelope in his hands Brad slid the contents out and instantly felt smacked in the gut. He passed one to Ted while he looked at the other, the breech of privacy of the one he held made him sick. He had never been against strategically planned sex in public, god, he and Danni as teens had made love on the beach right outside the back of his parents' house, they'd had sex in his car, a few different places over the years but this was a violation of their privacy.

'He can't save her' the block lettering written in the bold black ink of a sharpie marker on the yellow Post-It note said.

"I'm guessing that 'he' refers to you." Ted took the picture passing the other over from outside the house. "Good guess." Brad took in this picture. "Whoever took this probably did it from the mainland with some really expensive equipment."
"You sure?" Ted looked at it, closer it did look a little grainy.
"If someone took a photo from the road I would have seen them, there was no one there but the few fire trucks."

"And this one?" Ted handed the first one back to Brad.

"A boat." Ethan interrupted them. "I looked at them the entire way here, a boat with a telescopic lens."

"Makes sense," Brad agreed.

"Now will you take this threat to your daughter seriously and answer my questions?" Ted moved to stand in front of Ethan.

"I'll tell you whatever you need to know."

"Maggie, did I hear my father?" Danni came out of the kitchen where she had been baking while Daisy was out walking with Louise in the park, they'd asked her to join them but Ted had said it wasn't a good idea. "He's in there with Brad and Ted."

"Did something happen?"

"I don't know."

"Well if it did I deserve to know." Danni didn't wait to hear any argument Maggie may have tried to give her and opened the study door to see the three men standing there, Brad was holding papers in either hand.

"What's going on?" She stopped between all the men.

"We had another message from our perp." Ted answered for the two men who cared so much for Danni. "I want to read it."

"Don't show her." Ethan ordered Brad.

"This bastard's after me dad, I have the right to know what he's threatening and sending." Brad gave up any type of a fight when she snatched the photos from his hands, and the men watched as Danni took in the pictures. "Wow." She maneuvered slightly and sat on the arm of the couch which lined one of the walls. "I don't look too awful in that one." She made a weak attempt at a joke as she held up the picture of Brad and her having sex. "Danielle this is serious." Her father snapped.

"Yeah it is." She read the note to herself and then got up and passed them back to Brad. "But me getting pissed off about them makes this sicko's plan already working. I have something I need to get back to."

"Hey." Brad caught up with her outside the hall letting the door close behind them, leaving the other two to talk. "It's okay to show emotions Danni."

"Maybe but not in front of my dad."

"Why?" He followed her in to the kitchen and the smell of something he hadn't smelt in decades came wafting out of the room. "He's had so much going on, so much sadness. I'm trying to be strong."

"I think even he can deal with you getting scared."

"I'll be fine." She was pulling the oven gloves on when the timer went off, and he waited for her to do whatever it was she had been doing before continuing.

Lemon meringue pie.

He smiled seeing her put it on the cooling rack and take off her mitts. "I'm not saying I won't get quiet and upset when it's just you and me, but I will not show anything in front of him."

"What's with the pie Danni?" He ignored what they had been talking about. "Oh, I wanted to make you something, and for some reason all I could think about was lemon meringue."

"So, no one told you?"

"Told me what?"

"I haven't eaten one of those since my seventeenth birthday."

"You haven't, why not?" Her blue eyes looked up at him and studied his smiling face; he could tell when she'd figured it out as her mouth opened slightly. "I had no idea."

"It was my childhood favorite; you used to help your housekeeper to make me one every summer for my Birthday, even though my Birthday's in October. We'd celebrate the weekend after Labor Day, and when you were probably twelve you started making it yourself."

"You've not eaten one since?"

"I could never bring myself to do it, and cheesecake became a favorite."

"Are you going to eat some of this one? I could make something else?" Her voice suddenly sounded flustered and soft. "I'll eat this trust me." He cupped her face with both his hands. "I'll only ever eat them again if you make them for me."

"For every one of your future birthdays." She whispered out as he kissed her very slow and sure.

"Excuse me." Maggie coughed from the doorway; she was holding the cordless phone from the study.

"Major Cole returning your call."

"Hold on to all thoughts and promises about my birthdays." He left her taking the phone from Maggie and going in to the living room knowing Ted was still behind closed doors with Ethan. "Major."

"Commander Johnson, my team and I had a chance to go over your friend's medical file and I think we can help her."

"Are you serious?" His legs felt weak, and thankfully the armchair was behind him so he dropped in to it.

"We'd like her to have a new MRI, a few scans to see if there's a possibility there's something going on there physically, but we would like to try to help Ms. Morgan."

"I can't tell you how grateful I am Major."

"Make sure you pay the medical bill, it's all I need to know."

"You have absolutely no worries there."

"My team and I work rotating shifts twenty-four hours seven days a week so when is good for you?"

"The sooner the better, if we can find out who thinks she knows something; our perp is stepping up his game."

"Then can you be in DC either later today or first thing in the morning?"

"We can be at Walter Reed at eight am."

"Perfect. I'll have an MRI booked soon after that and we'll get the process going as soon as possible. Will you both be able to stay Wednesday too?"

"I have to be back here Thursday, but sure."

"Excellent."

XXX   XXX

"That smells so good." Maggie sat at the counter looking at how happy Danielle looked since the ball less than a week before. "For some reason I had to make it, I didn't know why aside from I wanted to do something nice for Brad."

"What a nice thing, he'll devour it all I'm sure."

"I hope he enjoys it."

"Did something big happen for your dad to come in like that?"

"The bad guy took pictures of Brad and me at the beach house the other night, one rather eye opening for my father to see."

"Ted and Brad will figure out whoever is doing this Danielle."

"Oh, I know."

"This is all crazy." Danni said aloud as she took a seat on one of the bar stools facing Maggie. There was something comforting in her, motherly almost and like Louise and Daisy she liked them immediately upon meeting. "I feel sorry for you Danielle; you're still trying to gain a place in this world, especially in this city."

"You can call me Danni you know."

"I'll save that for a certain tall, dark and handsome male who cares a great deal about you."

"He does, doesn't he?" Her own voice sounded thoughtful to her ears.

"I know you don't remember, but I've been close to this family for a very long time; what happened to you affected so many people, Brad hasn't been the same in a very long time."

"Yeah, I get that now since seeing that photo album."

"Threats or not." Maggie smiled. "I'm glad you're here."

"Thanks." Danni paused. "I wish more than you guys were."
"What do you mean?"
"There's my dad and you, Brad, Louise, Daisy but that's about it."
"Not your brother? The dinner last night didn't help?"
"I think it's easy to guess, if I needed a kidney he'd say 'hell' no."
"He was always a quiet shy boy; you used to let him tag along whenever you went anywhere."
"Then any gratitude over being a nice older sister has evaporated into history along with my memories."
"You Danielle were always so strong and sure of yourself, like now. He was always in the shadows. I guess that's why he's attracted to Felicity."
"Don't get me started on her." Danni snapped.
"She still holds a grudge against you right?"
"Still?"

Waiting for an explanation Danni could tell Maggie was thinking through her response. "Give it to me straight Maggie; was I mean to her or something when we were kids?"
"No, you were never cruel to her, but you had something she didn't, and wasn't used to hearing anything but yes."
"The last pair of shoes from Saks?"
"You had Brad."
"I don't get it."

"Like your family and his, Felicity's family has been in the same social circle for years. She grew up with Brad, being in classes together through school. You came along and were his special summer friend, and then later, as I'm sure you know, you did the last year here in the same school. When she wanted Brad, you were the only thing he saw. A lot of girls wanted Brad because of how protective and close to you he was; wanting that for themselves."

"So, she's mad at me for not being able to get Brad?"

"I would guess so."

"I don't get it."

"This is all female intuition which, granted, I don't use much anymore since my late husband died, but she was one of the first females to call when Brad came back to town. I only know because even with his father alive he was doing a lot of work in the office, taking meetings and making sure John didn't stress himself too much against the doctors' orders. I think it was a week and Felicity called, they went to dinner, he complained she hadn't changed since they were teenagers, and every time she called he gave me standing orders to tell her he was in a meeting, she finally got the hint."

"How long ago was this?"

"Two years." Maggie shrugged.

"Peter's only been dating her about that long."

"She's been playing the field a very long time since her first marriage ended."

"I didn't know she was married before."

"A rich older guy from Germany, a small scandal in your social group."

"Why'd they divorce?"

"He died."

"I smell something wonderful in here." Louise's cheerful voice filled the space. "Danielle made lemon meringue pie."

"Bradford will love it."

"He does." Danni said.

"I get the feeling something happened." The older lady looked from Danni to Maggie. There was an air in the room. "There was another letter from the stalker." Maggie filled her in.

"Dear, I was hoping they wouldn't know where you were."

"They sent it to my dad."

"Oh my." Louise's face went whiter. "No wonder the two of you look so deflated."

"Might be because we were talking about Felicity." Maggie got up when the blackberry she had set before her began vibrating.

"What does Felicity have to do with this?" Louise asked Danni.

"We were talking about something else, why she and Peter have such a hard time with me being here."

"Felicity's a spoiled brat who should have been spanked more as a child." Danni started laughing.

"Good now that you're laughing."

"What's so funny?" Brad appeared and leant against the arched doorway. "You missed out honey; you should have been here."

"I'll tell you before I go back in the office then, Danni; we're going to leave at six am tomorrow and fly down to DC. I'll tell you more later."

"Major Cole is going to help me?" Danni's eyes lit up.

"They're going to run a few tests and see."

"This is big." Danni bit her bottom lip.

"Relax, and hopefully in a few hours I'll be done." He kissed the top of her head as he walked through the kitchen back to the study.

Louise smiled at her with the knowing look of the love in the room.

CHAPTER TWENTY-SIX

The study was filled again. Maggie sitting in his seat behind the desk, typing on his laptop Ted stood in front of the window while speaking on his cell, and Ethan was sitting on the couch, his head in his hands.

"What did I miss?"
"Not much Brad." Ethan sat up; if it were possible, it looked like he hadn't slept in weeks. "Ted got a call so we didn't get a chance to speak yet."
"Everything's going to be just fine Ethan; neither Ted or I will let anyone harm Danni."
"I know son." As Ethan leaned back Ted disconnected whatever call he had been on. "The forensic guys got a partial print from one of the pieces collected from the car bomb, nothing too complete to run through any databases, but we could compare it to something once we get a suspect; they're going to run it for any DNA evidence."
"What about the pictures?"
"A tech guy will pick them up in the next hour." Ted retook the arm chair where he had found comfort while being inside this strange office. "Why don't we get started?" He said to Ethan.
"Fine." Ethan swallowed hard. "But I know the person having an affair with Theresa had nothing to do with any of this."
"Who?"

Both men waited for Ethan to continue. "Mayor Spencer." That got raised eyebrows from both of them. "Felicity's father?" Brad asked for clarification.

"They were an item well before Theresa and I got together. She was his secretary at the law firm he first started with. His father disapproved of her because her father was a self-made man; you know how finicky our families are on those subjects." Ethan looked to Brad who nodded his head. "David Spencer was above someone like her, and he dropped her for his current wife to please the family. He married Julia a few months before I married Natasha"

"They had Felicity, I was born not long after, and then a year later Danni was born." Brad's thoughts spoke out loud.

"Theresa and I met when she began working for my company. I'd met her before because of her relationship with David, and I thought she was nice, pretty. After Natasha died I, well, I fell apart I suppose, and she was dealing with still being used by David; even married, the man couldn't keep his hands off her. We ended up in bed and thus began our relationship."

"But she never let go of her connection to David?"

"For a while after we were married she was content to be at home with Danielle, and to take care of the home. But she grew bored with my absence thanks to work, and then when Danielle started school, being alone didn't suit her and I found out she had been seeing him again. It almost broke us up, but the fool I was, I promised her the world, made more time for her, and a few years later Peter came along. Danielle was older and that seemed to help her, because she could do all the fun woman stuff with my daughter."

"And she went back to him?"

"I never had any proof, nothing solid, but I remember hushed calls, picking up the receiver in another room. I doubt the man was calling to check his punctuation. You'll find this out sooner or later, but that summer of the accident was make or break for us. One of the reasons I was in the city was the merger, but the other was that we were trying a sort of separation. I had no idea until Louise mentioned yesterday that Theresa was gone a lot, that the affair was still happening."

"Did you speak to a lawyer about this separation?" Ted was making notes with his blackberry. "Yes, Art Silverman, he handles all legal matters both business and personal."

"And how do you know the Mayor had nothing to do with the boating accident?"

"David's never been much, he barely scraped through election for his first term as it was. He's no Giuliani, but once news spread about the accident he called me. I had thought about hanging up, I had enough going on, but he was devastated. Whatever his relationship with Theresa, he really had loved her, she wasn't just a plaything to him."

"He could have...." Ted started and Ethan held up his hand to stop him.

"David and his wife were in Florida with her parents that week."

"We saw him at the ball Tuesday, he knows Danni's here," Brad said.

"After the ball, he left for the first game down in Port St. Lucie for spring training with the Met's, he always goes down seeing as he's one of the owners."

"I guess that rules him out." Ted sighed, what a waste.

"There was someone else around the time of the accident."

"Who?"

"I don't know; some private eye. Theresa said she saw him a lot, following in his car, places she went. I know he was a private investigator because he had followed us as a family once, and he told me he'd been hired to go wherever Theresa did."

"Do you know who hired him?"

"No, but I always suspected Julia."

"Julia Spencer?"

"Yes, it's all I know I swear." Ethan was having a hard time controlling himself now, his emotions were in shreds.

"Why don't you go and see Danni." Brad suggested softly to Ethan. "She needs her dad right now; she's trying to be strong in front of you."

"Okay." Ethan stood up. "I'm sorry I didn't tell you this before, it's not much, hopefully it can help you."

Once Ethan was out of the room Brad sighed noticing Maggie was still in the room, busy typing away.

"What do you think?" He asked Ted.

"The Mayor had to be involved, didn't he?" Ted shook his head. "I knew this was going to give me a headache."

"You can't do some quiet digging, corroborate the story?"

"Quiet? I need a judge to sign a search warrant for Mrs. Spencer's financial statements. Hell, anything personal in their lives and nothing stays behind closed chambers. That's if I can find a judge who'll even sign such a request on the little information we have."

"I might be able to help." Maggie spoke up.
"A kiss is in your future if you can." Ted told her. "Find the private investigator."
"Not so easy, do you know how many of them there are in New York State? And this was seventeen years ago, most of those guys are either dead or retired?"
"Do you know how many are trusted enough by the upper class in this city?" Maggie countered back.
"How many?"
"Two."
"That easy?" Ted shook his head again.
"I can tell you for a fact I can narrow it down, too." Maggie smiled as she leaned on her elbows on the desk. "You know who it was?"
"Here." Maggie held out a business card to Ted who stood up to retrieve it from her. "You're kidding me, right?"
"Nope."
"How do you know?"
"Aside from there being only two trusted, this one was used by Brad's father when he suspected the then head accountant of skimming off the top of the books. Mrs. Spencer personally called me the winter after we had used him asking for his number."
"You're shitting me Maggie." Ted said.
"No, I'm not."

Brad watched as Ted did as promised, walking around to the back of the desk and planted a kiss smack on Maggie's lips.

Maggie was blushing uncontrollably as Ted dialed the number and moved to sit back down. Brad got up, needing Maggie to do a few things for him. "Danni and I are going to DC in the morning," he told her as he scribbled a note on a pad beside them. "I need the spare plane fueled and ready." He spoke quietly.
"The spare? I'll call Mac."
"No, I'm going to fly the Cessna down. I'll file the papers with the control tower in the morning. I don't want to take any chances."
"Are you sure? You haven't flown in a few years."
"It's like riding a bike Maggie." He winked to her. "I hate to ask you to do this, but I need you to get to my place and pick up a few things for me." He handed her the piece of paper he'd been writing on and she smiled up at him. "I'll go now, want me to pick up some lunch?"
"And have less room for that pie waiting out there for me? No chance."

XXX   XXX

"Hey Dad." Danni said seeing her father emerge from the study. From the look on his face it hadn't been easy whatever it was going on in there. "Pumpkin." He sat beside her at the kitchen table, Louise had disappeared with Daisy a while ago, and Danni had been battling about whether to make something for everyone for lunch but didn't want to step on Daisy's toes.

"Do you want something to drink dad?"

"I would kill for a coffee."

"Sure." Getting up she started getting it the way she knew he liked it, straight and black. "I have to call your brother; he should know what's going on."

"I'd rather you didn't."

"Why?"

"I don't want him and Felicity looking at me worse than they already do."

"He might know something important Danielle."

"Please, let Ted's people do their job. If in a few days we have nothing new then we'll sit him down." She didn't want to mention the trip down to DC, her own hopes were so high she didn't want to raise his too, and then have this whole thing be for nothing. "Okay Danielle, your way for now." He gave up way too easily, had he always been that way?

"You look like you have something on your mind." She heard her father say as she placed the coffee down before him. "Just everything bad going on."

"How are you and Brad?"

"Nothing wrong there." She paused. "Aside from me not knowing everything he does about us."

"It's the now that matters honey, start from Tuesday and make that your beginning."

"I'm trying." Danni looked up hopefully when the study door opened again and she had hoped to see Brad but it was Maggie pulling on her coat as she came towards the kitchen.

"I have to go and run an errand, you guys need anything?" Maggie asked. "I'm good thanks." Ethan half smiled paying attention to his coffee.

"You know; some magazines or even the newspaper."
Danni figured it would keep her busy while Brad did
his work: it would also stop her mind from wondering
about the next couple of days. "Brad has today's
paper in the study on the desk; I left the latest copy of
people magazine I brought in this morning in there on
the coffee table"
"Do you think he would mind if I snuck in?"
"Not at all and do me a favor, two black coffees for
the men."
"Should I make them some lunch?"
"The only thing Brad is going to eat is that pie."
Maggie laughed as she left.

"You made pie?"
"Lemon meringue."
"Lucky Bradford." There was a twinkle in her
father's eye before he went back to looking in to his
coffee. Danni got the two mugs ready and was
absently thinking about something else as she walked
towards the study. She didn't hear the men laughing
behind the door, or even when the door was opened,
and before either one of them knew what was going
on Danni and Ted bumped in to each other, ending
with the both of them being covered in hot coffee,
Ted taking the majority of it on his white shirt. "Man,
that's hot," Ted said, brushing the liquid with his
hand, Danni with the partially empty mugs in hand,
still looked down feeling but not seeing where her
shirt had been hit. "Ted, I'm so sorry, I wasn't paying
attention."

"Neither was I." He gave her a smile. "Don't worry about it." He turned to Brad beside him. "Can I borrow a shirt man?"

"Of course." He took the mugs from Danni. "Danni, get one of the shirts from my closet before you change your shirt."

Wordlessly she heard Ted follow, and with their being little inside the closet she was able to find a shirt, not white like the one he had on, but pale blue. "I'll wash your shirt so it doesn't stain." Danni offered.

"You don't have to." He pulled his own shirt out of his pants, and Danni felt uncomfortable, even with the bedroom door wide open, she really didn't know Ted, and to see his naked skin. She looked away and Ted could tell why. "I'm wearing an undershirt." He told her. "Don't worry, I wasn't being inappropriate."

"Sorry."

"It's okay." Once off his arms the white undershirt wasn't touched, not a drop, which was amazing, but as she let her eyes remain on him she saw scars up his right arm. They looked old and she wondered how far they went below the material of his undershirt.

"It happened in Iraq." Ted's voice brought her from her distraction looking at him. "Oh Ted, I'm so sorry. That was really rude of me." Danni felt mortified.

"Relax no harm. I know how bad they look."

"Was it painful?"

"Extremely."

"I suppose you won't tell me how you got them?"

"Car bomb, not only did I get burning shrapnel land on my jacket, but a chunk of glass did this too." He pointed to his left cheek. "It was only second degree burns and if it wasn't for." Ted stopped and grinned as he began buttoning up the new shirt which fitted him as equally well as they did Brad and for the first time Danni noticed that chest wise, the two men were almost identical in width.

"Wasn't for what?"
"More a who than a what."
"Who?"
"Your boy in the other room."
"Brad? The two of you were together?"
"Yeah, and I just realized I can't tell you anymore than he saved my life that day, as well as the lives of three other men on my Team."
"If he saved you, why won't he like you telling me?" She put a hand on his arm to stop him from leaving the room, while he rolled up the sleeves to his elbows.
"Brad would be mortified Danni, he's never thought of himself as a hero, but that's how he was treated. Not to mention his years of secret missions he did in the Navy, which make him forget some things he can talk about with those he loves."
"You think he'd tell me."
"Can't hurt to ask, right?"
"No, it can't."

CHAPTER TWENTY-SEVEN

Watching Brad eat the pie was a treat for Danni; he didn't stick with one generous slice but two. He was willing to share with her dad and Ted but had whispered as she walked by, to hide the rest so he could eat it later when they were alone.

Louise reappeared with Daisy. Brad listened to his mother as she informed them that she was having dinner with Clive, Daisy was going to drop her off downstairs at her friend's apartment on the second floor, and was then going to see a movie with a friend. He knew his mother was trying to give the two of them some privacy, but he thought it silly seeing as even there the two of them could do whatever they wanted, they always had.

As he put his fork down he caught Danni looking at him from the counter where she was leaning, resting her chin on one palm as her elbow remained next to her other hand. There was something in the way she looked at him and he wondered what it was. He knew the look when she wanted him alone, that wasn't it; he knew how her eyes got when she was thinking naughty things; that wasn't it either, but it made his own mouth stretch in to a smile.

She knew something she wanted to ask him, that was the look.

He wondered what it could be. Something to do with the past, something she might have gotten a flash of, maybe the trip down to DC?

The sound of Daisy getting the door and Maggie's voice meant she was back, and soon they would have to get back to work. Ted was going down to the federal building for a while. Ethan would leave whenever he was ready and Brad was just looking forward to an evening again with the woman still looking at him.

Catching Maggie's quick look in the doorway to the kitchen he nodded to the other door closer to the bedrooms and got up leaving everyone in the kitchen. "Here." Maggie held out the garment bag.
"Find everything okay?"
"I'd check if I were you."
"Good idea, thanks." Taking it he went to the bedroom and was half done unzipping the bag when he heard the unique sound on the wooden flooring of Danni's flip flops. "What do you have there?" Danni put an arm around his waist as she came to stand beside him. "Nothing important." He took the hand touching his side and turned her so she was facing him, his back to the bag he was hiding from her view. "I beg to differ seeing as you're trying your best to keep me from looking." She tried to look around him but he was quicker and lifted her up, his strong hands on her perfect butt, her legs wrapping around his waist, and walking her to the nearest place to set her down, which wasn't the bed. He chose the window ledge, about a foot deep and perfect for cornering her.

Kissing down her neck made her legs tighten their clench on his hips. He was hoping to make her forget the bag but her slight chuckle as her body involuntarily shivered from his lips, made him aware she wasn't going to be so easily distracted.

"Brad." She whispered feeling his lips under her ear, his hands on her ribs while his fingers gently caressed the skin just below her breasts. "Yes Danni."
"What's in the bag?"
"What bag?" He kept kissing her, switching sides only stopping to answer her. "The one on the bed."
"I don't see a bag." He felt her as she laughed louder. "What's with the sly secrets?"
"What's with all the talking?" He stood straight disconnecting his lips and meeting her eyes. "You know all these questions are ruining the moment for me." He joked but he felt her shift slightly knowing she could feel his excitement filling his pants, like it did whenever he got to touch her, he'd been a walking flag pole just being around her when they were kids. "I don't think you're really having a problem with my questions."
"You found me out." He wiggled his eyebrows.
"So, what's in the bag?"
"I asked Maggie to pick a few more things up for me from my place, lending a shirt to Ted has me down one."
"Really?"
"Aha." He went right back to kissing her neck.

"Speaking of Ted." Again, he stopped but this time took his hands from under her shirt and kept only his waist connected to her. "Ted? Now there is a way to get me out of the mood." He moved his legs and turned to rest his butt on the ledge beside her. "Hey." Her hand on his head made him look at her while his arms crossed over his chest. "Don't be like that."

"You want to talk about Ted?"

"He is your friend, right?"

"So?"

"I saw the scars on his arm earlier." Brad dislodged his head from her hold and went to the bed, taking the garment back, opening the zipper completely, and taking it to the closet to hang, the contents still out of view from Danni. She'd seen Ted's arm, presumably she'd asked him and he must have told her.

Waiting for him to say something Danni slid down from the ledge and moved closer to him. He was moving back from his closet and was headed to the bed to sit she knew from his direction. She sat beside him again as he lowered himself. "What exactly did Ted tell you?"

"Little more than you saved his life and three other guys after a bomb exploded."

"All that huh?" She took in his posture, tight and bent slightly, his elbows resting on his knees, and his head looking to the floor between his spread feet. "How can I get to know you Brad if you won't tell me the important things?"

"I don't think this subject is important."

"I think it is."

There was a long pause and Danni felt a sigh building up inside her chest. She would have to let it go for now she knew, but she wanted to know everything about the man. She couldn't get to the past 'him', and she didn't understand his need to keep important things like this to himself.

"Ted was in an Army Ranger Team inside Karbala, Iraq. They were finishing up a routine sweep of the city. I was doing reconnaissance with my own orders but I was able to get communication to my superiors, who got me a ride with them; they knew little more than they had to make room for me. I didn't wear a uniform or camouflage gear like them, to this team I looked like a native." He paused. "Long hair and a beard helped with that."

"We left Karbala; we had to stop at a roadside checkpoint, and I was in the hummer behind the one Ted was in, which was the convoy's lead. We sat there for a few minutes and a car pulled up calmly beside them, going in to the city, and something about it got my attention. The Iraqi man was acting nervously but before I could say something, there was an almighty explosion and the glass on our hummer was showered with debris and...." He stopped, not wanting to say body parts. "I got out without thinking, the entire area was filled with smoke but I could see the hummer Ted had been driving. It was on its side, and there was fire building under the carriage; all I could hear was the men inside shouting, and the sound of the fire hissing to the ammo it was turning in to deadly explosions every so often. I ran over to it, climbed aboard, seeing the windows blown out. The four men inside were shaken and I opened the back door, helping the two in back get out; one broke his arm when the vehicle flipped. I had to get Ted and another guy through the front windshield which I had to kick in. I could see fire inside and the engine was smoking pretty bad.

I got out the third guy, some other guys from their team had come over and took him from me as I went back inside to get Ted. He was out cold, a piece of glass from his side window had stabbed him in the cheek, and his shirt was covered in small pieces of burning debris. I had to cut his seat belt and drag his dead weight out. A few minutes longer and we would have both been blown up in the hummer, because it exploded behind me, forcing us both to fall to the ground. Ted came to as we got him ready to transport on a helo from the medical base not far away. I told him who I was, that I wasn't a native but an American like him"

"You were very brave." Danni's voice sounded soft to his ears while his head battled the replaying sounds of that day. "Brave and stupid."

"Stupid no." She touched one of his hands as he sat there.

"What amazed me was right after that helo took off we all went back to what we had orders to do, as if it was nothing that had just happened. I sat in the convoy for a few hours, thinking any closer and it would have been a worse day than all the other pretty crappy days inside that country. I got to my destination and after forty-eight hours, I myself was being airlifted out after I'd done what I was there for. By that time I was actually on the same flight back state-side with Ted."

"I bet he thanked you."

"He sure did. I found out he had lost his wife in nine-eleven, she had been in tower two. He had been in the Army before joining the FBI, and because of his loss he rejoined. It was his second tour."

"Both of you are heroes."

"He's more of a hero than I am." Danni touched his cheek as he looked sideways to her, his posture still the same. "Why?"

"He was doing it for his daughter."

"He has a daughter?"

"Ted's a real family man, don't let his charm and looks fool you, compared to me he lives like a monk, and his entire world revolves around her."

"And now you're friends, I think that's nice. It must be a help to have a person around that knows the things you've done when you can't tell anyone those secrets."

"That's an understatement." Brad flopped back on the bed relaxing his head on his bent arms. "I was debriefed, and then I took two days leave before I had to report back. I came up here, Dad had just got the news about the cancer when I was leaving, so I wanted to see him. I will never forget the look on Daisy's face when she opened the door and saw me standing there, long hair and a beard. She thought I was some homeless guy who had snuck past the doorman and was asking for handouts."

"Your parents must have been worried sick about you."

"After seeing the way I looked I'm sure it got a little worse."

"Did you clean up while you were here?"

"Nope, I couldn't, those two days went fast, and I was back on a transport to the Middle East."

"Were you there a lot?"

"A good amount of time."

"So, when you moved back to New York you got back in touch with Ted?"

"I saw him before I moved back."

"Where? Iraq again?"

"No, he took an honorable discharge after his injuries. I suppose the fact he'd come close to leaving his daughter an orphan got the better of him."

"Then where?"

"In DC." Brad got up and walked over to the built-in wall unit along an entire wall between the window wall and the bathroom door. It held books, knick knacks, photo frames. He opened one of the drawers and took out a blue velvet case. "I was summoned to DC to get this." He handed it to her and waited as she opened it. Inside the lid was a card with the words like you'd find on a certificate of excellence. The large words 'medal of honor' stood out bolder than the rest. "I'm guessing this is really special." She noticed the previous president's signature in the bottom corner. "Not as special as the purple heart, but that one goes to guys who are wounded or lost their lives in combat." He'd meant it as a joke but even to his own ears it didn't sound at all funny.

"Oh Brad." Tears welled up in her eyes. "That was horrible."

"I'm sorry." He kissed the top of her head. "Ted was there at the ceremony and we met for lunch the following day. Seemed we had a great deal in common aside from what we had gone through."

"Like?"

"Well, for one. Losing the women we loved."

"Loved, as in past tense with me, even now?" She carefully closed the case hearing the slight snap it made. "Do I really need to dignify that with an answer?" He looked incredulous towards her, and she could tell from his eyes alone what he felt for her. She kissed him softly as an answer.

"There must be a small part of you that can't forget, you must have seen a lot of ugliness?"

"More than could fill a book."

"And you want to go back to that?"

"In a heartbeat."

"Why?"

"Someone has to do it, I can, I'm really good at it."

"Then you should."

"Until a few days ago it's one of the big things I could only think about."

"And now? What changed?"

"Having you back, I want us to work, I want you not just for now but forever Danni; and a small part of me worries what the life I would be offering, one as me being a soldier, would put you through. I'd stay here and work behind a desk for the rest of my life if it was what I needed to do to make that work for us."

Brad saw the emotions across her face. Her eyes were still wet, and with her eyes half closed he couldn't get a real read on what they would be telling.

"Then we should try and work out exactly how we can make everything happen then."

CHAPTER TWENTY-EIGHT

After lunch, the apartment seemed to get quiet.

Ted went out to drop off the photos and to find the private investigator, while Ethan returned to his office to try and get some work done before the end of the day.

Brad was locked inside his office; the only movement was when Maggie came out to get something or make a call without disturbing him.

Danni had looked through the refrigerator, trying to use her culinary mind to decide what to make Brad for dinner. Daisy kept a stocked assortment of delicious items, and although not organic, Danni wasn't about to complain, they were all so kind and helpful; and Louise tried her hardest to make her smile; and Danni believed Louise knew the one real way to do that, aside from resolving this situation was to keep Brad close to her.

Danni appreciated that.

By mid-afternoon and when she had finished the paper and flipped through the people magazine, Danni decided to call Sam to check in; she felt immensely guilty about not returning as planned. Being a Monday she knew Sam would be at home, the restaurant closed only on the first day of the week. It had been Sam's idea, seeing as a lot of their

suppliers were Italian and they also closed the same
work-day.

"How is New York treating you today babe?" Sam's
voice asked as the call connected. "Very well." Danni
laughed.

"Would that be the city as a whole or just one certain
resident?"

"I'll go with the certain resident."

"Oh, do tell."

"I don't know where to start."

"Well you told me last time we spoke about there
being a past, childhood friends and everything you
found out, but what about since you've been there?"

"I've never felt so close to another person Sam, he's
beyond anything I've ever experienced before, but
from what I keep learning I have felt like this before."

"Before the accident?"

"I've seen the pictures, heard the few things." Danni
let a moment pass and then said. "I've had a few
memories since being with Brad."

"Memories." Sam's voice rose a little. "Are you
shitting me?"

"No, there were just a few."

"What was the first one?"

"Knowing the face I've seen in dreams over the years
belonged to someone, but the biggest one was of
something that we did when we were teens."

"This is amazing Danni, you must be so thrilled."

"Aside from the stalker sure."

"Any luck with that?"

"No, we got some new threats today too; my dad got pretty raunchy photos of Brad with it."

"Sending raunchy pictures to your dad is pretty sick."

"Don't I know it?"

"I want to tell you something?" Danni had wanted to tell her dad, but knew this secret was safe with her best female friend in the entire world. "Is it something Oooh worthy?"

"I'm going to DC tomorrow, there's a doctor down there who might be able to help me remember."

"Remember as in?"

"Yeah."

"Crap Danni, that's, that's." Sam stuttered unable to find a word to do it justice.

"I know, right, I thought I was lucky enough to get Brad and now this."

"It's what you've always wanted."

"Do you know there's something I want now more than anything, more than my memories?"

"What?"

"I want to be with Brad forever."

"Oh Danni, I have a feeling you will."

XXX   XXX

"Where did you go?" She pouted as she came in to the living room tying the belt to her Japanese silk kimono. He sat on his couch, holding his cell wearing only his boxers. He'd left early; being the son of the boss was nice when you got away with stuff.

"I had to get a call." He pushed himself off the couch and looked at Felicity. He didn't deny that he liked her, but sometimes things just seemed to be more stressful with her around, with the latest with his family she had been so far from supportive, but he didn't want to anger Felicity, who was gifted with a quick temper, and a tongue which could scar down to the bone. It had been a long time since he had felt the compassion she showed him from a female. He could barely remember his own mother's face most days, and Felicity seemed to fill that void.

"Who called?"
"My father."
"Please don't tell me he wants to do another bullshit dinner with the loon?"
"It had nothing to do with Danni."
"Please don't say her name out loud, makes me want to gag." Felicity moved over to the side table and took two tumblers from the crystal set. She poured a vodka for herself and a scotch neat for Peter. She smiled inwardly as she poured her own, the decanter was actually filled with water but he had no inkling of that.

"What do you not like about her again?" He accepted the scotch and tried to think of how the nasty comments had started, and couldn't. "Aside from her entire 'holier than thou' persona? She's a nut job who plays it all for sympathy. I mean, look how she's wrapped Brad around her little finger, don't get me started on your father."

"Brad was always wrapped around her finger as you so put it. I always thought they made a nice couple, he was always nice to me."

"Please." Felicity huffed again. "What did daddy want?"

"I'm ordered to his office this afternoon; he has a meeting ending at five and wants me there before he leaves."

"Maybe he's going to hand the company to you finally, so he can take care of your sister's problems."

"I don't think he's retiring anytime soon Felicity."

"Well he should, you're ready for it I know you are."

"Your faith in me is comforting but I have some more years before I get the big office."

"We should work on your father, maybe as a wedding present?"

"Felicity, I won't have you planting any seeds in his head."

"Who's he going to leave it to, your sister?"

"My dad has enough years left in him to go on working."

"If you say so."

"If you want to get in to my dad's good graces as I am, then you'll think about being nice to Danni."

"That is never going to happen."

XXX   XXX

He was so grateful when the afternoon was finally over, a little earlier than usual at four but still, it felt like those four walls were going to squash him as they came closer towards him.

There was a great deal to get done before Thursday's board meeting, and he was going to be away the two days before it. Again, Maggie had offered to reschedule the meeting, but he wanted to get it out of the way. He could get some last-minute things done in DC and then there were the things Maggie was taking care of, the presentation layouts and report packets.

Walking Maggie to the door he was aware how quiet it was, the sun was hidden by the neighboring buildings making it darker than normal inside. There was a smell emanating from the kitchen, which he couldn't wait to investigate, and he'd caught a sneak peek in the doorway to the kitchen as he walked past. Danni was busy doing something but seeing her, even without connecting visually he got hot knowing the next few hours they would be all alone.

"Thanks for everything Maggie."
"You know you're very welcome Brad, it's an honor to work with you especially times like this."
"I think you're a little biased." He opened the front door.
"Possibly but that's my right."
"I suppose." He laughed slightly. "So we'll be communicating via phone tomorrow, if anything comes up."
"I'll take care of it Brad; you just make sure Danni gets what she needs."
"Keep your fingers crossed."
"I'll add her to my prayers tonight."

"Night Maggie."
"Night Brad."

"All done for the day?" Danni asked from where she was taking something out of the oven. "No." He waited for her to put the roasting pan on the counter. "I have a very important woman I have to entertain and satisfy."
"Someone special?" Danni placed the oven gloves on the counter and leaned against it like he was, so they were facing. "I seem to think she is."
"What a special lady."
"One I plan on cherishing."
"Is that a promise?"
"For as long as I live."

XXX   XXX

"I thought you were coming over tonight?" Peter said as he poured another scotch in to the glass as he sat on the couch in his living room. It was almost nine, he had tried calling Felicity for the past two hours since getting home and she was just now calling him back.

"I have some things to do."
"I called your office; your secretary said you haven't been there all day."
"I can't work from home?" Her voice sounded pissy, and he rubbed the glass on his forehead. "Of course you can, I just thought we'd be having dinner tonight."

"We'll have plenty of dinners together once we're married." She told him in her stern voice, the one which, when they had started dating, had scared him a little.

"So what did your father want?"
"He was explaining Danni is staying a few extra days."
"She was meant to go home tomorrow."
"I'm guessing she and Brad are getting closer."
"Then what does that have to do with you?"
"He wants to have me take my sister out to lunch."
"Why would you do that?"
"Spend some time together; have me give her a chance."
"What a waste of your time."
"He said I should try and get you to be nicer as well. I explained you are your own person and you do what you want."
"How ballsy of you." She bit again at him.

"You might consider at least acting nice."
"Give me one damn reason why."
"Dad's threatening to send me to London to work on the FTSE, basically three thousand miles away, and for half the pittance I get paid now."
"He would never send you to London."
"Seems he would, he's already spoken to Keith over there about my position. Either I give Danni a chance or I'm being sent away."
"Son of a bitch." Peter was glad in a way that this was being done over the phone. "That little bitch has been a thorn in everyone's side for years and now this."

"It isn't that bad."

"Who are you trying to kid?"

"All you have to do is smile Felicity and keep your thoughts to yourself while in her presence, and this will blow over. She'll be back in LA soon enough."

"Not soon enough for me, she should never have come back."

CHAPTER TWENTY-NINE

Seeing him fly the small plane was an experience as the noise from the engine filled the small space and she was grateful for the headset and microphone so they could talk to one another.

The best part of the morning so far though was not the looking out at the Eastern Coast, being told where they were and stuff, but what had taken her attention since coming out of the bathroom that morning was how he looked.

"What do you think?" He'd asked standing there in the middle of his room, gleaming in this way she'd never known possible. All pressed, starched and stiff, wearing what he had told her was the only suit he'd ever thought he'd ever wear.

And man did he make it look so good.

"I think I've never seen anything so beautiful before in my entire life," had been her reply.

"We'll be landing in ten minutes," he told her as she looked out at the cities far below them as they flew over. "I can't believe we're flying in this small thing." She hadn't had the heart to tell him she hated planes; that it was taking everything she had not to grip the seat arm rests, and not keep herself tight in her seat. He'd looked so handsome, so excited to take her aboard his little toy, she had smiled and swallowed her fear.

Once they landed and Brad was taking their overnight bags, she allowed herself to release the breath she'd held for forty-five minutes. She made her way to the small door of the plane and waited as he placed his uniform white hat on his head. With those dark glasses covering his eyes he looked like a different man, a strong formidable type of man, and she knew if she were a bad guy coming upon that, she'd probably run a thousand miles from him.

There had been a dark sedan waiting for them once they made it across the tarmac of the private air strip, and had there been a dividing section between them and the driver, she might have been tempted to lean over and kiss this new man who, with confidence oozing from every pore, still held her hand tenderly inside his own.

Since waking up at four-thirty that morning Brad had been walking around wanting to be a lot more intimate with Danni. After dinner and a shower together he had made love to her before insisting they get some sleep, knowing they both needed to be awake, and he figured the more conscious she was, the better the procedure might go. He was determined that this was going to work, he couldn't allow it not to.

Having been to DC many times and a few times visiting people over at Bethesda and Walter Reed he knew his basic bearings around the hospitals and grounds. He had the driver drop them at Heaton

Pavilion, also known as building two, and made sure he had the driver's number so he could call when they were ready to go to the hotel, and then told the man the name of the hotel they were booked in to for the night-the local Hilton, ten minutes away.

Like a civilian hospital there was no security on the main entrance and only a woman in an army uniform ready to give directions to the lost at the reception desk. There were many people already milling around the halls and elevator, and they found ward 61 easily, Dr. Cole's office even easier. It was not unlike the other doctors' offices, a waiting room filled with uncomfortable chairs, and people waiting, reading the crappy fair in magazines. There were maybe seven other people in the waiting room, all alone, no one speaking to anyone else. None wore anything resembling a uniform, and no t-shirts or sweatshirts connecting them to a branch. There was only one female aside from the desk nurse, who was in uniform, and busy typing while she looked at a computer screen.

"Excuse me." Brad said.
"Do you have an appointment?" She didn't look up at either of them.
"Danielle Morgan, she has an appointment with Major Coles."
"Good, you're early." Finally, she looked up as she reached behind her for a clipboard from a shelf to one side of her. "Fill these in, we need proof of insurance and we'll need your Military Number Commander."

"I'm actually paying for the treatment." That made the woman's eyebrows rise. "I'll need a credit card or blank check to run to ensure...."

"Trust me when I say simply you won't need to ensure anything, but here." He took the wallet from his back pocket, extracted his gleaming black American Express card and passed it to the nurse, whose name he noted was Brenda. He tried to remember she was just doing her job, and it had to become tedious doing the same thing every day, he himself could relate a hundred percent.

"I'll run this and you can have it back," she said and Danni took the clipboard walking over to a section of empty seats, Brad joined her, and sat there with his cover on his lap. He wished he'd thought to bring the paper, because he'd been there seconds, and with Danni busy he was looking around the off-white painted room trying not to look at the people waiting. "Commander." He heard Brenda say. She was holding up his credit card, and he left his cover on the chair to go and get it. He smiled, remembering that morning when Danni had taken that flat white uniform hat, and placed it on her own head as if it were a beret, God that had looked hot!

"If I could have you sign this too." Brenda placed a receipt needing his signature while she held on to the black American express card. He heard the waiting-room door open and signed, ignoring whoever it was, more than likely another patient. "Sergeant West." Brenda sighed loudly, and Brad had to look out the corner of his eye to see the man in civvies like everyone else apart from him, and he was beginning to feel really overdressed. "Please Brenda I'm begging you, I gotta see the doc today."

"And I told you 'no go'."

"Damn it." The man banged his fists on the counter as Brad was putting his card back into the wallet and to his back pocket. "I'm serious Brenda." Brad took in the mannerisms of this guy quick, he was sweating, fidgety and obviously on the edge. "Look, Sergeant, I feel for you, I do but rules and regulations are for everyone, I can't bend a rule for you without feeling sorry for everyone else around here, plus I could lose my job."

"I'm not going anywhere until I see the doc."

"Please, Sergeant don't make me call security again."

"All I'm asking for is what I'm due."

"And I'm only telling you what I've told you the last three weeks, Sergeant."

"Jesus, I almost hit my wife last night." If possible, the already silent room went deadly quiet.

Brad felt a soft hand on the middle of his back and turned to see Danni looking nervous with the finished paper-work. Brenda looked relieved to have something else to focus on, as the large African American man looked ready to explode. "Sergeant." Brad said, and the man looked at him. They were roughly the same height but the man was definitely a foot wider, and Danni could see heat in his face and she feared he was going to explode.

"What?" The man asked but Brenda interrupted.

"Miss Morgan." She pointed to a man in scrubs who had appeared behind them. "Evan here will take you downstairs to have your tests run before you see Dr. Coles."

"I'll be right here." Brad promised and took her small purse for her without having to be asked. "Can I buy you a cup of coffee?" Brad said to the man. "Why do you want to do that?" The guy frowned.

"You'll be doing me a favor; my girlfriend is probably going to be a while."

"I'll be back," he told Brenda who sighed as she kept on typing.

"I'm hoping you know where the cafeteria is." Brad tried to joke.

"Yeah, I know this place better than I know my own place."

The pace was set as they made it through the corridors towards the cafeteria. "I'm Brad by the way."

"Will."

"So, which division were you in?" Brad asked.

"Rangers." The man's tone was just flat; Brad didn't think it had anything to do with boredom but more frustration. After a pause, he said. "How many tours did you do?"

"Three." Brad was about to ask something else when the man said. "I suppose a water boy like you hasn't even been close to any action."

"Actually, I'm not serving on any ships."

"Pentagon, DOD?"

"SEAL."

"So, you have seen action?"

"For almost four years I spent nearly all my time there."

"That place is evil." They reached the double doors which were open and the many people inside made it a little noisier than the base mess hall Brad thought it felt like.

"I don't suppose there's somewhere outside we can enjoy our coffee?" Brad paid for the coffee's and a couple of Danishes. "There's a garden out that side door." Brad followed and once outside he needed his glasses again from the early morning glare, but kept them off so as not to seem rude.

Once seated on a retaining wall overlooking the cafeteria picnic tables Brad asked. "So you were giving Brenda a hard time in there."

"Every day for the last three weeks."

"How come?"

"I've been back state-side for the last two months; after the initial five weeks of therapy I'm told I don't qualify for any more medical assistance from the Army because I opted for a honorable discharge and have no physical injuries."

"What were you being treated for?"

"PTSD."

"You have nightmares, mental flashes? I occasionally even think I can smell the same thick air."

"All that and I miss the action, the camaraderie I had with the unit. I can't seem to get my head around this being the safe zone, the non-scary world."

"Lose many guys?"

"Some, I'll never forget them, but it was more the place that got under my skin, you know. The way women are treated, the decay of war." Will stopped speaking but looking into the half-finished polystyrene cup. "We were sent in to help look for casualties inside a village, my last tour. I have a harder time getting the faces and gnarly body parts out of my head of all those innocent little children."

"It's always harder with children." Brad agreed.

"My wife tells me I ignore our son, I'm not the same with him anymore."

"How old is he?"

"Six."

"He reminds you of those in Iraq."

"Deep down I know that, but with everything else."

"What else?"

"You don't want to hear my woes."

"I'm not going anywhere."

"I can't sleep well, everything keeps me awake, fear of going back to that place. I can't hold down a job because I'm too tired or I'm under qualified. I've only ever been in the army. I know how to fire a weapon and motivate my team. With not being able to hold a job, we're having to live with my wife's parents, which causes stress. Like I said before, she nags me about not spending quality time with Miles, and then because I can't afford to pay our way."

"I'm sorry."

"I felt like I was making progress here, seemed to be ironing out the things that haunt me, but then after five weeks I'm told no more, without being in the service I'd have to pay, and without a job." His words trailed off. "Half of me is still living in Iraq, the other is freaking out; I'm ruining everyone's lives here. They may have been better off if I had come back in a pine box."

"Don't say that." Brad placed a hand on his shoulder. "No one is better off like that, not you or your family."
"That's what it feels like."
"I know."
"How'd you deal with it?"
"Still a work in progress." Brad let out a short laugh. The dreams and memories would probably always haunt him. "You meet your girl here?" Will asked him. "No, she's never served."
"But you got her in here, without marriage?"
"It's a really long story."
"I'm not going anywhere." Will told him like he had said earlier.

Brad watched Will listen to the entire thing, everything about the past and his history with Danni to that morning, and arriving in the hospital. "Well, Major Coles is a great doc; he'll help her I'm sure."
"Thanks." Brad felt the phone in his pocket vibrate, and taking it out to see the screen he saw it was Maggie. "Can you give me a moment?"
"Sure thing."
"Maggie." Brad stood up and walked a few feet away. "I'm not interrupting anything, am I?"
"No."

"I wanted to just let you know that everything here is okay. I'm in the office and Ted said he would call me if anything comes up."

"Thanks Maggie." Brad suddenly got a rush of adrenaline as he thought something through. "I need your help with something, good timing."

"Anything."

"I want you to put together an account for a friend of mine, take twenty grand and deposit it in there."

"Name?"

"Will West, retired Sergeant. One of the big banks here in DC; I'll have him go there later and prove ID and whatever. Then I want you to call down and ask for Ward sixty-one here at the hospital. Ask for a Brenda and tell her the charity will be paying for whatever medical assistance Will needs with them."

"Okay." He knew Maggie was writing everything down.

"Call Brenda first then text me when you have the account info."

"It's being done now." Disconnecting, he saw Will getting up to throw his now empty cup in the nearby trash. "I'm going to get back, bug Brenda some more." Will told him.

"I'll come with you, hopefully Danni is done."

Back in the waiting room there were less people waiting, but the place was still so quiet, and there was no sign of Danni. Both of them had walked towards the reception desk and Brad could see Brenda's internal sigh that Will was coming back also.

Before either of them could say anything to her the desk phone rang, and she answered it in the official tone and as she remained quiet listening to whoever was on the other end he knew it was Maggie, and was keeping his smile internal. Brenda began jotting something down, and after a few minutes the call was over.

Brenda looked up between the two men; the call was the first she'd ever received like that, and it was a little more than a surprise. "Happy to see me Brenda?" Will joked expecting her usual comeback. "I'll get you some new paper-work to fill in Sergeant. We can make you an appointment after. If you aren't busy we can possibly fit you in today." Though she spoke to Will she gave Brad a glance. "I didn't expect that response." Will looked at Brad.
"Surprises happen, right?" His own cell beeped and he looked at the text as Brenda returned. "Can I borrow a pen?" he asked, but was given the item without a response from her. He took out his wallet, finding the spare business card for the organization his father had started, and he was very passionate about; it was men like Will they tried to help, and he was going to see he could do it for him now, he jotted down the information on the back which Maggie had sent him, and then added his cell number to the front where the charities numbers were.

Will was leaning on the reception desk filling out the paper work when Brad turned from the sound of a door opening and saw Danni walk in with a man in uniform and a white lab coat. She gave him that toe

290

curling smile, and as they came closer he saw it was Major Coles she was with. "Nice to meet you," he said once the introductions were made, before he made his own to Danni, and Will who was still filling out his paper work. "I was telling Brad, the doc is good," Will told her as the Major was walking away to speak to another patient. "He said we're going to start right after he confers with someone" Danni's excitement was still there he could tell.

"Will, I'm going to take Danni for a coffee now, but I wanted to tell you something."

"Shoot."

"There's an organization I head; it's actually a charity started by my father a long time ago, but anyway, that's who called Brenda, we're going to cover your medical help completely."

"You're gonna pay?" Will's forehead furrowed so deep his eyes were almost closed. "Here." Brad handed him the business card. "That's the name of the organization, and I wrote my number on there. On the back is an account number for an account over at First National Bank; it was opened ten minutes ago for you, and the money in there is for you to help get back on your feet."

"Are you kidding?" Will took the card.

"Not at all, I'm fortunate enough to be in the service still, and come from a family with money. I know what you feel Will, and no one should be left behind because some bureaucrat who's never served, has some money-saving scheme. I have the means to help you, and I hope you'll accept it."

"I don't know what to say."

"There's nothing to say." Brad held out his hand, and Will shook it eagerly as if a thousand pounds of weight had been lifted from his shoulders. "Give yourself time to heal, and get strong, and give the charity a call, I personally know the boss, and we're always looking for men with your experience and knowledge to work with us."

"You're offering me a job too?"

"It's yours, if and when you want it"

CHAPTER THIRTY

Standing in the middle of a room covered in those large light-up wall machines you saw on television medical shows, which the faux doctors always placed x-rays on, Brad looked with confusion at what Major Coles had been pointing to, and explaining in animated detail, since bringing both him and Danni in there.

They'd had to wait an hour and a half once Danni had returned from the tests she'd told him about in explicit detail over coffee, after she had asked what had transpired between him and the man who had seemed so tense when he'd arrived in the waiting room. Major Coles himself had come looking for them, finding them not far from the retaining wall where he had also been sitting with Will earlier.

Now, both Major Coles and a civilian doctor, a Stephanie Monroe, were there with them. "I've never seen any evidence personally of this but I've heard about it," the Major had said. "This is very promising." Stephanie had smiled to Danni, and he knew from the hand he was holding that she was comforted by that last comment. "You can see here the scan taken at the time of your accident, that there was significant damage from the temporal lobe area, which is why you've been unable to remember anything from before the injury," Coles started. "What we see from today's MRI is that over ninety percent of the damage has healed over the last seventeen years."

"Is that normal?" Danni asked.

"We've talked this over, asked a few colleagues here in the neuro wing." Stephanie was bubbling over. "There are a few published cases known about self-regenerative healing. I googled it quickly, and there have been some cases out west, of people who suffered heart damage repairing over time the dead tissue, normally left to wither away. They've found a connection with the nuclear testing and radiation fallout which stored a certain cocktail of gasses inside their systems."

"But I wasn't alive in the what, forties and certainly not on the West Coast." Danni scoffed.

"The interesting thing we noticed from what you filled in this morning on your paper work is that you own an organic restaurant and obviously you eat food from that, it is possible to make a far stretch and presume maybe wherever the foods were from may have been rich in these chemicals which have enabled your body to self-help itself to get better."

"So, there's another pro to my life choice?"

"Possibly." Coles smiled as he nodded.

"We talked this over and we think the only thing you need is a way to kick start what you haven't used in a long time, but have in the past few days experienced the beginnings of." Stephanie explained.

"With being hypnotized?" Danni looked at the two doctors.

"We both have appointments for the next hour and then Stephanie is going to start the process, while Brad and I sit in the neighboring room listening. We can make sure that way that everything you remember really happened." Coles turned to Brad. "I'm going to need you for the next hour to write down everything pertinent we may need as guiders. A small timeline so to speak."

"I can do that."

"And Danni, we're going to have Ethan take you down to a room we use to relax patients before we start."

For what felt like an entire day, and harder than when he had sat inside a classroom back in Annapolis trying to learn everything he needed to become an officer, Brad sat there alone in a plain room with a few tables scattered around, trying to make sure he had everything that might come out in her memories. There was little he didn't know about before they had met as kids, hard not to when Danni had gone on and on about her best friend Michelle that first summer, Michelle this and Michelle that, Michelle did things this way, not like him; and mainly that was because he was a boy. The thought made him chuckle. As they had grown older it was the first week of vacation she spoke about what she and Michelle got up to during the school year; and when they were fifteen he had finally met the fiery red head best female friend of his best friend.

He didn't get a chance to see Danni before Major Coles took him in to another room where he saw Danni through a one-way mirror, getting settled with Stephanie. "She looks nervous." Lewis had told him earlier to call him by his first name except he couldn't, that rank thing always sat in his head. "No,

that's her anxious face." Brad took one of the two seats while he noticed Lewis turning something on in front of the window. "Steph' has an earpiece in so she can hear us. If at any time you hear something Danni says which never happened, then you'll need to step in."
"Got it."

Danni had spent a little less than an hour, sitting in a room scented with fragrances she couldn't distinguish, and candles, and soothing music like the stuff Sam played while they did yoga. The lighting had been dim and the blinds had shut out the morning sun. The room certainly put you in the right headspace as you sat on the overstuffed armchair.

It felt like she had floated from that room to the equally comfortable room which looked like a living room complete with fresh flowers, and a beautiful painting of a nighttime sky on the wall, filled with pinks, purples, oranges and some blues. Danni wasn't sure in the second room where she should sit but she naturally went towards the armchair, probably because it looked just like the one in the last room.

"Okay Danni." Stephanie was sitting on the other arm chair opposite her separated by a long rectangular coffee table. The couch was empty but looked inviting also. "How about we start?"
"Sure." Danni heard her own voice and it sounded so soft.
"I want you to close your eyes and relax your body, let everything relax starting with your head, then your

shoulders, arms, feel your breathing even out and all the way down to your toes." Danni heard the woman's voice as her body felt slightly heavy, and her head like when she woke up from a nap, able to fall right back asleep or wake right up.

"Now Danni, I want you to imagine a room, a room with one large open window and a door either side. The door to the left is to come back here and the one on the right takes you back to those memories."
"It has pale yellow walls." Danni said.
"Good, now in the middle of the room is a chair, I want you to choose someone from your life who makes you feel comfortable and safe; we are going to use that person as an anchor to your memories."
"Brad." In her mind, she saw him smiling at her.
"He's there wearing his Navy uniform." She knew there was a smile on her face.
"Good now, we're going to have you bring three other people with you."
"Who?"
"I want you to imagine you at five, eleven and seventeen."
"I'm there." She felt comfort from seeing the three hers with Brad.

"Very good Danni, now I want you to hold out your hand to the five-year-old you, she's going to lead you to that door on the right. I want you to let her take you, okay."
"Okay."
"Go through that door and tell me what you see."
Danni heard the doctor's voice as she felt as if her

entire body was floating towards that white door. She felt the hand inside her own, and as the door opened a burst of sunlight came out, washing her as it blinded her for a second. "I'm in Southampton."

"At your father's summer house?"

"It's the first day we went there; we just drove down from Connecticut."

"Tell me what's going on Danni."

"I'm following me up the stairs with my dad; he's so excited to show me something." Danni's breath caught as she felt an excitement deep inside her watching the five year old version of herself laughing as her dad joked and tried to make her happy. "I complained all the way there in the car. We'd left really early, and I wasn't happy about not getting to see my friend Michelle, we grew up next door to each other in Connecticut and I didn't want to not see her for six weeks. I cried in the car all the way to the state line, when dad started telling me about his best friends he had grown up with in New York City, they were his best friends, and he hoped I would be friends with them too, they had a son, a year older than me but he was a nice boy, and I would get to play with him."

"I'm in my room now." Danni felt light headed as she twirled around seeing the room as if it were for the first time again, but she knew the familiarity of it.

"Tell me about it."

"It's lilac, the bed has a white canopy and the windows look towards the house next door. I even have a bathroom and the biggest walk-in closet I've ever seen until then. The bed is pretty, it's a big-girl bed and there are some new stuffed animals on it. My dad has put my suitcase inside the closet." Danni watched the smaller her looking around the room, noticing the quiver in the bottom lip. "I loved the room but it made me a little sad."

"Because?"

"It was the first strange place I'd ever had to sleep in."

"What are you doing now?"

"Theresa just came in telling my dad their friends had arrived."

"And?"

"He kneels down and tells me he can't wait to see his friend John, and would I like to meet them, I tell him 'yes' but in a soft nervous voice."

Danni was quiet as she followed the three of them down the winding staircase and out the back of the house. She could see a man her father's age over by the low wall separating the yards from the sand, green one side, soft and golden on the other. "I can see a man and a young boy who's sitting on the short wall, reading something. There's a woman over on the deck, actually there's two. I think the one standing is wheeling the other." Danni paused. "Louise looks so young and pretty, she had shoulder length dark hair back then." Looking back to her father she noticed the man shaking hands with him. "John was handsome too; I think Brad looks a lot like him except Brad has stronger, beautiful features."

"Which Brad?"

"Oh." Danni was watching her little self. "The one now, the younger one is too cute. His hair is short on the sides but longer on top and he's dressed like his dad in khaki shorts and a white polo."

"What are you doing?"

"Watching me watch Brad, I remember how nervous I was because I didn't have any friends who were boys. Boys were those stinky loud people who filled half of the class room."

"I knew a few of those." Stephanie laughed.

"I'm sitting next to him and I know what is going to happen now." Danni felt her lips smile. "I'm going to sit there and stare at him until he looks up from his comic."

"How long does that take?"

"Moments but it felt like hours, our dads' words sound like noise in the background, and finally Brad looks at me and smiles."

"Does he say anything?"

"Yeah." Danni laughs hearing the boy say them again. "He said so you're Danni, I thought for sure you'd be a boy."

"What did you say?"

"You don't like me because I'm a girl?"

"Carry on."

"And Brad said, 'I like that you are a girl', especially when I was so pretty."

CHAPTER THIRTY-ONE

Brad sat there for two hours listening with a host of emotions running through his system, which he was trying to hide from the Major beside him, and was hoping he was keeping them to himself.

A few times Coles had asked him if he was sure everything she recalled was right. He'd nodded and said. "If it isn't I'll tell you." But it had come out like a whisper as she went from using the five-year-old 'her' to replay the first time they'd met through the first few summers they were together, to the eleven-year-old 'her' who probably revealed more to people they didn't know than even Danni would be uncomfortable with.

He listened as Danni spoke about the summer she had turned twelve. That vacation he had fallen off his new boogey board and almost cracked his skull open on some rocks, but it was the end of the holidays she was recapping, the winter months he had no clue about that stumped him. "I can't corroborate any of this." He told Coles.
"Let's see where it goes." Coles had said before letting Stephanie know through her ear piece.

"I always showed Michelle every picture from the summer, we would sit in my room in Connecticut and she would listen for hours as I told her every single detail from beginning to end. Then by Christmas she referred to Brad as my boyfriend but by spring vacation she was asking me why I wasn't going on any dates with guys in school, and saving my first kiss for a boy I didn't even know what he was doing at that moment, which would depress me a little, but I would start telling her the plan I was going to set in to motion to get Brad to kiss me, my first real kiss: I dreamed about it until summer."

"The summer I turned thirteen Peter and I had finished school early, as my dad wanted to take us with him to Tokyo while he was on business, and we arrived in New York right from there. It was a week before Brad would arrive, and I was still in full-on planning mode to get him to kiss me. There were lots of boys wanting to take me out, I had grown a foot since that last summer, my body had filled out, and I had persuaded Dad and Theresa to let me cut my butt length hair to just below my shoulders. I'd also got a load of new clothes, thanks to my growth spurt, and even though my dad wasn't happy, Theresa had let me buy my first bikini." Danni grinned. "See, usually we spent a great deal of time in and out of the water, and the years before if I wasn't in some dress I was in a bathing suit."

"Theresa was getting ready to go with Louise to Paris for the weekend, while John and my dad planned on keeping an eye on the three of us kids. I was beyond anxious to see Brad, and having to wait a week killed me. The morning they were due to arrive I had snuck over to their house. Even after nine months Brad's room still smelt like him, and I set a present I'd got in Tokyo on his bed. There was a picture of the two of us on his bedside table; I remember picking it up and hugging it to my chest."

"I was in my room waiting when I saw John pull the car in to the driveway. When Brad got out he looked over, blocking the sun on his right with his hand to his eyes and waved knowing I was there."
"You had never kissed Brad before?"
"Maybe a peck on the cheek a few times, a hug here and there, he'd never shown me any sign he saw me as a girl or he wanted anything more than a friend."
"But you liked him."
"I liked him a lot." A laugh. "I ran down those stairs as if someone had lit a match up my...." Danni stopped. "Well you know where. My dad yelled for me to stop running in the house as I opened the front door, letting it slam closed behind me, and I ran so fast across that yard, seeing that Brad had started running towards me. He'd grown so tall and wider; the summer before he'd begun shaving, and I could tell even at fourteen he had morning stubble. Anyway, I launched myself up and he caught me square on his chest hugging me so tight, and I could have died happy right there and then."
"He kissed you?"
"No, but it didn't matter, one of his arms held me while he leant back slightly to see my face, when he poked my nose, he got this fascination from seeing my eyes cross, and he said he had been dying the entire drive down because he had missed me over the winter."

"It sounds like he liked you too."

"At that point I could only hope, but I did think I noticed something in his eyes when he put me down, seeing me in a bikini top and shorts. I was very proud of my C cups back then."

"I'm sure you were." Stephanie nodded as if she too had something like that in her past. "We spent a few days just the two of us hanging out and goofing around, before we let the summer really begin and a few weeks in there was this barbeque a friend of Brad's was having, and Brad asked me to go with him. I was super excited as I would be able to wear the dress Theresa had brought back from her trip to Paris. I hadn't shown Brad but I loved it. He was at a Yankee game that afternoon, while I got ready and then about an hour before he was due back it started to pour and I was so annoyed. I saw them return and I threw on my red slicker over my dress, I had pulled my hair back in to a pony-tail because, thanks to the humidity it had frizzed, and wearing only my sandals on my feet I ran over to find Brad had been told the barbeque had been cancelled."

"So, you weren't able to show off your dress?"

"Louise I guess had been told by Theresa about my excitement, and after I wiped my feet in the kitchen doorway she was there in her chair. Brad was upstairs drying off, and getting dressed for dinner. Louise told me she knew about me wanting to show off my new dress and had made reservations for Brad and me over at the country club we'd been to so many times, but never without the parental units. She asked if I would model the dress so she could see it. So I unsnapped the slicker and she held out her hand to take it as I twirled slowly and let her see."

"It was my first real little black dress; it was a thin cotton with a layer of delicate sheer material over the top, which was embroidered with black cotton in designs of little flowers. It only came halfway down my thighs, and was straight across at the top with these impossibly tiny straps."
"What did Louise think?"
"She told me I looked beautiful, that I was my mother completely."
"You never knew your mother?"
"No, she died in child-birth, and I'd only seen a few pictures over the years. It had been Louise who had told me, when I was little, all about the woman I looked like."
"Not your dad?"
"He always got so sad talking about her that I didn't bring it up with him. But when I knew Louise had been my mom's best friend I had asked her."

"What did Brad say when he saw you there?"
"He was quiet, just looked at me but I knew he liked what he saw."
"How?"
"He gets this intensity in his eyes; it's as if they get so much darker and richer. He was wearing a pair of tan slacks and a blue shirt. His hair was still wet, and he coughed before he spoke-which made me laugh inside. Louise told us to have a good time and Brad gently took my hand and we went out to the car waiting out in the driveway. Charlie had an umbrella

ready and walked us to the back door he opened. I can even tell you what we ate that night."

"Which was?"

"I'd been having this aversion to red meat, and had decided to get chicken carbonara, while Brad got a steak with a side of veggies and a baked potato. We talked easily while we waited for our food, and when the waiter put it on the table the smell of his steak was mouthwatering, I think he knew what I was thinking, and called the waiter back without even asking me and said if it wouldn't take too long we would like another of his dinners, a spare plate, and my food wrapped to take with us."

"A spare plate?"

"He shared the food on his plate while we waited for the new one."

"That was sweet."

"Very sweet."

"It had to have looked funny, these two kids sitting amongst the adults, not doing anything to annoy anyone. But unlike the rest of the room we weren't sipping cocktails or wine, we had two large root beer floats. The steak was amazing, as good as I had imagined from the smell, and I didn't care about looking like a pig when I devoured my second half. Brad sat there watching me, and he always had a smile when he did."

"On the way back to the house later, I knew Peter was sleeping over a friend's house, and Dad and Theresa were in the city. So, when Brad wanted to have me watch a movie with him I said yes, but as we left the mainland we noticed how dark the strip was and Charlie told us power had been lost, thanks to a downed tree somewhere near the country club. Brad told me I should definitely come to his house so I wouldn't be alone at home in the dark, and I didn't argue. I had slept over many times before. He had a huge bed and we'd never had a problem sharing in innocence."

"Both John and Louise were in the living room, the rain was still heavy and you could hear it hitting all the glass surfaces and even the roof sections now and then. John gave Brad a flashlight, and a handful of batteries as well as a lighter for the candles he had already put up in the bedroom to light. I gave Louise the meal I hadn't eaten but ordered as it was one of her favorites, and she said if only the microwave was working she would have heated it up, because she always had room for it. I laughed as I held Brad's hand, and he used the flashlight to light the stairs up to his room. Once inside I sat on the end of his bed and waited for those candles to come to life."

"It was so perfect that night, the rain hitting the glass like a chorus in the darkness outside, while it drowned out the usual sound of the waves not far away. The candles made everything surreal in their soft light, and once he had them all lit around the room he turned off the flashlight casting us further in to the burning glow. Then he came and sat down next to me."

"It sounds like a perfect night for...." Stephanie started, but Danni interrupted.

"Don't get beyond the memory."

"Sorry." Stephanie apologized as she looked towards the men she knew were looking and listening through the one-way glass, giving them a smile. "Brad told me he had never had so much fun at dinner, that he always had fun with me, and that he sometimes forgot we were best friends and thought I was more like a-I stopped him because I knew I would be devastated if he said like a sister. But he shook his head and said he knew what I thought he was going to say but in truth he actually was going to say, 'like a girlfriend' and my entire body froze. He took my hand inside his again, told me he didn't want to scare me, but that's how he looked at me, he said he had been on a few dates during the winter, but he always seemed to compare them to me, and none of them came close."

"My voice was shaking like the rest of me, I wanted to tell him I felt the same; that I had planned for months to find a way to get him to kiss me, but when I was presented with that opportunity I felt closer to tears and nerves than anything sane."

"Tears?"

"Of joy, there was nothing more that I wanted from him than to kiss him, and instead I just nodded slightly and before I knew it Brad leant in and kissed me softly on the lips."

"I bet your toes curled."

"Everything seemed to curl and then retract. My heart was beating so fast I thought it would leap out of my chest. I followed his lead, like I said I hadn't kissed anyone in an adult way before, I knew the basics from Michelle so when he opened his mouth slightly I followed, and before long it was so intense that I didn't think I'd be able to hold my body up. We lay back together and when his tongue softly touched mine I think I moaned loud enough for everyone in the next town to hear."

"He was above me softly leaning across me as our legs lay side by side, I was too nervous to open my eyes to begin with, for fear it was really just my over active imagination, but when I did he was looking back and I could see the rain hitting the roof of glass, and his eyes were just...." Danni paused. "Brad gently pulled away and whispered in my ear before he kissed down the side of my neck, he told me he loved me more than anyone; sometimes he thought he would explode if he didn't get to kiss me, touch me. Ever since the morning they'd arrived and I'd run across the grass to him in my bikini he had been trying to pluck up the courage. I said I was glad he did as I found my voice and let him know I had planned on kissing him too, that I loved him the same if not more than the way he did for me."

"We spent the next few hours making out. John caught us kissing when he came up to see if I was staying, or if we had gone back to get something for me to sleep in from my house. It was late and I knew Louise was probably in bed already, I had vaguely heard Daisy going to her room at the other end of the hall. I was mortified John had caught us and I know Brad was the same, because I suppose we both knew things would change in the eyes of our parents if they saw us kissing. But he didn't say anything about what

he had seen, and when Brad said he would lend me
some shorts and a t-shirt so I wouldn't have to get wet
going over, and then John just said goodnight, and
left us to what we had been doing. Even after we took
a break to change in separate rooms we went right
back to kissing, and for the first time I fell asleep in
his arms."

"Did John ever say anything?"

"The next morning it was Louise who said something
at the breakfast table. She was, I think, as happy
about us kissing as I was."

CHAPTER THIRTY-TWO

Stephanie had stopped Danni moments after telling the story about their first kiss, and was walking her through returning to the safe room, and back to reality.

"Danni's going to remember everything she talked about?" Brad asked Coles. "She should, they were all there; just her mind needed a door to open to them."
"Should?"
"I'm positive she will but she might get a little frustrated as her mind organizes everything in order. I'll give Danni a couple of tablets to help her relax tonight and in the morning, we'll get to the end of her forgotten past." Coles promised.

Brad waited for Danni to come through the door to them, and without words she walked to him as he wrapped her in his arms. He thanked the two doctors, and they were down in the sun waiting outside the building for their car before Danni said anything.
"That has to go down in history as the weirdest experience ever." She was a little upset; he couldn't see her eyes as they both had on their sunglasses, but he could tell. "How does your head feel?"
"Confused."
"But you remember?"
"It's like this one time Sam and I went up to San Francisco, and drove over the Golden Gate Bridge while the fog was thick, and came out in to the brightest sunshine on the other side. I totally

remember the stuff I know I told Stephanie and the rest, the in- between stuff is just melting into clarity."

Danni felt him gently squeeze her hand, and when the car pulled up before them they got in, and she took comfort in resting her head on his shoulder. "I thought I was going to burst in to flames with embarrassment when you were talking about the first night I kissed you" Brad admitted close to her ear.
"Really?" Her blue eyes looked up to him.
"It's not that I forgot, I'd never forget; but to hear you talk about it, to hear how you so desperately wanted to kiss me, I guess I never really understood that until now."
"You were my first kiss Brad, and I'm hoping you'll be the last man to do it when we're old and grey."
"I think that's something we can certainly plan on."
Tenderly he kissed her on the tip of her nose, and content, she snuggled further in to his body.

"I think I'm gonna take a fast shower, and lie down for a while, before we go out to eat," Danni had told him as they walked in to the suite. It was a well decorated, comfortable space, but it was sterile in its impersonality. "I should make some calls." He put his bag down and took out his cell which had been turned off most of the afternoon. He should at least check in with Maggie and Ted. He was hoping his friend had some good news, like the stalker was in custody.

Seeing Danni come in to the seating area from the bedroom with just her jeans and bra on, his fingers almost stopped pressing the buttons, but he wanted the calls out of the way, and if he was lucky they'd be short and sweet so he could make it at least to help her rinse shampoo out of her hair.

"Was the doctor able to help?" Maggie's voice sounded happy, and it made him comfortable. He knew if something had come up to stress her she would have tried to hide it so as not to get him involved: but he would have known. "She has everything from five through thirteen years."
"Get out, for real?"
"I heard it with my own ears."
"Are you still at the hospital?"
"No, at the hotel; how was the office today?"
"Slow and quiet, without the boss ordering us around." Maggie joked. "No, really it went smoothly and I spoke to Ben. He has only a few suggestions in changes, and seems to like his staff, but said he'd know better once he gets a chance to meet everyone personally."
"How are the details for Thursday coming along?"
"Smoothly, oh before I forget, that package came in that you called about, from the Bronx."
"Excellent, do me a favor and put it somewhere safe in my office. I don't suppose you've spoken to Ted or my Mom today?"
"Neither."
"Well, I should call Ted then. Thanks Maggie, and I'll call you tomorrow before we leave if we don't hear from you."
"Enjoy your night Brad."

Quickly dialing Ted's number as he heard the water turned on in the other room, he stood up and walked towards the bedroom where he saw Danni's bag on the arm chair inside, the clothes she had been wearing neatly lying over the back of it. "How did it go?" Ted asked, like Maggie he knew how important the trip to DC was. "Working well so far. I'm hoping all the embarrassing teen things were revealed today," he said with a laugh. "Well that's good news man, I wish we had some for you but I'm still searching for this PI."

"I didn't think it would be so hard with Maggie's help."

"Neither did I, but the guy doesn't seem to like to answer his cell phone. I have the tech's looking to see if the guy has a GPS on his car. If not I suppose I'll be sitting outside his apartment until he comes back here."

"You're there now?"

"Sure am."

"You know Ethan's curious about your sudden trip to DC."

"You spoke to him?"

"No, your mom did, she told him you had a meeting, and decided to have Danni tag along instead of being separated with what's going on."

"And there Mom was thinking she couldn't do anything to help."

"She's a smart woman your mother."

"Yes she is." Brad started unbuttoning his dress shirt. "So I don't know what time we'll be leaving here tomorrow."

"No big deal, want me to meet you at the airport?"

"If you're free?"

"Unless something big happens and I'll call you if it does. Look, I should make some other calls, tell Danni to relax and I'll call tomorrow."

"Give Anna a hug for me."

"Night Brad." The call was ended, and throwing the cell on to the unused bed Brad stripped the rest of his clothing fast, and was in the bathroom seeing Danni inside the steam covered glass-walled shower before she turned the water off, and slipping inside he got a wide bright smile. "I was praying you'd find your way in here."

XXX   XXX

"I'm so glad you could join me for dinner." Louise told Ethan.

"Turn down an invite from my oldest and dearest friend?" Ethan smiled over his wine; they were at an old Italian place where they had gone when both John and Natasha had been alive. "With the kids away it was suddenly lonely inside my apartment." Louise admitted enough; it was hard keeping the real reason for the trip from Danielle's father, but she understood why the decision had been made; the man sure had dealt with enough of his own heartache.

"How do you think things are going between them?" Ethan asked.

"I think with every moment they're together it becomes obvious to both of them that not to continue would be a very big mistake."

"I'm almost too scared to wish for them to marry. We had planned so hard for that so long ago and disaster tore everyone apart."

"Nothing bad will happen this time." Louise took Ethan's hand. "Bradford will never let that happen."

"I know."

"They are still so perfect for each other."

"They always looked good together." Louise agreed with a nod

"The only thing in the way is their locations."

"Danielle mentioned that, she and her partner have been talking about opening new places in other cities so wherever Brad wants to be they could settle."

"I have a feeling my son is still leaning towards going back to his Team."

"John never wanted Brad to have the life he did, he loved Brad's desire to serve his country, and not that Brad has openly complained, but I can tell he doesn't have a passion for filling his father's shoes."

"No, his passion lies with being a hero and I'm proud of him too. I just don't know what I would do if I lost him."

"I know."

"I just wish there was someone Brad would trust to step in to that position, who the board of directors would be happy with."

"I think the obvious solution has been overlooked."

"Which is?"

"There are two people who together could do everything."

"Who?" Louise frowned.

"You and Maggie; you love the social side as well as the fun you have with what you do now, and Maggie knows the business like the back of her hand. You want Brad to live out his life then let him do it without feeling guilty for abandoning the ship. You know when he retires from the service and he wants to come back, then you'll both be ready for that."

"You are a very clever man."

"Now, I am going to bet you dinner that our children will be married by the end of the year." Ethan held up his glass.

"I'll take your bet and make it shorter: I say by the end of this summer."

"If only I was as happy about Peter's choice in life partners."

"I thought you liked Felicity."

"Hardly, she's a piece of work, she always has been and since coming back from Germany there's been a glint of something I can't put a finger on, but it concerns me, not to mention how my son has been since they started together."

"He does seem to drink a lot."

"That's what I'm talking about."

"Well, I've never liked her either." Louise sighed.

CHAPTER THIRTY-THREE

Man, was he tired!

So okay, since getting back together with Danni the sex had been amazing but there had seemed to be something renewed inside herself which had spurred the most exhausting night of his life.

He wasn't about to complain, there was never going to be any of that, if she was even half of last night in bed for the next fifty years.

Smiling in to his coffee cup Brad sat in the same seat as yesterday, as Stephanie had Danni up to the seventeen-year-old her. In a few hours they would be leaving to get back to Manhattan, and hopefully they could call Ted and tell him who this stalker was.

Of course, he'd need a steady supply of coffee in his system or he'd never get the plane off the runway.

A few things Danni had talked about; the year before that last summer she had been in the same school as him for the first time, and that had been a real treat, seeing her all year round was better than anything. So many of the guys who'd never met Danni but had heard the stories and not believed she'd existed, had been awed, and that had boosted his ego big time.

"Tell me about the week before your seventeenth birthday." Stephanie had led her to that moment and a sudden memory plummeted to the pit of Brad's stomach. There was something he hadn't been quite honest with Danni about, and he hoped if she remembered it then it wouldn't be too big of a deal, but that nagging thought in the back of his head told him he should prepare himself for whatever was to come.

"Brad and I had a major argument."
"Did the two of you argue a lot?"
"Never before."
"Then what was it about?"
"I was having this huge party the following weekend, and he was due to go down to Annapolis for his first orientation; way more important than a stupid party, but I was so mad he wasn't going to be there."
"At sixteen I bet it felt so huge."
"It was back then. I loved him more than words, more than anything in the world, and it was just the beginning I knew; orientation and then he'd be gone for an entire year. We wouldn't talk everyday like we did, I wouldn't be able to just take a cab to spend the night with him, and I was so worried I would lose him, and myself, when he left. I was proud of him for making it in to the school, but my anger came from knowing he would grow out of love for me."

"I was a stupid child and even when he came over the Wednesday night before, the night before he was leaving I was still pissed. I got angry at myself for being that way; and I just, he was trying so hard and I was so grateful when he began tickling me, because everything seemed to melt away; and before he left we had sex and then he made me open my gift."

"What did he give you?"

"A new charm for the bracelet he had given me years before."

"What was the charm of?"

"A heart, it was in platinum and looked like one of those candy hearts with the words on, it said 'mine always'."

"That's a very nice gift."

"He was going to have it soldered on when he got back at the jewelers, so I wouldn't lose it. He left as the sun was coming up, and the moment he was gone all of those fears came back, and along with it my bad attitude. I hated being at the beach house without him, and I snuck over to lie on his bed when no one would miss me, I felt closer to him there. Some of my new school friends came over Friday and slept over, helping me to relax and get ready for the party Saturday. We had the house to ourselves. Dad and Theresa were taking Peter to see a show in the city. Then they were staying over at the place Dad was renting a few blocks from Brad's parents' apartment."

"I think we started the party midafternoon. All I know is one of the girls had bought a few bottles of vodka, and I had always been an easy drunk. By the time the real party got underway I was beyond drunk, and one of the girls was telling me this guy from Brad's year above mine was watching me. She was telling me I should forget Brad, who couldn't even be there for my party, and have some fun. So I went over to the guy and I just kissed him, I didn't say anything, just kissed him."

"What was his name?"

"Colin Jenkins. He and Brad were not friends; Colin was the basketball star while Brad got more notoriety from being the football star. It irked Colin, and with the vodka and beer in me, I saw that as a very stupid way to get some petty revenge on Brad."

"A kiss is only a kiss Danni."

"We had sex." Even in a different reality Danni felt the hot tears coming down her cheeks as she watched herself humiliating everything she had with Brad. "It was mainly a blur, and I cried so hard after. I wished I had been nicer when Brad had called me that morning, because my sensible half knew how hard it had to have been for him to call me, but the selfish side wanted something evil."

"I cried for days after, my dad was so worried and I told him and the look on his face killed any hope that Brad wouldn't find out and not hate me. Dad said I should just be honest and tell Brad when he got back, and maybe I'd be able to keep Brad as a friend. It was the first time I felt as if my dad was disappointed in me, and I didn't like that either. I knew my parents and his were planning us being together forever, and until that stupid party I had thought that would be my future, had dreamed of that; and I had blown it acting like a spoilt brat, not thinking about how hard this was on Brad too, he was going to a tough school away from everyone he loved."

"I heard his parents' car pull in their driveway around dinner time and I cringed inwardly. I lay on my bed, wet tissues all over the place, and prayed someone had already told him and he wouldn't come over. But later that night he was knocking on my bedroom window and I couldn't look up at him when he came in, I wanted the earth to open up and swallow me."

"Did you tell him?"

"He was so worried finding me in tears, he begged me until he was almost in tears himself, and I blurted it out. I started off with how I had wanted him so much, how there had been vodka and beer and once that was out I knew he had pieced things together. We'd tried drinking liquor a few times and I couldn't hold anything. The moment that clicked in his eyes I told him to get out, that he should have taken the hint of me not wanting to see him and go. I told him he should break up with me, that he deserved better than a brat who would do something so cruel, and that he needed a woman who could love him completely."

"Did he break up with you?"

"No, I watched as his face so filled with pain and hurt changed to anger, as he walked back and forth in the middle of my room, he snapped a question at me, wanting to know who it had been, who had I fallen so easily in to bed with. I told him it was Colin which made him even madder and I thought he was going to leave. I was still crying, but without making a sound. His face was red, his eyes redder, and he sat on the end of my bed, his head in his hands as he told me I was the only one he had ever trusted with more than his heart, and it was broken, torn over what I had done, but he couldn't dump me."

"Couldn't?"

"I was the center of his world, I was all he ever thought about, and he had done some serious thinking while away and he knew where my anger had come from. Even at that moment he knew why I would have sex with someone else, but he had decided something on the way home, something I had mentioned, and he had always answered me with a kiss."

"Which was?"
"He wanted me to marry him, we'd joked it was a long way off, that we'd goof it wouldn't happen, but I had told Brad I was thinking about changing my college plans, I could apply to the liberal arts center at Georgetown, and I could have dad buy me a car and I could drive out to see him. He'd be in his second year then, and if I did summer credit classes, I could graduate when he did, and then we would be able to go to wherever he was stationed. I wanted to be with him, near him."
"Did he ask you to marry him?"
"He did, Brad had asked his dad for advice on the ride back, and Louise had insisted they stop in Manhattan and gave Brad the engagement ring that had been her mother's and that night he had it in his pocket. He had come to my room to ask me the one thing since the first kiss I had wanted him to ask, and there I had told him I'd been an unfaithful brat."

"He took my left hand, held the shiniest ring in his other hand between his thumb and finger, I just stared at it through my tears. He said he could forgive me, continue to love me and the decision was now mine. The tears came out heavier, and I said 'yes', I also told him I would never be unfaithful again."

"Your parents must have been so happy."

"Dad was staying in the city; he and John had a merger going on, and Theresa was away a lot that summer. I called dad and he was very happy. John and Louise cracked open a bottle of champagne, but I turned mine down until Brad whispered in my ear that I was allowed to drink with him around, because then he knew it was his body I would be getting naked later."

"And that was the Tuesday night?"

"Yeah, Brad and I spent Wednesday and most of Thursday together until Theresa came home. We told her, but she wasn't as excited as we were and seemed preoccupied."

"Do you know why?"

"I'd heard whispers since the Christmas before, she and Dad were having problems, something about moving to New York had been a mistake, as he should have known it would start again."

"What would start Danni?"

"Theresa was having an affair."

"Do you know with whom?"

"No, but I knew it was someone in our social group, someone Dad knew too."

"So what happened after you told her?"

"She needed to get some things together for the trip, Peter had been hanging out with us and she said he had to go with her which made him complain and she snapped at him, I'd never seen her lose her temper before, and I just took Peter's hand and we all went outside to the beach to let her calm down."

"Did she calm down?"

"I heard her shouting to someone; I presume she was on the phone as no other cars were in the drive." Danni paused. "Yes, she had to have been on the phone as a few minutes after her shouting started she came to the back door and yelled that one of my girlfriends was on the phone for me."

"Who was it?"

"It had been Felicity." Danni stopped to shake her head this time. "She was in Brad's year, and I always got the feeling she never liked me. Butut the year we spent at the same school she was mostly nice to me. It had been her vodka bottles which had been part of my drunkenness at the party."

Without asking in the other room, Brad pressed the intercom button so Stephanie could hear him, and asked her to ask a certain next question.

"Danni, can we just go back to your party, who was it that told you to get together with Colin?"

"I, um." Danni's closed eyes seemed to squeeze tighter. "Felicity."

"Okay, now tell me about that phone call."

"Felicity was calling to see how I was, she had called Monday, and Theresa had told her I was upset. She was worried, as I never called back, and I told her the cliff notes version of what happened when Brad had found out, that he had asked me to marry him and I had said 'yes'. There was some noise on her end of the line, and she said her dad needed her and she would call me later."

"Did she call you later?"

"No."

CHAPTER THIRTY-FOUR

"Daisy, did I hear the door?"
"Yes, the doorman called me to let me know he had sent up a delivery." As Louise came in to the hall she saw her assistant carrying a very large box of Godiva chocolates a dead giveaway as they were in the tell-tale golden box.

"Who an earth would send me those?"
"They are for Danielle."
"From who?" Louise maneuvered her chair so Daisy could get past, and in to the kitchen where she sat the box on the center island. "I'm not opening the card." Daisy took it off handing it to Louise as she went to get some water, as it was time for Louise to take her pills. "Oh, dear God," Louise muttered as she looked up and yelled for Daisy to stop making her drop the glass. "We need to get out and call Ted."
"Louise?"

The second Louise's words died from her mouth the entire room flashed with an almighty explosion, which pushed Louise's chair back until it hit the wall, and Daisy whacked her side in to one of the cabinets, feeling the heat from the flames and a sharp pain in her arm. "Louise," She shouted over the sound of the fire alarm, and through the thick smoke in the room, as she moved holding her arm, to the small door at the end of the cabinets. Inside was a small fire extinguisher and Daisy wanted to get the flames doused before they had a chance to spread.

"I'm okay Daisy." Louise shouted. "Are you hurt?"

"I think my arm is broken."

"I'm going to call the fire department." Louise heard the sound of the extinguisher, along with the smoke moving as the fire was put out. Then Daisy appeared, Louise held her breath seeing her assistant with blood on her shirt sleeve, as she used the other hand.

"You're bleeding," Louise rolled closer.

"So are you." Daisy saw not only her boss's face and the blood stain on the wall, probably from Louise hitting the back of her head, but her cashmere sweater covered in a black film, and the redness in her eyes too, as if someone had taken out the white and replaced it. "I'll be okay, we should call Ted." Louise carefully turned her chair and rolled down to the hall phone. She coughed from the thick air, and as she picked up the receiver, she heard Daisy coughing too. "Ted, thank God you answered." Louise coughed again. "Can you come here right now, there was a package for Danielle and it exploded."

XXX   XXX

"We had to meet my dad at the mariner where the boat was kept, around noon. She insisted right after breakfast that we go down to get the last few things; Peter needed new water shoes, and she had seen a pair of sunglasses she wanted. I didn't want to go, no need explaining why, and I was putting on the sour puss again, hoping by the time we got to the marina I would have persuaded everyone to leave me in Southampton."

Danni sighed. "Dad was a little quiet when he got there, and Theresa was trying a little too hard to be nice. We were just getting ready to leave when one of the deck hands from the club came running down towards our boat. He had a package in his hands, and said it was for me, some kid had asked him to bring it down."

"What was inside the package?"

"I don't know, when I went inside the boat I threw it on to one of the bench seats, everyone at the marina knew Brad, and if it wasn't from him, then I didn't want it. I suppose maybe I worried it was from Colin, and I didn't want anything to get between me and Brad."

"Dad untied the lines and we were underway. I kinda hid out in my bunk. It wasn't so big, the boat, but there were three separate bedrooms. I stayed there thinking about Brad, and looking at my ring for hours, until I was told to join everyone for dinner. The tension between dad and Theresa was thick, and I was glad to sneak away to my room again. Peter came in to bug me about sleeping on deck, and I turned him down. I wasn't in the mood, especially to see a sun rise without Brad."

"I went to sleep early. Dad woke me and it was still pretty dark. He wanted me to join all of them to see the sun come up. I moaned and rolled back over. Theresa came in I don't know how long after, and told me to suck it up, that this was family time, and it meant a lot to my dad. Begrudgingly I crawled out of bed, finding my sweatshirt, and I was just opening the door when...."

Danni's body started to shake as she began to hyperventilate. Stephanie knew, as did the two men in the other room, that this was the moment of the explosion. "Danni, I want you to use that door to get back to the safe room," Stephanie told her soothingly. "It was the package, not the boat. Theresa was holding the package, telling me to not leave my stuff lying around." Tears streamed heavily down those smooth cheeks. "I was the one that package was for." "Danni, leave and go to your safe room." Stephanie repeated.

Sitting a little quieter Danni slowly opened her eyes and it seemed like everyone else, the three of them, let the breath they'd been holding in. "It's okay Danni." Stephanie took her hand.
"I know."
"I think my job here is done. I'll go and get Brad for you." The doctor got up, and Brad did the same in the other room.

"I'll give the two of you a few minutes, and I'll come in," the Major told Brad, and slowly he made it to the room he had only seen from the window. More than what she had just remembered about the accident, he was freaking inside about how she was going to be about the small thing he had not told her.

"Hey." She was still when he spoke, and he watched her get up and walk in to his arms. "Why didn't you

330

tell me about us, the important part?" He closed his own eyes hearing her question.

"When I went to that hospital, the doctors said you had such bad injuries, that I should go in to your room and say goodbye, but I couldn't. They had taken off your ring and bracelet, your dad gave them back to me after I'd been in there. I didn't want to hear you were gone, I didn't not want a chance to speak to you again, and your dad assured me if you woke up I'd be the first person he called."

"It took two years."

"And your dad called the moment they had finished with their tests, and told me you weren't our little Danni, that nothing inside remembered any of us. I asked him to let me know if that changed; I could get out of school for a few days and be there."

"Aside from not getting those memories back, what happened?"

"He called my dad, suggested I let you be for a while. You were going to a school out West, you didn't need me pushing you to remember me, us, that we were in love."

"I wish you had."

"So do I. But I had lost you once, half of me with you. If I had gone to see you, upset you, not found what we had, I probably would never have recovered Danni."

"I know."

CHAPTER THIRTY-FIVE

After thanking the doctors, Danni had felt different as she walked in to the sun outside the hospital building, like a new version of herself had finally grown too big for the bubble she had been living in. She had been a little upset finding out that Brad had actually asked her to marry him, and not one soul had told her over the last fifteen years. But on a deeper level she knew she understood, and just hoped one day in the not too far away future he might ask her again.

Brad had turned his cell off when they'd started the session, and once outside the building he turned it on with the task of calling the driver and car back to take them to the air strip. They'd made sure to pack everything up that morning in the hotel room, and checked out. He was looking forward to getting back to New York, but would even more once he called Ted to tell him the interesting pieces of information.

Not that he wanted to think about it, but he had a nasty feeling everything pointed to Felicity now he knew what he knew.

Instead of beginning to dial he saw he had missed quite a few calls, nearly all of which were from Maggie. So instead of calling for the car he called her cell back, fearful of what could be so important.

"Are you on the plane yet?" Maggie sounded winded.

"I wouldn't be calling if we were." He joked. "We just got out of the last session and are headed for the airport."

"Well you have to get back as fast as you can, I'm going to have one of the company drivers drive me to meet you, so call here before you get on board."

"Maggie what happened?"

"A package was delivered for Danielle and it exploded."

"To Ethan's." He looked at Danni as he spoke, and her face went from thoughtful to anxious. "No, to your mother's."

"Jesus, don't tell me."

"Your mother and Daisy are okay, Ted's with them down at Lenox hill."

"And the apartment?"

"I just left there, there's a team of Ted's guy's there, and it was mainly just the kitchen and a few walls, which were damaged, Ted wants all of you in a safe house."

"We'll use my place; He can arrange a couple of agents to sit front and back."

"Any luck with Danni knowing who it was?"

"A few things she said make me suspicious of someone. Can you do me a favor and call Ethan? Just tell him I want to see him when I land."

"He's with your mother, but I'm going there next, Charlie's driving me right now."

"I'll be at the strip in an hour and a half, unless we hit anything in between."

"We'll be there."

"What?" Danni asked as he hung up.

"Another explosion."

"My dad?"

"My mom's place."

"Are they okay?" She touched his arm.

"They're at the hospital; we should get our asses back there now." Without waiting he called the driver, and within thirty minutes they were in the plane and taking it down the runway, as they left whatever happy memories of getting seventeen years of Danni back behind them.

XXX   XXX

Maggie was pacing at the side of the runway where Brad and Danni would be landing soon; she had persuaded Ethan to come, but along with them Louise had insisted, as had Ted. The only person aside from Charlie who had no idea for the real reason for the DC trip was in for a real shock.

Having made sure there was an agent with Daisy, whose arm was broken and would need to be casted, as well as a few lacerations being sutured, Ted had promised Louise after his call from Maggie, that she could join them to the air field. Louise herself needed observation in case she had a concussion, and the staples in the back of her head where a mean looking cut had appeared were the only evidence she had been hurt. Maggie had collected clothes for her to wear, since what they both had been wearing had been taken to the lab to join whatever the team had found and whatever was left inside the apartment.

The soft noise of the far-off plane engine made Ethan squint towards the end of the runway, seeing a small twin engine plane descending with its gears down. "That should be them," he said. He wasn't sure why he had been summoned, unless while they had been down to DC Brad had persuaded his daughter to marry him without all of their family there. Though he would be ecstatic, he would be a little upset he had missed out on walking his daughter down the aisle. A long time ago he thought he would never do this and even now he feared if they couldn't keep her safe after the apartment attack, that he never would.

Danni watched with butterflies in her stomach when she saw the few people waiting for them by the hanger as Brad skillfully brought the plane closer to the runway. They'd been talking nonstop since they left the hospital, and the more Danni used her new old memories the more she thought Brad was right; Felicity either knew something about the events or was solely responsible for them. Together they had figured out as a team how to deal with everything and as they descended lower she sent the text message to Ted they had put together so he alone knew the plan.

Landing was the sign of the end in a very long two days for Brad, emotionally he had been so exhausted from everything, he could sleep for a week. But he had to keep his head about him for a few more days. Then regardless of what may have come up, he was getting on the bigger plane to California late Friday. Nothing was going to stop him and Danni leaving for the golden sands of San Diego.

"I have so many butterflies; I haven't felt so anxious to see anyone since arriving in New York last week." Danni stopped inside the closed door.

"Just remember those four people out there love you."

"I know, it's just now I remember everything I felt for them, which is trying to merge with the last couple of days, I mean Maggie was always so nice to me when we were little, but she made it out as if we just knew each other in passing."

"Well, she knows what we really went to DC for; the only person you are really going to shock is your dad."

"Are you sure I can tell him now? We could wait until later when everything is over."

"I think now would be a nice surprise, which might make him less suspicious about our other plan."

"Okay, I'm ready." Danni squared her shoulders as she hefted the overnight bag she insisted on carrying, over her shoulder.

While the plane had been parked, the hot sun bouncing off the metal hangar nearby, and the black asphalt making it glary, the car was in the shade of the hangar and Danni pushed the glasses back like a head band so she didn't trip or something equally embarrassing, and she saw the four smiles clearly and returned them. She held the one her father gave her longer as he came closer; the man she could now say in all honesty was the world's best dad, a man who had given her everything in thirty-four years, and all the opportunities his money could buy.

As Ethan got a foot from his daughter he noticed one very startling thing about how luminescent her eyes were, their blue hue sparkling all the way to the center. "You look good." He frowned to himself as he hugged her, not that Danni had ever not hugged him in fifteen years, but this felt like the teenage hugs she gave where one hand gripped her other wrist to hold on very tight. "A few days with a very charming man can do that." Danni leant back slightly, looking into her father's dark grey eyes. "Of course, knowing what you went through just to get to my first real ballet recital makes me love you."

"And what did I go through?" Ethan played along looking back.

"A speeding ticket, a flat tire and a toll you paid with a fifty because you didn't have anything smaller on you."

"You've been telling tales again." Ethan laughed to Brad who shook his head as Danni finally let her strong grip around his shoulders loosen some.

"Brad didn't tell me." Danni said softly but with a smile. She lent her mouth close to his ear and said. "How would Brad know that when I was three I asked for the first time about mom, and you had tried to tell me but your tears were too heavy?" Ethan's body jerked as Danni slid from him and she stood before him. "I remember everything dad." She said the words she had wanted to say to him for so long and he had wanted to hear even longer.

"How?"

"It's a long story, how about we get back to the city?" Brad suggested and his mother squeezed his hand tighter. After he had shaken his head at Ethan's earlier statement, he had gone over to his mom, and checked her head, kissed her cheek, and then spoken to both Maggie and Ted briefly, while holding her hand.

In the air-conditioned limousine Brad sat one side of Danni as her father sat the other, and everyone was waiting for her to explain, especially her father, as he had no clue. "You tell dad." Danni told Brad who just nodded, as she let go of one of his hands so she could hold her father's using both. "A friend of mine in the Navy had a patient who had suffered a TBI with a different outcome, but after a call to her I found out there was an experimental technique that they were doing on service men and women to overcome whatever they were now living with. I got the team leader's number and called him. Major Coles listened to what we told him and said he would like a look at Danni's medical file which we arranged. Then he agreed to let us go down to Walter Reed to be a part of what they are doing."

"What technique?" Ethan asked.
"Hypnotism." Danni answered that one.
"Are you serious?" Ethan was floored, mentally; as Brad had been explaining he had been looking Danni over, looking for any sign she'd had some serious operation performed; and here it was she'd been hypnotized! "Very Ethan! Danni spent almost ten

hours the last two days walking back through her life."

"And you remember everything Pumpkin?"

"I think so, some I'm still working out in my head, and others I got while I was asleep last night. Stephanie, the doctor who hypnotized me, and Major Coles, said from looking at a new MRI that the damage caused to my brain had started healing which they couldn't account for medically. However, they explained my brain hadn't used that area for so long it just needed a jump start."

"I don't know what to say." Ethan looked from his daughter to Brad.

"Just enjoy it." Brad said softly. "Trust me when I tell you, hearing all those old memories, especially from Danni's perspective, is gut wrenching enough."

"Thank you." Ethan held out his hand for Brad to shake.

"You should thank Stephanie, I just flew." He tried to crack a joke.

CHAPTER THIRTY-SIX

The joyful chatter continued all the way in to the city and from text messages Ted and Brad sent each other, pretending they were actually speaking to other people, one of which was Maggie's cell, but Ted also continued communication with his forensic team. Their plan was almost set, and once again Ethan would be out of the loop, but then so would Louise, and with nothing changing too much to what had been decided on the plane, even Danni knew more than the other two.

While the limo dropped off Louise, Danni and Ted tat Brad's house, Brad went with Maggie to the office, and they dropped Ethan off at his own office. He was going to get his son and make sure both Peter and Felicity were going to join them all for dinner, also to make sure the two of them were prepared to act better than the last dinner they'd all had together. Danni had asked her father to keep the good news to himself as she wanted to surprise Peter herself, and he agreed, hoping it would change Peter's mind to the sister he had once been in awe of.

He had called up to Norma from the lobby, and told her he would be up shortly. He was going to stop by his son's desk first. On the fourth floor the sound of the usual bustle was soothing, and he found Peter at his desk on the phone. When his son saw him, he hung up the phone instantly. "I've been trying to reach you, I heard about the accident at Louise's. Is everyone alright?"

"Everyone?" Ethan sat the corner of his hip on the edge of the desk, while he crossed his arms. "Well didn't Brad take the last few days off? Danni was there too and then there's Louise and Daisy."

"Everyone is fine; actually, Danni and Brad have been in DC."

"But Louise?"

"Will live, she has some staples in her head."

"Man, what's going on? I heard it was an explosion."

"How did you find out?"

"Felicity."

"And she knows because?"

"I don't know, someone must have told her, maybe it was on the news?"

"It wasn't on the news Peter."

Peter sat there looking up at his dad while his thoughts were running through his head. "What are you insinuating? That Felicity had something to do with this?"

"No, of course not." Ethan shook his head and sighed. "Look, we're all having dinner together tonight as a family."

"Okay, your place?"

"At Brad's."

"Sorry, it's just that you said family."

"The Johnson's are our family Peter; at least they always have been for me and now with your sister and Brad."

"Did he pop the question?"

"Not that I know of yet but I wouldn't be surprised if it happened soon."

"So, dinner tonight." Peter groaned inside he knew what Felicity's reaction to this would be.

"Yeah, and we should talk briefly about that." Ethan stood up from where half of him had been lazily relaxing. "I'm done with asking you and your fiancé to treat Danni with some respect. Every time both of you behave as if she's a piece of shit on the bottom of your shoes."
"Dad."
"Don't interrupt me Peter." Ethan's voice growled deep, low and serious. "If for some reason you can't control yourself, or Felicity then my threat about sending you to London will come true and you'll have flight reservations for Friday. If you think I can't control your life then quit the company, go out on your own without any of my credit cards or connections." Ethan didn't wait more than mere seconds before he asked. "Do you understand?"
"Yeah, I get it." Peter's fear made him mumble.

Waiting for his dad to leave his desk area, he looked around as he picked up his cell and dialed Felicity. She would know what to do, how to deal with this new threat. She was always going on about him getting the company someday, and he hoped with this on their shoulders that, just maybe, she would behave tonight.

XXX   XXX

Before the call from Louise, Ted had finally got the PI on the phone with a promise to talk later which was perfect seeing as he was now cooped up inside Brad's house, keeping an eye on Louise and Danni, who were just pottering around waiting for everything. One woman who knew more than she let on to the other.

Sure enough, Julia Spencer had hired the PI back that summer to watch Theresa. The PI was proud of the fact he had been able to find the proof the woman wanted, and when Ted had asked why the woman was still with her husband, after the mayor's obvious unfaithfulness, the guy had laughed and said in his experience, half the time these upper crust women didn't want the proof so they could use it in some divorce settlement, but so they could get whatever they wanted if their spouses wanted their indiscretions kept from the tabloids.

Interested in only one thing, Ted had stood in the foyer of the house watching for the delivery man, and checking that the agents out front looked as inconspicuous as possible. He asked, "While you were watching the Morgan family, did you note anything out of the ordinary? Anyone hanging around."

"Besides me?" The guy had laughed before pausing to think, and Ted waited patiently. "Well, there was a girl I saw a few times, not really doing much but watching the house, and a few times when the woman and two kids were out she'd be around."

"I don't suppose you remember what she looked like?"

"You're kidding, right? I knew exactly who she was and I just figured she was keeping an eye on that Johnson woman like I was for her mom."

"Her mom?" Time for Ted to play dumb.

"Yeah, the kid was that daughter of theirs. I met her once at the house when daddy dearest was out; scary thing, like she knew more than she should."

"You're sure?"

"I'm positive, actually, if you give me a day I can look through the files at home; I keep everything from each case I work, and I know I got pictures of her from when I was working."

"That would be awesome, thanks."

With the PI promising to get those pictures, he put his cell back in his pocket, only to feel someone walk up behind him, and he knew it had to be Danni. "I can tell from your face you got the next piece of the puzzle."

"You and Brad are more on to something than I think you realize."

"It makes a lot of sense."

"How's Louise?"

"On the phone with Maggie."

"When the team gets here we'll tell her they are going to be serving the dinner you're cooking tonight."

"How many?"

"Two."

"I kinda wish Sal was cooking so I can be there for every moment of this."

"You won't miss anything but if you happen to, then we're recording everything."

"Sneaky."

"I'm hoping this goes quick. I promised my daughter I'd be home before she goes to bed tonight; she has some form I need to fill out for school."

"How old is Anna?"

"Eleven."

"I bet she's pretty."

"Because of my stunning looks?" Ted grinned.

"And that." Danni poked back.

"She looks like her mom."

"I know how hard that is for my dad, it must be hard for you too."

"Sometimes."

"At least you have a small part of her in your daughter."

"I always think the same thing." Ted noticed the grocery delivery truck pull up at the curb. "Brad told you about how we met, about why I was where I was."

"He did."

"Good."

Letting Danni lead the man with the two large plastic totes inside to the kitchen, he waited with the door open as his team got dropped off, and they brought in their own couple of large duffle bags. It was going to be interesting trying to keep Louise out of the loop, but he had thought about suggesting she lie down upstairs for a little while. Then when Maggie got back with some fresh clothes she could shower and be her usual regal self for dinner.

XXX   XXX

With enough money giving you a great amount of luxury Brad had stood inside the apartment he had grown up in, looking at the kitchen, while a contractor explained what would be needed, fixed and how long it would take. A couple of days at most, that included redoing the entire floor, replacing the island counter top, a few cabinet fronts and the walls and ceiling. "If you can have it done by Monday morning I'll give you a forty percent bonus on top of this quote." Brad had offered this and the man had raised his eyebrows, and said they could start immediately. He'd call some of his men in and figure out what could be done during the night hours, saving the noisy jobs for when people were awake.

Asking his mother's friend Clive to keep an eye on the work-men, he and Maggie had gone to the office. There were a couple of things inside his father's safe he wanted to get, things he had asked to be taken and hidden a long time ago. After the office, they stopped to collect Daisy who was more than his mother's live-in assistant, and told her to expect some help until she was better, because Brad was not going to allow her to continue doing all she did for his mom, while injured. On their way back to his house they dropped Maggie off at the subway to Brooklyn. The following day was going to be long, and after the day Maggie had dealt with, he figured she was owed a few hours to herself.

But she had made him promise to call the moment something happened.

Arriving back to his place, seeing all the people inside, he had left a bag on the floor near the stairs, being told by Ted as the sun was going down that dinner was due to start in an hour, and that his mother was in her room getting ready. He could hear Danni's laughter in the kitchen and found her in there with two very attractive looking women, both wearing black skirts and white shirts. He introduced himself knowing they weren't hired waitresses, as everyone would be told, but really two of Ted's crime scene techs.

"I missed you." Danni had been chopping something, and it had been so precise and perfect to watch. She had stopped only for a second to turn her head and kiss him. "I missed you more." He whispered in her ear, before stealing a perfectly sliced carrot. "I think a shower before dinner is something I need, I don't know if it's my imagination but I feel like I smell of the smokiness of the apartment."

"You do a little." Danni admitted. "I have the pork in the oven, and I'll start the vegetables in a moment, so I can come join you, if that's okay?" Danni wiped her hands on the kitchen towel, and took in the look Brad gave her. "What?"

"Do I really need to answer that?"

"I guess not." He must have known Danni thought, the heat in his dark brown eyes was sizzling.

CHAPTER THIRTY-SEVEN

Danni had been busy in the kitchen when her father arrived alone and when Brad had come in to watch her put the finishing touches to the simple pork roast she had asked just to make sure that her brother was really coming with Felicity. She was worried the woman might be suspicious and bail out. "She's smart enough to make a bomb." Danni had argued. "She's also stupid enough to want to gloat in her righteousness."
"I hope so."
"Don't worry, from what your dad was telling mom your brother was served a very stern ultimatum about behaving as well as Felicity."
"Poor Peter."
"Yeah, poor thing." Brad was cut off by Ethan coming in to see his daughter.

Having set his mother and Daisy in his dining room ready once Ethan was done speaking with Danni, he had joined the women, and five minutes before the time they had asked for the last two guests to arrive, the doorbell rang and Ted took his place at the table.

"Peter, Felicity." Brad smiled with as much false friendliness as he ushered them both in. "I brought something for dinner." Peter held out the bottle of red wine. "Why don't you take it on through there, Danni's just finishing up the food."
"Danni cooked?" Felicity raised a manicured eyebrow while her voice only held surprise. "She's been having fun in there since we got back from DC."

Leading the way Brad stopped inside the kitchen looking towards Ted who just nodded back. "Something smells great." Peter seemed too nervous with the bottle in his hands. "Hey Petite." Danni using the pet name she'd used when Peter was small, made Peter stop for a moment but he didn't respond, and Brad was sure the kid's head was thinking it was either a fluke or maybe something more.

"Hello Danielle." Felicity's tone may have warmed a few degrees, but now they knew a few things it made them all do nothing more than smile. "Felicity, lovely to see you." Danni said as she put a rather deadly looking carving knife down. "I'm glad you both could come tonight."
"We wouldn't miss it." Felicity answered again. "I'd love to see Louise; my parents have been so worried since we heard earlier."
"Let me lead you to her then." Brad motioned and Peter remained in the kitchen looking at his sister.
"How has your visit in New York been?"
"I'm having a great deal of fun."
"It's nice you and Brad are back together."
"You think so?"
"I always liked him when we were kids, and you never told me to get lost when it was just the three of us."
"I know." Danni just winked, and before Peter could ask the question on the tip of his tongue, Danni had turned to the two women floating around waiting for instructions.

"Louise, my parents wanted me to tell you if there was anything they could do." Felicity took the empty seat beside the woman leaving the other one beside Danni on the opposite side. So Ethan had to sit on the end, on the same side of the table as his two children, leaving Brad who was at the head with Daisy to his left; Ted took the empty seat at the opposite head of the table.

"Tell them I thank them very much but Brad has been a rock and has taken care of everything."
"Brad always was a good guy." Felicity looked down the table at him, and inside he was dying to vomit, but that wasn't what the outside showed. "We should dig in before all my hard work goes to waste." Danni hefted a serving dish from the center of the table, and passed it to Ted beside her. It was the meat platter, and once he started with that and had it passed to Louise, he was given the vegetables. "This is very nice, being all here together." Danni spoke up continuing the conversation which had been interrupted. "So how do you and Brad know each other?" Felicity had been introduced to Ted, but all she had been told was he was a friend. "We served together." Ted answered.
"You're Navy too?" Felicity had taken two neat thin slices of the pork, and passed the plate to Brad as Daisy couldn't hold it steady, with the injured arm in a sling; and it had been Brad, not Felicity, who had thought to put a few slices on Daisy's plate.

"Army." Ted finished with the vegetables, sending them on the same clockwise journey to Louise. "Well

350

I give you and Brad kudos' doing such a dangerous job." Peter, sipping the water, had decided on not drinking: he would get in to less trouble that way. "I still don't get how your kitchen exploded," Felicity said, and everyone except Peter looked at her as if she had brass balls. At least the ones in the know did. "It was a package," Daisy said. "A package?" Peter stopped buttering a dinner roll.

"A box of Godiva chocolates to be exact." Danni looked at no one in particular. "I think I'm missing something." Peter gave up, it sounded so absurd. "Someone sent Louise a box of exploding chocolate?"

"They weren't sent to me." Louise locked eyes with the younger woman opposite her, who meant a lot to her. "Then who?" Peter followed the older woman's eyes to his sister, and when he looked back at the table, Felicity's face was like stone. "Me." Danni felt her father's hand on hers.

"Who did you piss off?" Peter again the only one asking anything.

"For a while I wasn't sure," Danni answered her brother. Brad and Ted were both watching Felicity who was the quietest person at the table; even her appetite had seemed to disappear.

"You know who did this?" Ethan's attention focused on the two men at the ends of the table, and then quickly Danni. "The doctor was able to help?" Louise asked her own question.

"What doctor?" Peter asked.

"I was in DC the last couple of days seeing a doctor." Danni looked around their father to her brother. "A doctor of what?" Peter continued thinking part of his confusion in the kitchen earlier was being answered. "Could I get some more wine?" Finally, Felicity's voice filled the air; and one of the waitresses took her glass using a cloth napkin and left the room. The second waitresses had poured a fresh glass and handed it to Felicity, before taking the bottle around the table topping everyone off except Peter who hadn't touched his.

"He's an Army doctor." Danni explained for her brother. "Major Coles specializes in severe brain injuries."
"You had some procedure done?"
"I had some treatment."
"And?" Peter was waiting, hoping his boyish hopes that his sister, after all the years, remembered him; how much he had loved and idolized her. He'd lost his mother and sister that day and even the time he'd spent before college with Danni, she had never been the same and it had hurt him deeply. "I have probably as many memories back as I'll ever get." Danni's eyes watered up a little looking at her timid younger brother that even with the years of hostility and distance she still madly loved. Knowing what they'd had before made it all the more emotional. Like her relationship with Brad she really hadn't ever understood it after waking up until now.

"You remember?" Peter prayed it was true.
"Your fear of spiders?" Danni told him softly. "How you'd sneak in to my room in the middle of the night and snuggle because you'd heard a thunder storm;

that Brad taught you how to boogie board, even though it scared you to death; and me helping you with your homework?"

"Man." Peter was glad his head was clear, no alcohol blurring this revelation. "That's wonderful Anni. I wondered in the kitchen when you called me Petit."

"Well you always were short for your age when you were little."

"And you stood up for me when the kids in my class picked on me."

"Isn't that what big sisters are for?"

"What else do you remember?" Felicity asked as she gritted her perfectly white teeth. "I remember my first day at the school you and Brad went to." Danni held her contempt and anger inside for the woman sitting opposite. "You were not happy that I had started and you supposedly accidentally spilt your perfect coffee down me as you bumped in to me before second period."

"Why would I care if you joined the school?"

"You are the only one who knows the answer to that." Danni said back.

"You were jealous." Brad said.

"Me? Jealous of Danielle?" Felicity laughed with an icy tone.

"I always noticed how you glared at her when we all hung out." Peter blurted out. "Excuse me?" Felicity roared, glaring at Peter.

Ted's cell began beeping and he took it out of his pants pocket. "I have to take this." He got up going to the kitchen and Felicity was still waiting for Peter to grow a pair, he'd always been weak and maybe that's why he appealed to her, she could be in control. "Did Ted tell you about this doctor?" Peter ignored his fiancée.

"No, Brad heard about him."

"Wow, after all these years and you were finally able to get part of your life back." Peter was amazed; he didn't care how the doctor had managed it, it was probably something personal seeing as he didn't see any signs on his sister that she'd had brain surgery. He would never forget the bandages and how she looked after the boating accident; he'd suffered nightmares for years.

Ted returned to the dining room feeling his blood pressure start to rise a little. He'd asked his tech to take the glass and run the prints from Felicity's glass and compare them to the partial ones they got from the bomb which had blown up the SUV. There had been little left from the exploding chocolates and the boat basically washed away any evidence with the waves and Theresa Morgan's body.

He didn't say anything but he walked to stand behind Felicity and he leant forward, putting a hand either side of her body, his face close to her head. He asked in a very controlled voice, "Tell me why you did it." Danni's hope they were wrong went out the room, while Brad had to control himself from getting up and dragging the woman out of the house. "Why I did what?" Felicity's hand was steady as she took another drink of wine, trying to ignore the strong man standing behind her, and blocking her in. "Blow up Brad's car."

"Blow up what?"

"Don't play dumb with me, smarter people have tried."

"I have no idea what you're talking about." On instinct, she tried to push her chair out to move, but it was blocked by those jean clad thick strong legs she had admired earlier when they'd been introduced.

"You blew up my son's car?" Louise moved her wheelchair from beside the woman. "I didn't blow anything up. I work for a cosmetic company; how would I know how to do anything like that?"

"You were always an A student in chemistry." Brad said.

"And I'm sure a few hundred people in New York too."

"I have a match with the print we found from the device to the glass you were using tonight."

"A print?" Her facial color paled a little.

"And I'm sure if we went looking at everything you own, everywhere you go, things you've bought lately, that we'll find the items used."

"I doubt that."

"Are you suggesting Felicity tried to hurt my sister?"

"I'm not suggesting anything." Ted exclaimed.

"If you are going to accuse me of such a ludicrous action I think I should remind you of who I am. I don't think there is a judge in this city who would grant you a warrant to search for whatever you're looking for, and my father can sue anyone who tries to ruin his family's name."

"How about I tell you a story?" Danni got everyone's attention. "It's about a teenage girl who is so insecure and in love with a boy who doesn't even see her. Now her father is having an affair, and being the controlling person she is she just can't stand not getting anything, so she blames the girl who keeps her from the boy she madly wants, and tries many ways to break them up, including pretending to be her friend to get her drunk while she's upset, and forcing her on to another boy so the one she loves will be heart broken." Danni got up and walked to stand between her father and brother.

"But it backfires, her plan is ruined when she finds out the boy she thought would come running in to her arms decides to forgive the girl he loves and ask her to marry him. It makes her so mad she is blinded and needs to do something to get the girl; do something so the boy won't love or want her anymore. So, she makes something, a small bomb; she delivers it to the marina where the girls family is about to leave for a weekend boating trip, and asks a deck hand to deliver it to the girl."

"I don't have to listen to this." Again, Felicity tried to get up, and this time Ted placed a strong hand on her shoulder, holding her there. "Stay." His voice was just as firm. "I was never in love with Brad, I never got you drunk, you fell in to bed with Colin with no hesitation." She snuck a look at Brad. "And I certainly didn't make a bomb to give to some guy who then gave it to you."

"But you were at the marina that day." Peter felt sick.
"No, I wasn't."
"You were there, I remember seeing you in that red car your dad bought you."
"I was in Florida with my parents."
"No, I distinctly remember your mother telling me you had stayed in Westhampton with the house keeper." Louise sighed.
"Okay, but me being in the neighborhood doesn't mean it was me."

"You made the bomb that killed my step mother, your fiancé's mother and almost killed me." Danni continued. "I'm in a coma, Theresa isn't screwing your dad anymore and you feel you have a chance with Brad; except he leaves New York and until he returns two years ago you don't see him. But when you do, those strong urges return, and you don't like it when he makes it clear, by ignoring you, that he has no interest."
"You might think Brad is a God but please...."
"What I don't understand is, 'why Peter'. What do you gain from screwing him up?"
"You were always worried Danni might remember something." Ethan said something for the first time.

"What do I care if your crazy daughter remembers anything?"
"No, you got close to me because of your own sick sense of self preservation." Peter had to get up from his seat. As he walked towards the living room, his back to them, he said. "Aside from your mother spending more money than your dad has, and the

campaign money he had to fork out last election, your father lost a great deal of money in the stock market, I found out accidentally when your father asked me about some investments he was looking to get a quick buck with." Peter turned back to them. "Aside from Brad I'm the only trust fund schmuck left who isn't over the age of ninety, married or completely obnoxious." He paused. "At least I wasn't completely obnoxious until I got mixed up with you." He stared at the woman he had loved, and hated in the past two years. "You marry me, you stand to gain everything my family has, you've been pushing for dad to hand me the company as a wedding gift. How can I be so stupid?"

"So, she blew up the boat, you say she blew up Brad's car too?" Peter wanted to know. "I didn't do anything." Felicity spat.
"I got a threat saying I should never have come back, the Friday after the ball, I didn't think about it until Brad and I had gone down to Southampton for the weekend, and during the night someone blew up the damn SUV. Another message telling me I had been warned. Dad then got a couple of photo's telling him Brad couldn't keep me safe, and then the trip to DC saved me from being in Louise's house for the third bomb."

"Did someone set the SUV to go off or was it something else?" Peter asked. "Why?" Ted's forehead creased.
"It happened Saturday night, right?"
"How did you know?"

"We were supposed to have dinner together and Felicity called me telling me she had a headache. I called her apartment and she didn't answer; it had to be around midnight to check on her. When I got no answer, I called the doorman it just seemed strange and he told me she had gone out a few hours before."

"Have you ever seen her with a camera, some telescopic lens one?"

"Felicity borrowed one from a friend at the office, used his dark room too." Peter cringed inside. "She has the penthouse apartment in her building. She has the rooftop so she has a little patch of vegetation up there and stuff. If you're looking for anything I would check the shed up there."

"Thanks Petite." Danni knew how hard this had to be for him.

"I need some air."

"Felicity Spencer, you are under arrest for the murder of Theresa Morgan, attempted murder of Danielle Morgan along with the stalking, threatening and making of explosive materials." Ted roughly pulled Felicity to her feet and used the cuffs he'd had in his back pocket, knowing he'd need them. "I'm going to enjoy seeing you prove all of this." Felicity bit out.

"I think we have enough to get any judge to give us what we want, especially seeing as the FBI has a little more pull than the NYPD."

"FBI?" Her eyes flared.

"Sorry, did we forget to mention that?" Ted's laughter made the rest of the room light up a little.

CHAPTER THIRTY-EIGHT

Danni had waited until Ted had escorted Felicity out to a waiting car followed closely by the two women carrying everything they had bought in, before going out to the cool evening air where she saw her brother sitting on the neighboring steps of a darkened brownstone.

"Hey." She sat beside him.
"For what it's worth, I'm sorry for what she did."
"Me too, you lost more than I did, all these years you knew everything, I'm trying to just deal with what has happened today."
"You must think I'm an idiot."
"Never." She put her arm around her brother's shoulders, pulling in the larger manly frame to the place so many times in her memories she had placed her younger brother.

"I'm also sorry for how I've been towards you."
"Peter, I understand, I really do."
"Do you?"
"There's a man inside that house who has had to go through exactly what you have, and since being back I've learnt to understand how hard it was on all of you, I'm sure I wasn't easy to get to know, how frustrating it must have been."
"All I ever wanted was my sister back."
"And you have her now."
"Maybe dad can give me a few days off, we could hang like the old days and get to know each other again."

"I would really like that Petite."

"Good." Peter turned his head and kissed his sister's cheek. "I think I'm going to get out of here and go home, I have some things to deal with figure out."

"Then be here for breakfast in the morning, Brad has a big meeting after lunch and I'm sure he'd love to get to know you again as well."

"I'll be here."

Waving her brother off she heard the door behind her open and she looked back to see it was the man she loved so much she almost lost herself inside the feelings. "Is Peter okay?"

"He'll work through it."

"Good."

"This is all over, isn't it?"

"The bad part yeah."

"So only the good from now on?" Turning and standing on the step above Brad she wrapped her arms around the wide shoulders the same height as her. "You better believe it." Brad kissed her quickly and then picked her up and carried her back inside the house.

Ethan, Louise and Daisy were all still in the dining room, when they came back in. The looks on their faces were a mixture of shock and outrage. "How long have you known?" Ethan had asked both of them.

"We've suspected since this afternoon." Brad sat down with Danni sitting beside him now holding his hand. "I'm sorry about your apartment and getting you both involved." Danni apologized to Louise and Daisy.

"Dear Danielle, I have survived a car accident, the death of more loved ones than I want to remember. It would take a lot more than a sick woman's act to hurt me."

"And you're sure it's that horrid girl who did it all?" Daisy scratched the top opening of the cast.

"Positive."

"How is your brother?" Ethan asked Danni.

"Upset, but he'll recover; you should join us for breakfast before work in the morning."

"Sounds like a great idea."

Danni had cleared away the little bits of food leftover as Brad brought in the dirty dishes. Louise had wheeled herself out to say goodbye to Ethan while Daisy insisted on at least loading the dishwasher if not being able to do anything else. Once everything was cleaned up, the lights turned out and the house locked up, Brad had helped his mother with the chair lift carrying her wheelchair up to the first floor, and making sure she had everything she and Daisy needed, before joining Danni upstairs. He had carried the small bag with him he had picked up from the safe, and found Danni lying down on the bed on her back wearing a very alluring short pink silk night gown.

"Now that is a sight I could certainly get accustomed to." He placed the bag on his bedside table as Danni rolled on to her side leaning her head on her hand.

"Then you should." She grinned.

"Were you thinking about anything in particular?"
"No, just really sorting everything out in my head."
"Think you're all done?"
"I don't know if I'll finish for at least a week."
"Need any help?" He pulled the shirt over his head knowing with a toss of the arm where it would land, close if not actually inside the hamper. "Not with that but there's other stuff you can help me with."
"Tell me more."

"Do I have to tell you?" Danni laughed softly, watching as the man before her took his jeans off, she knew now the differences between both of them, the integration of the two Danni's were starting to coexist nicely in her head, and knowing now the old Brad and then this version was so nice.

"Before I help you in any way possible with my body I have something for you." Brad sat beside her and took the bag from where he'd placed it, while sitting there in his black jockey shorts. "What?" Sitting up herself Danni moved so her thighs rested across his legs. "Here." He passed her the first velvet pouch. Tenderly she opened it and took a hold of what felt like a thick chain. Once outside of its protective pouch she could take it in completely: it was her charm bracelet, the white gold chain, with the little pieces of history. The heart shaped piece, the pair of ballet slippers, the Aztec style sun, the wave, the small key and the teddy bear. Each one meant something to her, more than it would have a few days before. "I asked my dad to look after that. The hospital had cut it off but he had it fixed just in case."

"It looks just like I remember it." She undid the little clasp and liked it when Brad took it from her so she could put it back on to the right wrist. The weight of it as she jingled it felt familiar.

"Thank you." She couldn't stop looking at it and missed seeing Brad take another smaller velvet pouch from the bag, before dropping it on the floor. "This was yours too; I'm hoping you want this back just as much." Danni felt her breath catch, she knew what else the doctors had given him and the pouch felt empty, it was so light. Slower than taking the bracelet out she slipped two fingers inside and felt the ring; the image of it when it had once sat on her ring finger came to her mind as she closed her eyes and pulled it out. "I love it more." She held it, looking at the three diamonds on the platinum band. There was a vintage look to it, but then it had been Brad's grandmother's first, and that had never bothered her. She would take a rubber band if it just meant one day they would marry and be together forever.

"You giving it back to me now, does it still mean the same thing as the first time?" She asked for clarification.
"That I want to marry you?"
"Do you?"
"Seeing as you asked sure." Brad grinned.
"I'm serious, you want to do this?"
"Very Danni." He took the ring from her fingers and slipped it on her finger.

"Because once we agree to this, there are going to be a lot of changes; and I just want to be absolutely sure."

"Then I'll remind you what I promised you when we were much younger and marriage was talked about."

"Which is?"

"I'll love you until you're so old I'll have to change your adult diapers." His laughter was muffled by her playfully hitting him with one of his pillows.

Brad got her back by proving he knew where she was ticklish. He had her howling with laughter when he said. "I have the party in San Diego Saturday. We could leave Friday lunchtime, fly to LA, show me around your life and then drive down Saturday and I'll show you my other life."

"I like the sound of that plan." Danni's breathing was labored even as her body recovered from his fingers assaulting her rib cage. They now found their way to the hem of the nightgown, and so feather light those same fingers ran upwards along bare skin.

CHAPTER THIRTY-NINE

Brad had to be grinning like a fool.

From the moment Danni woke up Thursday morning every person she saw she immediately showed them the ring they had already seen her wear once before, but back on her hand. Louise and Daisy had been the first to experience her excitement and then when Ethan and Peter arrived Brad had seen the happiness for their daughter and sister regaining the last thing she had once lost back.

He'd had to leave mid-morning to get to the office. The dreaded board meeting was at one, and he had stuff to catch up on before that. The only saving grace was that out of the five remaining board members from when the company was first started one was his mother. She had taken the fifty-five percent of the shares and kept them against many of the other board member's advice after his father had died. A friendly face amongst the older men was a small comfort.

Maggie had wanted to know everything, so once they had the daily items covered, mail sorted and papers signed he had sat with her at lunch; while he told her in more detail about DC, the dinner, and that he and Danni were engaged again.

"Your mother should be here by now." Maggie got up knowing that in reality Louise had been in the building for an hour. This was one of the reasons she had persuaded Brad to eat lunch in his office and relax. Louise, as controlling board member, had called an early meeting behind closed doors, and this was the only way Maggie could think of to keep him from finding out. "I believe she was bringing Danielle, I think she wants to make sure your fiancé knows how wonderful you are at work."

"Or to share in my humiliation."

"Now, now." The phone began ringing in the outer office, and Maggie leant across his desk to answer it. "It's Ted," She whispered as someone knocked at the office door, which had been closed. She went to open it as Brad took the receiver.

"I got the tour." Danni beamed as Maggie opened the door. She had chosen a simple summer dress as the sun seemed to be enjoying a day out. It felt like the first day as a complete person. "Let me see the ring," Maggie whispered as Danni held out her hand. "Congratulations."

"Thanks Maggie," Said Danni throwing her arms around her.

Both of them let the man behind the desk take the call, Brad said very little, and once he hung up he gave them the quick update. Felicity had spilled everything once her lawyer had been able to speak to her. She had been advised to plead guilty and take the offer on the table. Twenty-five years in the federal prison in upstate New York with no chance of parole. They had been able to keep it out of the press but in a few hours, it would hit all media outlets, and it looked like Mayor Spencer might step down as the city's mayor. Maggie felt like Felicity should have gotten a harsher punishment, but Danni was just glad the fear was gone.

He also told them dinner was going to be at his place again that night. Sal would cook again, giving Danni a chance to relax. Ted was going to be there with his daughter now the case was solved and he could breathe until the next one, and Maggie of course was invited, as well as Ethan and Peter, his mother and Daisy.

Danni held his hand when they walked down the corridor past other smaller open offices, to the old dark wooden paneled walled conference room. The table inside sat twenty comfortably and it wasn't the room which intimidated, it was the men. Once, after the first board meeting, Brad had joked to himself that those four crusty old men should be put face to face with the people trying to hurt and destroy the country; they may just succeed where missiles couldn't!

Seeing the five of them already in there and the conversation was nothing he hadn't expected; but seeing the smiles on their faces had not been something. Sure, the profits were up from last quarter, he hadn't completely screwed up, and the projects in the works were making money; but smiling old men were creepy.

Danni went and sat down in a seat beside Louise who was like the ring master to the board. On the way in Louise had explained why they were going in early. It had been hard for Danni to contain the secret and she figured her face had given nothing away, which was good. Maggie was sitting by the door, and the visual aids of graphs and projections were on the easel behind him, all fresh from the printers, and he saw the five reports, smaller printed versions, in a pile, in the center of the table in front of the members. She wondered why they hadn't looked through them yet.

"Bradford." The oldest man on the board sat opposite his own mother said. "Mr. Cohen."
"I'm afraid Bradford that we have something very important we have to speak to you about," he said. Had they looked at the numbers and been disappointed? Even his mother his biggest fan? What had he not done right? "You know we gave you a hard time the first board meeting, we were a little disappointed in the report, but that was two years ago and young man, I know for a fact your father would be the proudest man in the room if she were here. I know I am proud of you," Mr. Forster said, and Brad knew he'd never seen the white haired thick mustache man smile before.

"Ah, thanks." Brad was unsure how to take this.
"But we know how this was not your life plan." Mr. White joined in.
"And though we think you did an amazing job we have to fire you." Mr. Petrelli's words made Brad step back feeling like he had been smacked in the gut.
"It's not as bad as you think." Louise spoke up. "We are firing you for your own good. We all know if you didn't feel so loyal to your father you'd still be in the Navy."

"But who is going to head the company?"

"We met earlier than you asked us to be here, and we already took a vote." Mr. Petreilli explained.

"You did?"

"We are placing Maggie who unquestionably knows how to run the company, as your replacement; Louise will help out with the charity side of the company. We have all confidence that between them they can keep things up and running." Mr. White looked at one woman and then the other as he spoke.

"We called the base Admiral in San Diego and made sure you were able to return." Mr. Forster started. "He's expecting to see you Saturday morning. We know you won't be a SEAL forever, and when you're ready to come back then there will always be a place for you here as the head of this company."

"You called my admiral? But I may not want to be in the Navy anymore." He stole a look at Danni. "And we'd know you were lying." Louise said.

"Then I suppose I should clear out my desk." He let the corners of his mouth rise slowly. He had thought of nothing but returning to active duty for so long.

"Yes, you should." His mother told him.

He'd shaken hands with the men and kissed his mother's cheek before returning to his office with Danni. Maggie was sitting at her desk, and Brad let go of one woman's hand and took the other. "I want a visual of you sitting behind that desk looking thoroughly bored," he kidded, taking Maggie gently steering her to sit where his father and he had taken prized place. "Will you miss this, honestly?" Maggie asked, feeling the soft worn leather beneath her. "I'll only miss you."

"I'll miss you too."

It had taken Brad mere minutes to collect the personal items he had in the office, and then with a rejuvenated feeling he had Charlie drive him and Danni back to his house. He hadn't planned on having the rest of the day or the week off but everything now put a whole new spin on the future.

Without a fear for Danni he had let her google a place in lower Manhattan which sold organic free-range items, and watched as she climbed in to the town car Charlie drove to go get the items. She argued about having Sal cook for them, she really did love being able to do those things, and he wasn't about to stop her.

Brad wanted things in motion; he wanted an idea of what he could offer Danni, what he could entice her with. He knew she loved him, had realized those feelings, whether known or not, from the past had been there the past week and a half. But now he was free from the family business he could hopefully go back to one of the teams in California. Then there was just Danni and the business she loved a hundred and some miles away in Santa Monica. He didn't think it would be fair to either of them to do the commuting relationship, he would have to be near base, and with her hours they'd hardly see each other.

But he would give everything up if Danni wanted to stay in Santa Monica.

He dialed Coop's number, wondering if the team was even around. "Cooper."
"It's Johnson."
"We were just talking about you BUD."
"All good things I hope."
"That depends on if the call I got from Admiral Clark is right, and that he needs to know if the team could use a thirty-five-year-old Commander who's been doing the soft life for the past few years."
"What did you tell him?"
"Well, my XO and I think this Commander needs to prove it with a few tests, but we don't have any doubt he'll pass, and be on the Team soon enough."
"Sounds like the best news ever."

"Speaking of news. I heard a certain Mayor's daughter was arrested last night at your house."
"Yes, she was."
"And?"
"She was the one who killed Danni's step-mom, hurt Danni and then tried to kill her or at least scare her off this week."
"So, Danni going to DC helped?"
"She remembers enough."
"And you and she are?"
"Engaged."
"I had heard that too when your friend Maggie called me to get the name and number for the Admiral."
"Maggie called you huh?" That made Brad smile.

"Now you don't have that huge desk to sit behind, are you going to be in Cali this weekend?"

"We wouldn't miss it. I'm actually planning on going to Santa Monica with Danni first and then drive down."

"Whenever you get here you know there's still room at your place."

"I was hoping you'd say that." Brad had asked Coop to move in to his house on the beach years ago when he'd bought it, and when he'd left not wanting to sell seeing as he'd hoped to return before too long. "I'm looking forward to finally meeting your Danni."

"I'm hoping meeting everyone won't put her off, I don't think she understands how serious our job is."

"The women will take her under their wing and not let her go, I guarantee it."

"You could be right." He agreed, imagining that image. "Do we need to bring anything for the party?"

"Only beer or wine."

"It's just Danni is a chef."

"Then whatever she desires to make, I know the grill will be going and I'm sure Patti and Mary have been cooking up a storm."

"It sure will be good to catch up with everyone."

"In good time, I'm going to schedule a few tests for first thing Sunday morning so be warned."

"Thanks."

Danni arrived back at Brad's to find him asleep in the living room. It sure had been a stressful week and she let him sleep while she started in the kitchen. She had ideas up her sleeve and she lost track of the time until

Brad successfully snuck up behind her, and scared her half to death. "What are you making?"

"Dinner."

"Smart ass." She felt his fingers work up her sides and she tensed, knowing he was about to start tickling. When he didn't, his fingers just sitting there, she turned her head to look at him. "I have to keep you on your toes now you know everything I might try."

"You certainly got more cheerful from that nap."

"A little nap does wonders."

"I know."

"Also having you here, knowing I can go back to the service."

"Did you call Coop?"

"I sure did."

"And?"

"I have to sit a few tests to prove I still have what I need."

"I bet you'll pass with flying colors."

"I hope so; it's been long enough to be out of shape."

"Then why don't you go down and work out for an hour? When you are done we could have a little fun before everyone gets here."

"I will, I want to ask you a few things first."

"Like?" Danni felt him move to stand leaning his lower back on the counter, his arms folded across his chest. She wiped her fingers on the kitchen towel, waiting for him to talk. "I have a house in San Diego, if I get back on to the team I obviously want us to live there and start fresh but I also know that would mean me asking you to give up everything because I can't do the commuting relationship, not with you Danni. I need you with me whenever I'm lucky enough to be home, but like I've said before, that's selfish of me. I know. I need to know you aren't dazzled by everything and you are okay with leaving LA, your life and job?"

"To live with you, marry you and hopefully have a few kids?" Danni felt her cheeks heat up as she continued. "To be able to be more than your best friend and lover? I can live in San Diego very easily. I see it as losing very little compared to what you are offering me."

"Your company?"

"Can be started in whatever city I want or I could do something else."

"Like?"

"Be a wife and mother, stay home and make that house of yours warm with love and nurturing, just like I had once dreamed of doing."

"Danni." Pulling her towards his length, his hands on her hips, he placed his forehead against hers. "I'll support you in anything you want to do."

"Like children?"

"Yes."

"And I'm going to support you as well, I want to learn all about this way of life and embrace it. I have a wedding to plan for, and so much to do."

"You should ask the wives of the team about the wedding, have them help. If we have a service wedding there are traditions we do."

"I'm going to have so much fun."

"And Coop said aside from the usual beer and wine everyone brings, he said you should make whatever you want."
"Then maybe I'll make some desserts."
"Some?"
"You'll see."

Maggie had been the first to arrive and she had perfect timing. After showing Danni how much he loved her up in his bedroom they had showered and he had just pulled his t-shirt over his head when the doorbell rang.

"Maggie." Brad said, hearing footsteps behind him, and Danni stopped. "Hey Maggie."
"I'm sorry I'm early but I have a few things for Brad to sign, and the itinerary for you." She tapped a file on her thigh as Brad closed the door behind her. "I should get back to the kitchen. I'll leave you two alone." Danni disappeared. "Let's go in to the living room." Brad waved her in and then followed, allowing her to choose where she wanted to sit first.
"I'll start with the boring stuff." Maggie opened the file. "I have insurance papers for you to sign. I figured you could use the payout and get a new car in California."
"Thanks." He took them as well as the pen Maggie held out.
"I also have the checks for the contractor at your mother's apartment."
"Okay."

"I arranged the jet to be ready for you at nine; the flight plan has been given to the tower. I presumed LA was your first stop."

"It is."

"Do you know you haven't stopped grinning since I got here?"

"I know."

CHAPTER FORTY

For the first time she could remember flying didn't scare her half to death.

They were about twenty minutes from Los Angeles and Brad had left her to go up to the cockpit for a moment to speak to the pilot.

Something that surprised her after her feelings about being in New York to begin with, was that even after five hours she was still a little sad about leaving.

Dinner had been wonderful. They were like one very large family; something she hadn't known but remembered had been during her summers growing up, when the Morgan's and Johnson's got together. It had been so nice to see Ted relaxed and meet his daughter Anna, who was a dark haired younger version of her father.

She had noted how Louise looked a little sad when the talk started about Brad being in California again, but the moment the wedding was mentioned, there seemed to be a renewed woman with a purpose more than working her late husband's job which didn't seem to make her anything but happy.

Hugging both her dad and brother the night before had been hard. She was just feeling like she finally understood both of them, but they had promised to come out for a few weeks once everything was settled and of course, now that she remembered the city and her past, she wouldn't mind going back again either.

"You are looking thoughtful." Brad closed the door to the bedroom suite at the back of the plane where he had shown Danni upon arrival that morning. The old Danni's insatiable desire became joined with the older 'her' and they had done things a mile high from the ground, that would always be inside his head whenever he flew again.

"Just thinking things through."
"No second thoughts? You know if you don't want to." He sat beside where she was still wrapped inside the silk sheets. "Never."
"Good, because I wouldn't be so calm asking, if I even felt a hint you were thinking like that."
"You're stuck with me forever."
"How do you think Sam will be when you tell her?"
"Sad, but she'll be more ecstatic than anything."
"Do you want to go right over there first?"
"We'll be landing at noon, right?" Danni didn't know where her cell was, the only clock on her person.
"Yep."
"From LAX it's about twenty minutes, so it will be a good bet she'll be cooking but we can still go right there. Once the lunch rush is over she can sit with us on the veranda for a while. You'll like Sam."
"I'm sure I will."

The Greenery, as the restaurant was called, had people waiting around for their reservations, and not one person seemed to mind as they mingled in the bar area, not one person inside the place looked as if the food was anything but delicious, and the aroma was tempting. "Gary." Danni leant across the bar to hug the barman as Brad prepared to set his emotions on anything but jealousy. "I heard you were coming back today. How was the Big Apple?"

"Like the movies. This is my fiancé Brad, Brad this is the best bartender on the west coast."

"Fiancé? You'll have to tell me everything once the lunch rush is over."

"Plan on it. Is Sam out back?"

"She sure is."

"Give Brad whatever he wants and I'll have a red wine." She looked back to Brad. "I'll be in the kitchen."

"I'll wait right out here."

Weaving around the edge of the tables to the kitchen entrance Danni felt at home, but at the same time ready to leave for the life she was already building inside her head. On the way, she stopped and said hello to a few of the regulars she recognized, and also the wait staff. She wasn't sure if Sam had told them why she hadn't returned on Tuesday, and if any of them had read the papers like Brad's friend Coop obviously had then no one mentioned it.

There was an orchestrated madness to the kitchen, a familiar form of insanity. Danni knew where Sam would be; back making sure every dish looked perfect. At the beginning of the lunch hour they both would make sure the sauces, reductions and garnishes were right and tasted as good as they imagined.

"Busy?" Danni said resting her chin on Sam's white chef jacket.

"Run off my feet but I'm okay." Wiping her hands on a towel, Sam pushed the checked plate across to the waiting waiter, and turned to take in Danni. "Girl, either New York agreed with you or a certain man did?"

"I think both."

"Is he here?"

"I left him with Gary at the bar."

"Really?" Being nosy Sam wandered over to a porthole window in the swinging doors. "You mean that handsome piece of dark something holding a beer and looking right this way?" Sam felt Danni stand beside her, and from the corner of her eye the wave which explained why the man waved back. "He is gorgeous Dan; please tell me he has a brother."

"Sorry no, but he does have a lot of male friends."

"Could be even better." Sam giggled before moving so she could hug her best friend. "Welcome back."

"Thanks, but we should talk."

"If it's a deep and meaningful, you'll have to wait another forty minutes."

"Then I'll give you the first part of my news."

"Which is?" Sam grinned, hoping, after everything Danni had explained on their calls during the week, that she knew already. "Brad and I are getting married."

"Sweetie." Sam hugged her again. "I'm so happy for you."

"Thanks Sam."

"And I'm guessing that deep and meaningful has something to do with leaving Santa Monica?"

"You got it." Danni felt a little stir of emotion emanating from her friend.

"When we only have half those paying customers out there let me know, and we can all eat together. I'll even cook."

"Anything special on the menu?"

"Today you're in luck, all your favorites."

"Then I might just go crazy." Danni let Sam get back to the few dishes waiting for her, and made it back to the front, sure she had spoken to all the staff. "How's your beer?" She took the seat beside him.

"Good, I've never heard of the Tannery brand though."

"They are a small West Coast company, all organic of course."

"Of course."

"Sam wants to have lunch with us, so if you can wait forty minutes or so?"

"Fine with me."

Meeting Sam for the first time was not what he had expected. The woman was about ten years older than he or Danni, and also only about five feet tall. He felt like a giant when he returned her hug as they were introduced by Danni. He couldn't help seeing how different she and Danni were. Short dark hair, lip ring and a noticeable tattoo peeking from the bottom of her t-shirt, that he would guess was close to a half sleeve tattoo.

Brad would have been blind not to see Danni's half-sadness half-joy as they left the restaurant to go to her apartment. He let her drive the rental SUV, seeing as she knew her way better, and he felt a twinge of guilt. It put a certain amount of concern on him that his want and needs were ruining her life, but when she turned to look at him quickly and take his hand, to hold all of those thoughts and fears disappeared.

Her apartment overlooked the water, situated in a long building holding twenty of the same units. Some were two floors, some had balconies, and the entire long structure seemed to sit at angles like a straight walled snake length.

Inside was comfortable enough; he took in the picture frames on the mantel, the things which made him aware they were her whether she knew it or not. It was midafternoon, and on the way over he knew she was planning on going to speak to the apartment manager, and figure out what to take and what to leave. He had told her to wait until she saw his place; he would let her do whatever inside his walls as long as she felt at home there.

She had just left to go and get a few things from the store when his cell rang; he knew it was from someone on base as he recognized the exchange number. "Johnson."
"Hey Brad it's Lee."
"Lee, how are you doing?"
"I'm doing well, I hear you're heading back our way finally."

"I'm hoping to."

"That's why I'm calling. As team XO now Coop has me doing all his dirty work, and to the chagrin of a few men we moved up your tests."

"To when?"

"Can you be on base around eleven tomorrow morning?"

"Sure."

"Not that I would ever let on, but you're getting a weapon test, the O course and a test involving you and one of the Hell Week teams. Oh, and of course your physical with Jamie."

"Sounds easy enough, except for the last one."

"Then I should warn you beyond that, the Senior Chief is insisting he sit in on this one as his last hoorah."

"Thanks for the warning but I've dealt with worse, Chris and Jamie haven't been able to put the fear in me in a long time."

Still with a smile on his face when Danni got back he told her about the call. He also let her know she wouldn't be able to be there but Lee had said his wife was going to be at Max and Karen's place where the party was going to be held. Mary would be there, helping to get ready for the party, and the women would just love her help, a chance to grill her without anyone else around. Like everything else going on Danni took it in her stride.

Every time Danni fell in to bed with Brad it seemed to intensify her feelings and memories of the man, but she had things she wanted to do and knowing she could fix things at the house where the party was she got out of bed wrapping herself in her silk robe, and headed for the kitchen. She wasn't sure how long she had been working but when she felt his hands touch her hips, his mouth kissing her neck she shivered with the want of that release and the anticipation of just how it would occur.

"I wondered where you went."
"Just in here."
"Are you almost done? We should leave early if you want to see the house before I have to drop you off."
"I'll be okay; you should get to bed though."
"How much are you making?" He noticed all of the containers holding things he couldn't discern. "Not that much."
"If you say so." He kissed her cheek. "I figure we'll get on the road around seven-thirty. Traffic aside we should hit San Diego around ten."
"Let's leave at seven and then you won't be so rushed."
"Sure."

CHAPTER FORTY-ONE

Seeing the house which sat on a private stretch of beach had been eye opening. Not that Brad had said much about it, and certainly not anything about the size of it. Just as a guess she would say maybe six bedrooms.

"What do you think?" Brad came around to her side of the rental as he noticed her expression. They'd parked next to a black pick-up truck and she was guessing belonged to whoever was keeping the house in good shape which she knew was Coop. "Is this for real? Really your house?"
"It sure is, I've been renting to Coop since I left."
"Why?" Her use of the word he hadn't heard much in the last few days made him smile, and wrap an arm around her shoulder as they started for the front door, which opened and Danni realized her imagination had been nothing on the strong wide man with short dark hair who crossed his arms over his chest and smiled at them.

"Johnson." Coop was the first to speak shaking Brads hand before they did the manly quick hug. "Cooper Lee, this is Danni Morgan, Danni, Coop," Brad introduced them. "It's a pleasure to finally meet you Danni." Coop gave her a softer gentle hug and she liked him immediately. "Are all of the team built like you two?" She asked, looking between both men.
"Built?" Coop asked.
"I think she means our muscles." Brad chuckled.
"Mine are still bigger than yours." Coop retorted.

"Give me a few weeks," Brad kidded back.

"Well, I was about to head over to the base. Want to ride with me?" Cooper had moved so the two of them could come inside. "I have to get Danni over to Karen first so I'll show her around quick and then head out."
"No need. Give Danni the five-cent tour quick, and I'll drive you over. I made a map and wrote directions for Danni."
"How are you with directions?" Brad asked.
"Are they written in English?" She goofed, as she began walking further inside towards the back, where she was guessing the most important room was aside from the bedrooms. And she was right. The kitchen had an amazing view of the red stained wooden deck with the ocean in the background; if she squinted it would almost be as if she were back in Southampton.

"Coop redid the kitchen." Brad said behind her as she heard a set of heavy footsteps moving up the floor above and knew they were alone. "Himself?"
"He's good with wood; he did the deck out back and also the furniture. You should see the bed he made himself."
"Can I ask something?" She pulled him as she held his hand as he wanted to show her more, and he stopped. "Always."
"If you move back in, I mean we. Where will Coop go, I mean this place seems as much his as yours."
"You're right about that but come here." He led her through the house pointing out the living room, dining room, small powder room and family room until they hit two sets of stairs.

"Up there." He pointed to the left and also the end of the house if Danni was orientated properly. "Is Coop's apartment, it's very large and has everything he needs as well as his own entrance through the garage. Up there." He pointed to the right staircase. "Are the other five bedrooms and bathrooms."

"He doesn't mind?"

"Do you?"

"No, well I don't know him well but if he's like a brother to you he must be wonderful."

"I wouldn't ask him to leave ever Danni."

"I can't imagine you would and I wouldn't let you."

"Good." Leading her now upstairs she saw that three of the rooms were empty, one was an office and the last was a bedroom fit for a man, large sleigh bed, simple fabrics and a large arm chair and a flat panel TV on the opposite wall to the head of the bed. There was an en-suite bathroom with a his and hers sink as well as a small dressing room. "You can do whatever you want in here and of course any of the rooms if you don't like them."

"Aside from a little color I love everything."

"Good. I should also tell you there's a really nice Indian lady who cleans every Monday and Friday and when I was home I used to get the groceries delivered, there's a food store chain but we wouldn't have to use that because I know how you like to food shop."

"Johnson." They heard Coop shout from downstairs. "I should get going, are you sure you're okay to get to Max's house?"

"I think I can manage it."

"I should get a few things." Brad went over to the closet opening the doors to show a closet full of relaxed clothing, not a suit aside from uniforms in there and plenty of other clothes as well as plenty of room down one side of the walk in for her Danni thought. She watched as he threw in a duffle bag a black t-shirt, a pair of camouflage pants and a pair of heavy black combat boots. "Everything else I need is in the garage." He kissed her quickly on the lips.

"I'll come down, get those directions." She followed him and they found Coop waiting by the door.

"Here." He held out the piece of paper from a printer a map of the area she was headed to and from the quick look really detailed directions. "I put Karen's cell number on there too so if you get stuck give her a call."

"Thanks Coop." She turned to Brad. "Good luck."

"Not that I need it but thanks." He took her kiss and walking out of his door leaving her behind was nice, knowing one day she'd be there when he came home from some tough mission or just a hard day at the base.

Taking a quick look by herself around the house she started making mental notes of the few small things she would change to make it more homely. One big thing would be nice to have a child running around, maybe more.

XXX   XXX

Coop had ribbed him almost the entire drive over to the base twenty minutes away.

Of course, he'd got the low down on the Team and gossip you normally didn't waste calls on too. Normally the Team was full until someone died or retired. Brad was going to be filling the shoes of a guy who couldn't take the job, he had gone through HELL week with flying colors, but the actual doing missions had been rough on him and had requested a transfer back to the Marine squad he'd once served with. The Team had been a man down for a while and Coop seemed happy to fill it with his friend.

First stop at the base Coop had dropped him at the medical building. Before he could try to pass anything, he had to pass a physical to prove he was in good enough health.

This part of the medical building, was the wing off from the main hospital where sailors and marines were treated it was so quiet he wasn't sure if anyone was around, but as he approached the office he was looking for he heard a familiar voice and found Jamie, the SEAL Team's doctor talking on the phone to someone. She must have heard him as she looked back at him and smiled. "He's right here." Closing her cell, she walked towards him as he closed the office door behind him. "Hello Commander Johnson." Normally he would have saluted a fellow officer but Jamie had made it clear a long time ago that it wasn't necessary. Instead he gave her a quick hug. "Jamie, you look good as always."

"Not always but thanks."

Jamie moved towards her desk and he took a look around seeing the comfort of a couch and a few arm chairs as well as the institutional examining table and small sink with cupboards and jars filled with medical stuff as well as a light-up board which held a set of x-rays, but of what he couldn't tell with the light off. "How was DC? Did Danielle get the help she needed?" Her words brought him back as his mind had begun to wander across the photos of the teams. He was there in one, he'd have to find his copy and show Danni sometime.

"The Major and his Team were excellent; Danni got the majority of her memories back."
"That's fantastic Brad." He took in the differences to the Commander, it had been some time since he'd last seen her and like Coop, everyone looked just a little different, a little older. The long blonde hair she had once pulled back in a severe bun was shoulder length and down now. She looked a little younger but that could have been because she wasn't wearing the usual stark white uniform but a knee length hippy style flowing skirt and a black thin strap tank top. An expensive looking diamond necklace hung around her neck. "I should thank you Jamie. You helped me get Danni back."
"I did nothing but give you a name Brad, but you're very welcome. What was that moment like for you, that moment when Danni remembered the two of you when you were young?"
"There aren't words."

"Good answer, tell her things like that and she'll always love you."

"We're engaged again; see we were when we were teens."

"Oooh, then I can't wait to get to Max's house, and hear the women fussing over her."

"She'll be in her element."

Jamie had been shooting the shit with him for the rest of the time he was in the office. Aside from team doctor and an honorary member of Team Seven for life, she was also a Team member's wife and sometimes hearing her talk as if she were a guy hanging between classes, was a little odd, but it took his mind off the few shots she gave him, and when she drew blood.

"I'll see you at the party later, kick ass out there Commander."

"No one does it as well as you Jamie."

"I'm just a good sport."

"Thanks for coming in on your day off."

"Anytime and unless you have something on this blood work up I can pass you, I should know in the next hour I'll red flag it downstairs and remember, you or Danni need anything you call."

"Even Danni?" He frowned.

"You didn't hear? The admiral agreed to me being the physician for any of the wives and kids who wanted to switch, keeps everything in house and easier when the Navy has to foot the bill."

It was awesome to see the entire Team waiting for him over in the SEAL building. Some were dressed ready to go, while others were midway. He said hi to everyone and there was only one guy he didn't know, a petty officer first class. Espinoza as they walked out towards the pool area asked how he liked the Major, and Brad had told him everything, knowing the man had also been treated at Walter Reed by the team.

"You ready?" The soon to be retired Senior Chief asked, waiting poolside.
"Born ready."
"Hoorah." Chris responded back.

XXX   XXX

Danni drove with ease to the address on the paper given to her by Coop. His directions had been perfect and it felt like he had even made sure to keep her to back roads, which was nice when you were looking for a street name or something.

The house stood alone in a modest neighborhood. All of the houses seemed designed the same in the suburban area, but with each family's unique touch they couldn't have been any more different.

There were a couple of cars and SUV's already in the oval driveway, and she parked behind, hoping she wasn't blocking anyone in. Anyone arriving after would have to park on the street also.

Taking just the two bags she used to hold cold items, she walked up to the front door which was open; but the screen storm door was closed. Pressing the doorbell, she felt nervous about meeting a group of women who were so close already, when a tall dark-haired olive skinned woman appeared with a smile. "You must be our newest member Danielle." The storm door was held open for her and Danni smiled. "Please, Danni."

"Sure Danni, I'm Karen, Max's wife, this is our house and make sure you make yourself at home, okay? Can I help you with your bags?"

"Actually, I have a couple more in the car; if you could take these I can go and get them."

"Certainly." Danni went back the way she had entered and upon return Karen was there again. "I just wanted to make sure you didn't need any more help. Did you bring the entire food store?"

"No, just a few things."

"Few?" Karen shook her head with a smile. "I was told you were a chef by Coop. I should have known." There was a laugh Danni shared. "Come on, there are some ladies waiting to meet you."

The kitchen was smaller than either her own or the one at the new house. But it felt warm and cozy as the other four women she was introduced to made her feel at home, adorned her with oohs and ahhs about the desserts she had to finish off after her bags had been emptied she had been taken to the other room to be introduced to a few children of very varying ages, happily watching a Disney movie in the living room.

Trying to keep everyone's name straight was hard. Karen, Mary, Patti, Emma and Mel had all made her laugh so hard with stories and information about the

Team; nothing cruel or bad, no mean gossip and Danni liked that. She explained how she knew Brad, saw the looks of delight as she neared the end of her story; and then received congratulations that were so honest when she was done. Brad had been right; the Team women were wonderful and each one had offered to help her with wedding plans and getting settled.

A few hours after her arrival a few more women arrived with their children and it became quickly apparent that the kids were like brothers and sisters to one another, and seemed to have their own buddy system, with the older kids, one of Patti's sons and Mary's oldest daughter being the ones in charge. The smaller, baby aged children were always in ear shot, and it seemed natural that there was somewhere the sleeping babies went, a monitor ready for any of them to respond to.

The two women who arrived had been introduced as Veronica and Jamie; both had been over at the hospital where they worked. It had taken someone to explain the sibling connection to Jamie and Mel, aside from a few similarities they seemed nothing alike but Danni liked both of them. She was beginning to see the women who formed closer friendships, and she seemed to feel more comfortable with Veronica, who she talked to endlessly, as they moved from the kitchen now everything was ready for the men to arrive out to the back yard.

"They should be here soon," Danni heard Mary say. It seemed that Mary was going to be the new den mother with Patti's husband retiring. "Who?" Danni asked trying to keep track of who was who, who was married to whom and all the other little things she knew would come with time. She had laughed inwardly earlier when Mary had given her a phone number list for the Team. It told her everything she needed to know, but didn't want to sit there holding it as she put face to name and relationship.

"Kirsten and Sarah." Jamie said holding her glass of wine; most of them were drinking, aside from Mel who was nursing, and Emma who was pregnant. "Who are they married to?" She had thought she had accounted for all wives, knowing not all the Team were married and the few girlfriends would be arriving later. "Kirsten was married to the old team leader Daniel and Sarah's husband was Kevin." Even though Patti said the male names, she didn't recognize them. "They were both killed on a mission a few years ago," Jamie explained a little quieter in tone. Danni watched all of the women take a moment no doubt remembering the lost men. "Brad explained this, I'm sorry if I'm asking stupid questions."
"Don't apologize Danni, there are no stupid questions." Patti said softly. "I can still remember all the men who I've known, through my husband, that we've lost over the years, and I keep in contact with all of their families."
"They're very lucky to have all of you."
"See, she fits right in." Karen joked, getting up to open a new bottle of wine.

"Any ideas when you want to get married?" Patti decided the conversation was getting too serious.

"Soon." Danni hadn't thought about when, just soon.

"Patti here practically single handedly arranged all of our weddings." Mel said.

"You did?"

"It's a great deal of work, and if it weren't for her I would have gone crazy." Karen poured Danni more red wine.

"It's nothing." Patti blushed.

"Well, if you're free I would love some help."

"Danni, I would be honored."

"We all will help with whatever." Emma offered.

"I can definitely say I know a good caterer." Mel said with half a cannoli gone, and it was her third one in an hour.

CHAPTER FORTY-TWO

His legs felt like jelly and he had sweated more in one hour than in the last two years being gone.

"Ready?" Coop appeared at the door to the locker room. Brad was thankful for the hot shower after all of the tests. "I think so." He began throwing his dirty and wet clothes back in his bag. "I have something for you." Coop moved further in to the locker room and held out a rectangular strip of plastic. Brad took it and saw his last name on it. "Pick an empty locker and leave whatever you want in it."
"I passed?"
"With flying colors."
"I've been waiting to hear that for two years."
"I'm letting you have a week before I officially put you back on the roster so you can finish whatever you have to do. I figured you might need to get back to New York, LA maybe?"
"Thanks Coop."
"Let's get to that party."

Walking in to Max's house he said hello to the kids who had all sprouted since the last time he'd seen them. He couldn't believe Chris's oldest was in the second year of Annapolis, and the youngest graduating from high school, even Mary and Jamie's daughters seemed light years older.

Max had the grill going, the sky was dark, and the lights hanging around the yard made it look like they were at some tropical island. He found Danni speaking with Patti and a woman he didn't know, David, who was standing with them, introduced his wife Veronica, and then a beer was thrust into his hands. "How did you do?" Danni whispered in his ear while they were alone for a few minutes. "I got in." "Oh Brad." He saw her pride for him in the glow of her eyes.

"We have a week to get things together."

"Easy." She kissed his cheek.

Once the grill had done its job and stomachs were filled everyone was sitting around chatting. It had been Coop as Team leader who had started the speeches for Chris. He told the story of the first cruel thing the Senior Chief had put them through, making Brad recall the day, and even with the harshness of the training they had admired the man on the spot because his methods had taught them some valuable lessons they would always remember.

All of the men told their memorable Chris moments and then Danni listened with awe as Jamie said something perfect, as did a few other women. The one who almost got the women in tears was Kirsten. Danni had spoken to her after being introduced and the woman was lovely, friendly and had explained more about the life the women lead as the home crutch of normalcy the men needed when home. "Chris, I know if Daniel was here he'd be floored you finally put in your papers. I know he joked with you that the only way you would both leave was by force or death. I'm glad for you that neither is making you leave the Team. I thank you so very much for everything you've done for me since Daniel's death. You were a selfless rock in my time of need and I will always be thankful for your friendship, as I know Daniel cherished you for being that way too."

Brad had left during her words to get the box from the back of his car from New York. It wasn't heavy and aside from Maggie nobody had looked inside so he hoped it was filled with plenty of Yankee stuff.

Coop had given it to Chris from the entire team, inside was a signed shirt with the number seven on the back and SC above where the name would sit. There were even Chris's strips on the sleeves. He was floored you could tell. Then he pulled a few more items with the Yankee emblem on. Then there was an envelope he opened while everyone waited quietly.

"Senior Chief Chris Polanski." The man read aloud. "It was my honor to be asked to put together this box for you, as you know the Yankee organization has many charities. But one we hold dear and true is our commitment to service men and women just like you. I thank you on behalf of the entire Yankee's Team, staff and family here in New York for your strength and commitment. It would be my honor to have you, your wife and your two sons here for the day at the stadium as my guests, hope to see you soon, regards, Derek Jeter."
"WOW." Was a common response in the group.

The party went late in to the night and Brad pulled the SUV up outside of his house a little after two am.

Between the time difference and the afternoon he was beyond beat, but he hadn't had the heart to complain because all the way home Danni had been talking nonstop.

Being inside his house with her, holding her in his arms as sleep crept in fast, was like a dream, like his biggest wishes had finally come true and he knew he had fallen asleep with a wide grin on his face.

EPILOGUE

Having the help of the women who had become so special to her Danni had arranged the wedding for a very special day. A month and a half later on June fifteenth, it wasn't just a date Danni had pulled out of a hat or while playing darts with a calendar as the board but the day when as five and six year olds they had met for the first time.

Now as Brad drove home with Danni beside him he knew she was in for the biggest shock, it was her birthday and they had been out for lunch so that Coop, the men on the Team and all of the women and children of the Team could get the house ready for a surprise party.

He had a very nice surprise of his own waiting too.

Danni noticed the amount of cars in their road as Brad pulled in to the driveway as always beside Coop's truck, her own parked the other side. "Is there something going on inside the house?" Her face had lit up and Brad just kissed the tips of the fingers he had been playing with while driving. "Go see." He had to be stealthy to keep up as even with those heels of hers she moved fast. He was behind her just in time to hear over thirty voices shout. "Happy Birthday."

She was overwhelmed. Her dad and brother were there as was Louise and Daisy. She hadn't seen any of them since they'd all flown out together for the wedding and she loved seeing all of them mingling with the Team again, her brother had on his last trip taken a liking to Sarah, even when Brad and Coop had explained to Peter about her losing her husband Kevin. Danni knew for a fact Sarah and Peter had been talking since then and would have to ask later when they were going on a date.

Most of the party had been on the beach, the kids had fun playing and while Brad stood holding her from behind she hoped now she was off her birth control that by his Birthday in October they could celebrate a pregnancy also.

When those who had to go home left after the party, their family in their guest bedrooms; Danni had been enjoying another slice of birthday cake standing at the counter in a pair of Brad's old shorts and one of his old Navy t-shirts. They were so soft and comfortable she had stolen it for lounging in when she'd been doing laundry. She heard both Brad and Coop come in from taking out the last of the trash from the party and Coop unusually said nothing before disappearing and Brad came over to take a piece of the cake which he let her feed him.

"I have a special gift for you."
"I bet you do." Danni winked.
"No, it's something special that Cooper helped me with."
"And?"
"He'll be back." Danni tingled with anticipation as she waited. Before long their friend was back carrying something impossibly big and flat. "What on

earth is it?" She noted the light brown paper taped over it. She guessed it was a painting as the one Louise had cared for of her mother was now inside this house hanging in the guest room Louise used. "Open it." Brad laughed at his wife. He watched her rip with as much gentility as she could contain herself with and then the look of astonishment over what it was.

"Oh guys." Danni's eyes welled up with tears as she looked down at a painting sized print of the one picture that had captured her so hard back in New York, the teenage them looking at each other with so much love and everything else. "I know how much this picture means to you and I know you wanted something for above the fireplace in the living room." "We have to hang it first thing." She gushed, wiping her eyes.
"I can do it now," Coop said as he'd sneakily as part of the party preparations already put a hook in for it.

"Coop made the frame himself." Danni heard in her ear as they followed Coop. "How's that?" Seeing it hanging there Danni was speechless.
"Thank you." First, she hugged Coop who disappeared after, while she went to Brad who was looking closely at the picture. "I did good huh?" He tried to joke, a small part of him would always remember the years Danni didn't know, the wasted time. It was still a little hard to see the picture but he knew it meant the world to her and she meant the world to him.

"You did better than good."

Visit

Cjsummerhayes.com

For upcoming events, news and releases.

The next installment of SEAL Team 7 April 2018

www.ingramcontent.com/pod-product-compliance
Lightning Source LLC
Chambersburg PA
CBHW071150250626
47159CB00001B/53